A MILLION DIFFERENT WAYS TO LOSE YOU

The Horn Duet

P. DANGELICO

A MILLION DIFFERENT WAYS TO LOSE YOU

Copyright © 2017 by P. Dangelico. All rights reserved.
ISBN-13: 978-0692919705 (P. Dangelico)
ISBN-10: 0692919708

Published by P. Dangelico
All rights reserved. No part of this book may be reproduced or transmitted in any form, including electronic or mechanical, without written permission from
the publisher, except in the case of brief quotations embodied in critical articles or reviews.

This is a work of fiction. Names, characters, places, events, and incidents are either the product of the author's imagination or used in a fictitious manner. Any
resemblance to actual persons, living or dead, or actual events is purely coincidental.

This book is licensed for your personal enjoyment only. This book may not be re-sold or given away to other people. If you would like to share this book with
another person, please purchase an additional copy for each person you share it with. Thank you for respecting the author's work.

Second Edition July 10, 2017
Cover Design: Najla Qamber, Najla Qamber Designs
Proofreading: Judy's Proofreading
www.pdangelico.com

To everyone that read and reviewed my first book, thank you. Without you this wouldn't be nearly as much fun. Now come in, get comfortable, let me tell you a story...

Praise for the Horn Duet

Recommend "...romance that crackles with erotic tension...Dangelico's debut romance hums along at a brisk pace thanks to a pair of engaging leads and a well-drawn cast of supporting characters." *-Kirkus Reviews*

Four Stars Hot "Sexy, intriguing, suspenseful and heartwarming, *A Million Different Ways* will grab hold of readers' emotions and leave them wanting more. Sebastian is a broody, swoon-worthy alpha male, and Vera is a beautiful, courageous heroine. These two characters will pull at your heartstrings in this emotional and dangerous tale." *-RT Book Reviews.com*

"A steamy, character-driven romance novel with an international flair. The great strength in A Million Different Ways is the characters - and not merely the characters of Dangelico's two leads, but all the supporting characters as well. Dangelico is definitely a romance author on the rise. A Million Different Ways is filled with heartbreaking emotion, danger, sensuality, and characters you'll want to hear from again - there are a million different ways you'll love this book!" *-Self-Publishing Review*

Five Stars "I loved a *Million Different Ways*. Loved. It. How's that for a review? Author P. Dangelico has certainly done a fantastic job creating characters that her readers will care about, connect with, and continue to think of long after the last words are read. If that's not a hallmark of a truly great author, I don't know what is. I highly recommend A Million Different Ways and certainly look forward to reading more from a very promising new author P. Dangelico in the near future!" *-Readers' Favorite*

Prologue

Houston, Texas 1985

A HIGH-pitched wail woke him out of a dead sleep. Sebastian sat up abruptly, his Spiderman pajamas tangling with the bed linens. One at a time his eyes cracked open to find the room cloaked in absolute black. Someone had turned off his nightlight. That was the first sign that something was wrong.

All at once his heart was hammering inside his chest so hard it hurt, so fast butterflies filled his stomach. It didn't take long for his fertile imagination to run wild. Out of the darkness he thought he saw a claw reach out for him and his palms began to sweat. Gripping the sheet even tighter, he pulled it up to his chin.

That old familiar feeling was back. Loneliness. He was always alone, with no one to chase the monsters away for him. Sebastian knew what he had to do then, what he always did when he got scared.

He became Spiderman.

Spiders were the coolest. Spiders were small enough to hide, and some of them were even dangerous. Mr. Miller, his third-grade teacher, said that the venom of a black widow spider is fifteen times stronger than that of a rattle snake. They were real things. Unlike Superman, who was fake 'cause Sebastian never met any man that was nice, and strong, and liked kids.

A second more pronounced wail interrupted the silence.

His mother's voice—he'd recognize it anywhere. Without a second thought to those monsters, Sebastian jumped out of bed. Small, bare feet carried him as fast as they could down the endless hallway, headed straight for the shaft of light that filtered onto the carpet. Once he reached the edge, though, they stopped abruptly. They stopped because Sebastian was more scared of what awaited him inside that room than he was of the monsters lurking in the dark.

Spiderman doesn't get scared, he reminded himself. Spiderman doesn't need anyone. Gathering every drop of courage he possessed, Sebastian slowly stepped into the doorway.

Diana Horn lay face down on her sprawling California king-sized bed, small mewling sounds and hiccups emanating from her prone body. Her vintage, red Halston dress was ripped and her long, champagne blond hair spilled over the side of the mattress in soft waves. Sebastian's stomach clenched painfully.

"Momma?" he called out, his voice barely audible.

At the sound of a whisper thin voice Diana slowly lifted her face off the mattress. If there was ever a hot mess it was this woman. Tracks of tears melted down her face, stained black from the heavy eye makeup she'd worn that evening. Her lipstick was bleeding right off the edge of lips worthy of the front cover of Vogue magazine.

A boy stood before her, shifting nervously from foot to foot. She stared blankly at him while her alcohol fogged mind struggled to identify the child. As recognition hit her, so did a fresh set of tears.

"Scout? What are you doin' up, baby?" she slurred, the words tripping over her sloppy tongue.

"I heard you cryin'."

Reaching out, she clasped Sebastian's wrist and pulled him closer, close enough that Sebastian could smell the familiar stench of wine on her breath, coming off of her skin and her pretty hair. "My beautiful baby boy," she mewled and batted her fake eyelashes. Another round of sobs followed.

"Are you okay?"

With the heel of her hand, Diana swiped at the dampness on her cheeks, the makeup smearing across her face. "Oh, baby, what does that even mean?" Her son returned a confused scowl. "I'm fine," she said, waving a hand at him dismissively.

"I gotta go back to bed, or Santa won't come tonight," Sebastian mumbled.

"Santa? You still believe in that old fool," she chuckled, the sound ringing of bitterness. "There's no Santa. He's not real. Like love," she scoffed. "That ain't real either, baby."

Clumsily, she dragged herself into a sitting position and grabbed the bottle of Haute Brion Blanc off the nightstand. For a moment, solemn amber eyes made her pause, though the moment passed just as quickly. Then, after giving her son a weak smile that didn't reach her eyes, she tipped the bottle up to her full lips and took a long, slow gulp.

Sebastian's wide, worried gaze followed the track of wine that dribbled out of the corner of her mouth and snaked down her chin.

"Promise me something, Scout," she pleaded, her long red nails digging into the boy's slim shoulder. "Promise me you won't ever love nobody but me, 'kay, baby?" Her suddenly determined gaze bore into Sebastian's.

"Okay," he replied in a small voice.

Pacified, a flimsy smile spread across her face. "I knew I could count on you."

Clutching the bottle of wine, Diana rose off the bed and staggered around precariously on her Saint Laurent heels. Back and forth she swayed, her coltish legs as weak as her character. In an attempt to reach the back zipper of her dress, she jerked dangerously forward.

"You should learn that now, Scout. Loving anybody other than your momma will only bring you pain. Don't trust nobody. They'll only disappoint you."

The four-inch heel of her shoe caught in the hem of the dress. Slow to react, she stumbled forward and crashed onto her knees. The bottle of wine bounced as it landed on the floor. The remains of the rare vintage poured onto the carpet, soaking Sebastian's bare feet.

A horrible noise rose up from deep within his mother's chest. Horror stricken, Sebastian watched as she began to gag and choke. The liquid contents of Diana's stomach poured onto the antique Persian that had been purchased at Sotheby's for a record sum, onto her eight-year-old son's Spiderman pjs.

"Momma!" Sebastian screamed. "Momma!" His voice rose higher and higher as a puddle of bloody vomit slowly spread around his mother's inanimate body like a scene out of a Hitchcock movie.

Downstairs, a bloodcurdling scream jarred Ruth White out of one of the most peaceful nights of sleep she'd ever had. Unfortunately, this was nothing new. Her employer was a spoiled, overemotional creature. She should know, she'd raised Diana since infancy.

Grabbing her powder blue, terry robe, Ruth went to investigate whatever it was that woke her. She was angry enough to spit nails, and rightfully so. How many times had she cleaned up Diana's mess? How many times! And on Christmas Eve, no less. Mumbling to herself, she walked as fast as her bad hip would allow up the grand staircase to her employer's bedroom.

Her voice uncharacteristically loud, Ruth shouted from halfway down the hall, "Diana! I am telling you, I've had it—"

The rest of the sentence got caught in her throat as soon as she stepped into the bedroom. The oxygen left her lungs in a hurry and the brown skin on her angular face grew taut. Diana Horn lay face down on the floor—as still as death. Standing in a pool of blood, Sebastian was shaking his mother's limp shoulders. Ruth's tip-tilted dark eyes shifted to the bedside table where she discovered it littered with empty prescription bottles.

"Lucius!" she shouted. To her right, a young black man ran down the hallway, towards her. "Lucius, call 911! Hurry!"

Chapter One

Peaceful was the dark, the numbness seductive, stealing away any desire I may have had to return to reality. It was as if my body knew that it needed time to gather strength for what was coming. Time, that is, having become an entirely abstract concept. The consequence of which was that I remained suspended in between two worlds for what seemed like forever. Yet even in the dark, the memory of Sebastian, of the baby, called to me—a faraway lighthouse in a storm, beckoning me home.

"She looks so small. *Trop petit,*" a voice whispered. A woman's voice. I caught every other word, my mind struggling to keep up. My eyes felt clamped shut by a vise while a heavy fatigue pressed down on the rest of me. It threatened to drag me under by the ankles if I didn't resist. "The poor, poor girl."

The voice teased my memory. Synapses fired and connected. In a sudden flash it all came back to me. *Mrs. Arnaud.* "I brought some of the raspberry tarts she likes. The sooner we get her home, the sooner she can recover."

"When *is* she coming home?" said a woman with a clipped British accent. *Charlotte.*

"Not for a while."

I knew that voice. I'd know that voice anywhere—the pronounced rasp a balm to my battered soul. The abject despair saturating those four words, however, was a different matter altogether. The guilt it spawned raked its sharp claws across my conscience.

I was in no shape to deal with whatever had caused that soul-wrenching despair. So I let go. I relaxed my grip on consciousness once again and let the darkness carry me away to a place where nothing could hurt me, where pain and guilt didn't exist.

***

Shortly after I awoke in the hospital for the first time, bruised and in pain although relieved to know Sebastian had somehow found me, a routine began. Every time I opened my eyes for the twenty or so minutes of lucidity I was granted each day, I found Sebastian holding vigil in the same hard, uncompromising chair. I said very little and he said nothing at all. It felt like the words were being stored up for a showdown at a later date.

Reaching up, I felt around and discovered my head swathed in cotton gauze. The persistent ache in my head made it impossible to focus. I could've sworn there was a steel vise wrapped around my skull and that the devil himself was tightening the screws.

"Twenty-two stitches," a deep, raspy voice informed me.

My eyes crept open slowly, painfully, a shaft of light searing my eyeballs. Following the sound, I found Sebastian seated in his favorite chair. He was bent forward, his elbows resting on his knees and his hands clasped in a single fist. His tailored white shirt was wrinkled and his shirtsleeves rolled up, the sinuous muscles of his forearms taut with energy nourished by too much caffeine and not enough sleep. His gray slacks were rumpled. His expression, though, was not rumpled. It was perfectly smooth in fact, stone cold and relentless.

"Did they shave my head?"

"Yes."

The lack of feeling in his reply killed the smile growing on my face. "Oh well, I needed a haircut anyway."

Apathy stared back at me. There was zero amusement in his expression, not even a twitch of his lips.

"We need to talk before I disappear again."

He jerked back, every muscle in his body tensing. My careless words inadvertently cracked the surface of his deliberate ruse. And then I caught it, the pain and anger hiding under the thin shell of his calm exterior—a truckload of it.

"Disappear?"

"I *meant* fall asleep." I reached for his hands and felt him flinch when I made contact. The concern, now jumping off his face, made me feel bad about teasing him. The apology was on my lips when two knocks coming from the open doorway caused both our heads to turn.

Wearing a warm smile, Dr. Rossetti walked over to the side of my bed and patted my shoulder, the bones of which, now that I realized, were protruding in a frightening manner. "I'm glad to see you looking brighter. You've been in and out for about three weeks."

My gaze slid over to Sebastian and stopped short when I found his head hanging down, his attention fixed on the floor. I noticed the tense line of his shoulder, the knuckles that were mottled with anxiety. His fist tightened and the tendons on the back of his hands popped up.

Dr. Rossetti exhaled heavily. Something about it pulled at me, warranting my immediate attention. My focus snapped back to her. The air grew heavy. An ominous foreboding lurked in the corners of the room. When it began to circle the bed, the realization crashed down on me.

"There isn't any way to say this gently, Vera. You suffered a miscarriage."

It took me a minute to process her words, each one spelled out individually in my mind. And as the words coalesced, something inside of me extinguished, died with it. There was no despair, no anger—no feeling whatsoever. All that remained was a great desert as empty and barren as the Sahara, littered with the bleached bones of nascent hopes and dreams I didn't even know I possessed until that very moment.

My face was a placidly numb mask as I turned and met the turmoil evident on Sebastian's. He reached out and grabbed my hand. Lacing his fingers in between mine, he squeezed much too tightly for it to be comforting.

"I performed a D and C," Dr. Rossetti informed me, tempering the ever-present note of authority in her voice. "Both ovaries looked fine. You'll have no problem conceiving again."

My gaze jerked back to her. A terror, the dimensions of which I couldn't even begin to comprehend, spiked through the smothering blanket of detachment for a fleeting moment. I pushed it down and locked it away, the reaction automatic; the same one I always had when dealing with heart-shattering truths I didn't want to face.

Reading my expression, she quickly added, "More importantly you experienced significant blunt force trauma to the brain. There was enough swelling that we thought it best to keep you in a coma for forty-eight hours."

"Coma?" The word escaped me as a mere whisper.

"I'm afraid so." Dr. Rossetti softened the professional mask she always wore. "What was the last thing you remember?"

A knot formed in my stomach at the sudden recollection. I couldn't look at Sebastian as I spoke. "Blood…running through the woods and…blood."

Sighing deeply, Dr. Rossetti continued. "It seems your memory is largely intact. Might have some holes here and there, but those should close up quickly." Her focus shifted to Sebastian briefly, then swung back to me. "You were very lucky."

I thought I heard a note of censure in her voice. However, when I looked up, all I found on her face was sympathy. More likely the bottomless guilt that had begun to seep into my bloodstream was coloring my perception.

"When can I leave the hospital?" A sudden, urgent need to be gone from the antiseptic smell and the white tiles reflecting the florescent lighting made me speak more harshly than I intended. The persistent ache in my head didn't help either.

"You've recuperated remarkably well, faster than I had anticipated...let's play it by ear. It wouldn't be out of the question for you to go home in the next couple of days, predicated on the promise that you will remain on bed rest for at least another week." My expression must've been less than convincing because she continued. "You can't push yourself."

"I know." I would have said anything to ensure her cooperation. Still, she knew I was appeasing her. The polite smile she gave me conveyed her thoughts on the matter perfectly.

As I watched her walk out, a twinge of panic grew larger inside my chest. I was suddenly scared of being alone with the man I loved, scared of his censure, of his concern, of all the words that hadn't been said yet. The door swung shut behind her and the silence in the room immediately became as dense as quicksand, threatening to suffocate me by slow inches if something didn't give.

I turned back towards Sebastian and found the object of my affection staring back at me with what could only be described as concerned wariness. If I didn't know better I would say he looked almost scared of me, guarding himself, one step removed from actually being there. I couldn't stand to see it—and I couldn't hold his gaze.

"How do you feel?" His voice was gentle, the restraint in it unnatural.

"I'm fine," I answered, trying to allay his concern, even though somewhere inside of me I wanted to burst out sobbing. I wanted to rail and break things. I wanted to beg him to forgive me. But I didn't do any of those things. I couldn't. Because my feelings were locked behind an iron door.

"Then why won't you look at me?"

Reluctantly, my eyes climbed from the blanket I was busy picking lint off of, to his face. I took in every detail. The dark half-moons hanging under his eyes, the hollow cheeks, cheekbones sharper than ever. Exhaustion dimmed the bright sparkle I loved to see on his beautiful face. This had taken as much a physical toll on him as it had on me.

"I'm fine."

Staring back into those world-weary eyes, concern overrode everything else. I caressed his jaw, covered by a week-old beard. It pulsed with tension under my fingertips. I thought he would pull away, put distance between us, but instead he leaned into my touch. His eyes fluttered, his long lashes throwing shadows as my fingers skated over his angular features and traced the lines of worry across his face.

"I need you to come closer," I murmured. After a beat, he moved, pinning the chair he sat on to the side of the bed. "Closer than that," I whispered. His russet colored eyes opened and searched mine. He was that wounded creature I had met so long ago. *No sudden movements...talk softly.* When he hesitated, I patted the spot next to me.

"I'm too big. I'll hurt you."

"No," I countered, my head shaking at the irony, "you won't. You wouldn't."

I shifted to the far side of the bed to make more room for him, and patted the mattress again. In his gaze, glassy from exhaustion and stress, a silent war was being fought. I knew I'd won when he exhaled deeply. Right then I found that I could still feel something because the defeat I saw in the sloping lines of his broad shoulders dug its fingers into my heart and squeezed viciously.

He kicked off his shoes and lay down next to me. Face to face, we were on our sides, inches apart. He studied me for a long time without making a sound, his fingers brushing petal-soft up and down my arm. I wanted to kiss the caution and apprehension on his face away, soothe every hurt I had inflicted. Knowing that I had put it there heaped more guilt on a pile as high as Everest.

"Closer. I don't bite," I ordered softly, repeating the words he had once said to me. The side of his sensual mouth tipped up for the briefest moment. Then his head dipped down, close enough that we were almost nose to nose. "Closer," I mouthed. His sweet lips descended onto mine so carefully I barely felt them brush back and forth in a dry, chaste kiss.

I wrapped my hand around the back of his neck and felt him shudder under my touch. Ragged, broken pieces of air rushed out of him as I deepened the kiss. Sweet, tender kisses meant to soothe, meant to tease. My tongue traced the seam of his closed lips, begging him to join me.

His resolve failed. His nostrils flared and his hand lifted to my face, hovering, trembling with pent-up emotion. It must have taken the strength of Atlas himself to hold him in check, to stop him from crushing me with the violence of his passion.

"I love you," I whispered again and again, in between more kisses and caresses. A little at a time I could feel the words soak into him and unlock some of the rigidity from his muscles. When all of the fight had left him, he pulled back.

"Right now your health is my only concern," he murmured. "But I need to know what happened." Cupping my face gently, he forced me to meet the anticipation in his eyes.

Fragments of images, a jumbled mess of nonsequential events flashed in my mind's eye. The effort it took to organize those thoughts into coherent order made my head throb, a painful reminder that thinking was not a good idea following brain trauma. Especially since what I really wanted to do was forget everything that had happened. Unfortunately, there were no blind spots. I remembered it all too well.

"Bear said he saw you talking to Paisley outside the doctor's office."

"Yes. She knew..." I braced myself for the next words, the heavy pounding of my heart threatening to split my chest in two. "That I was pregnant. She told me that Isabelle had overheard my phone conversation with the doctor."

The more I spoke the more static his face became, cementing into an emotionless mask. I debated for only an instant whether to tell him the most damning piece of the story. "Isabelle told your mother."

I couldn't hold the eye contact. My eyes descended to the corded side of his neck, the tendons taut with anger, the only outward display of what was going on in his mind. He placed his index finger under my chin and gently lifted it. "What else did she say?"

"She said that if I didn't leave without a word to you, she would go to the newspapers, the tabloids. She would tell them I trapped you, that I was after your money. She said she would publicize every detail so that investors would lose confidence in your ability to run the bank." My voice grew more anxious with every spoken word. "Sebastian, she meant it. I'm scared of what she might do—to you, to the bank."

A heavy silence followed. His fingertips traced the contours of my face, reading the angles and depressions so delicately I thought I would shatter from the exquisite sensation.

"This is why you left?" he said. It was less a question and more a statement of fact. His expression softened. The information I'd just shared didn't seem to concern him. "You were trying to protect me?"

I replied with a slight nod, my voice deserting me.

"Do you know what scares the shit out of me?" His brow furrowed, a deep v chiseled in the middle. His chest heaved as he fought to control a tide of emotion. "A life without you." What I saw in his eyes made me want to shrink away. "I thought you understood that." The last sentence held a hard edge, a note that hinted at betrayal.

"I do but—"

"No. No *but*," he said, cutting me off. "Life without you is…" He shook his head, his Adam's apple rising and falling as he struggled to find the words. "Pointless."

There was an abyss of despair in his eyes. As I stood on the edge of it, I fully grasped how deep his feelings ran, how necessary I was to his peace of mind. The question was—whether I was strong enough to carry that burden.

Chapter Two

WHEN THE BODY EXPERIENCES AN overwhelming trauma, the brain shuts down, slips into a coma as to conserve energy and direct it at the healing process. Only later would I come to realize that the soul behaves in much the same manner when it needs saving, when it experienced a pain so great it shocks the system. The most vital part of me remained in a coma, while the rest carried on without it.

In the subsequent days, I moved through life completely detached, all my senses disengaged. And the more disinterested I became, the greater the palpable tension surrounding Sebastian grew, its tentacles reaching out to everyone and everything within his radius. With each passing day he grew more overbearing and more remote—apparently this was not incongruous—not to mention, more intolerable.

If I needed to use the bathroom, he was by my side in an instant, lifting me from the bed and carrying me there. If I wanted to stretch my legs down the hall, he was at my side acting as a human crane. He undressed and dressed me as if I were a two-year-old—he officially crossed the line with that one. By day four of this I was ready to conk him over the head with the chair I always found him in when I awoke.

"Why aren't you at the office?" I did nothing to conceal my irritation.

He looked up from scrolling through his cell phone, a scowl hardening his perfect features. "I'm not going anywhere until you're home—where you'll be handcuffed to my bed, and barricaded behind a steel wall fifty feet high with a hundred armed men guarding you."

I crossed my arms over my chest because, lying in bed, I couldn't very well stamp my foot and scream the way I wanted to. "Why do I get the feeling that you're not joking." The raised eyebrow he returned was his unequivocal answer. "What about the audit by the DOJ? The bank will suffer if you keep dancing attendance on me."

"Dancing attendance?" he repeated, smirking. "I'm not *dancing attendance* on you. I'm making sure you don't sneak out of here on some fucked-up, misguided attempt to help me."

"Language," I said with a grimace.

His long fingers raked through his hair. It was getting so long he could've pulled it into a ponytail. Reaching over, I sifted my fingers through it.

"Shit…keep doing that," he purred, his eyes briefly falling shut. After a deep sigh, he added, "The audit's postponed. They were reasonable about it, considering I wasn't in the best state of mind when I spoke to them."

How long would the unintended consequences of my actions haunt me? Then again, the alternative had been unthinkable. And the risk hadn't lessened. I still didn't know what damage Paisley could inflict. I had been literally in the dark for weeks.

"I'm sorry," I said, a pathetically inadequate phrase that would be ever present on my tongue in the weeks to come. His eyes returned to me, assessing, searching. For what, I wasn't certain. The only thing I was certain of anymore was that I didn't want to cause him another moment's worth of pain as long as I lived. "What are you going to do about Paisley?"

The look that flashed across his face made the fine hairs on my arm stand up. "I took care of it." His eyes narrowed into two golden slits, unfocused and far away—the predator always lurking beneath the surface of his civilized demeanor. My instincts warned me not to ask any more questions.

"You need a haircut," I said, while I continued to pet him. "Between the hair and the scruff, you look more like a sexy pirate than a banker."

His sensual mouth twitched and twitched until finally lifting up on one side. It was the first time since I'd awoken in the hospital that I could detect even a small measure of humor in his expression. I would've done anything to keep that smile on his face. "My sexy pirate," I murmured suggestively.

All at once his expression sobered. He looked me squarely in the eyes, and said, "I love you." It sounded like an admission I had coerced out of him. As if defeated, he reluctantly surrendered his feelings. It never occurred to me that hearing those words from him could make me feel bad. The urge to close the distance between us grew overpowering. I was out of bed and onto his lap so fast it took him by surprise.

"I was wondering if I would ever hear those words from you again," I said, wrapping my arms around his neck. "Although it doesn't sound like you're happy about it." Nothing felt better than being in his arms again. The sense of relief I felt was beyond words. It had been years since I'd called any place home. And even then the feeling had been a fleeting one, almost but never quite right. I knew then why—because nothing had ever felt like this, like being close to *him*. He was the home I'd always longed for.

My fingers dung into his rock-solid trapezius muscles, working the stiffness out. The love and doubt dueling inside of him could be felt under my fingertips. He was the last person I wanted to hurt. And yet, I had. Knowing I was the cause of all that stress stung. He hugged me tightly, and I kissed him gently, brushing my lips against his until he surrendered not just his feelings, but his body, too.

A forced cough coming from the doorway sought our attention. Bear stood just inside the room. "Mrs. Redman is here."

Underneath me, Sebastian's entire body turned to stone. A second later I was unceremoniously dumped back onto the bed.

"Sebastian—" I pleaded warily.

"Don't," he grunted, his alert gaze pinned to the open doorway.

On cue, an enormous bouquet of white peonies and lilies appeared. It obscured her face completely. Only her long legs, balancing unsteadily on four-inch, nude colored Louboutins, were visible. Her bright blond head shifted to the side, into view, and with a brittle, forced smile she drawled, "Hello."

I'm surprised Sebastian's gaze didn't pulverize her on the spot.

"Sebastian—" I implored, not in any mood to witness a murder.

But it was in vain. He was lost to everything other than the presence of his fury, the emotion emanating from every fiber of his being. I could have set myself on fire and he wouldn't have noticed.

Rising out of the chair slowly, he suddenly looked four inches taller, his countenance grim as he walked up to her. Every muscle in my body instinctively braced when he reached her. Without any acknowledgement, he gently took the vase of white flowers out of her hands.

And then...an explosion, the violence of which resonated throughout the room and down the hallway. I jerked in surprise. Diana screamed, her bony fists flying to cover her mouth. What remained of the vase, which had shattered against the wall, now lay scattered all over the floor. I sat there slack-jawed while my gaze climbed from the shards of crystal, broken stems, and petals strewn about, to the two of them.

"I need to apologize to Vera," Diana feebly insisted, her voice cracking and breaking. Her plea went ignored. He dug his fingers into her flesh and roughly yanked on her arm, maneuvering her out the door. Her wide, frightened eyes met mine for a brief moment before he had her turned around.

"Outside!" he shouted as he shoved her into the corridor.

"Make sure he doesn't kill her, for goodness sake!" I hissed at Bear, who was gone before I even finished my sentence.

The shouting commenced immediately.

"How dare you come here," he said in a hair-raising growl.

"Scout...baby—" Diana sobbed, interrupting what was sure to become a litany of swear words and accusations.

"Don't you *ever* call me that again. If you were a man, I'd knock your fucking teeth out."

The shot of adrenaline made me lightheaded, my heart thundering inside my chest. I had to put an end to this—for all our sakes. I didn't exactly have sympathy for her, however, for better or worse, she was his mother. Something I never had.

The one-two punch of weakness and fatigue clung to my limbs, acting like weights strapped to my ankles. Despite them, I still managed to crawl out of bed and shuffle to the doorway, clutching onto the wall for support.

"I just want to apologize to both of you," Diana wailed in a juvenile voice.

"I didn't think you could stoop any lower."

"You don't mean that," she managed with a pronounced tremor.

"You're the reason Vera lost the baby. My child is *dead* because of you! Do you understand that?! Do you understand what I'm fucking telling you?!!" he raged.

I implored my legs to move faster. It took all the strength I had just to make it to the doorway, my hospital gown soaked with sweat from the effort.

Orderlies and nurses ran by the open doorway, headed straight for the bloodbath. With the last drop of strength I possessed, I pushed through the crowd clustered around them and watched as Bear stepped in between Sebastian and Diana, his wooly mammoth-sized body the only thing keeping it from turning it into a crime scene.

My knees turned soft and the little muscle I had left in my legs trembled.

"Sebastian," I tried shouting; only a weak imitation of it came out.

"Crawl back into the hole you came out of and stay there— or I'll make you wish you had." Hurtful words were coming hard and fast now.

"Sebastian!" I shouted, louder this time.

"You are fucking dead to me. Do you hear me!" I was pretty certain they could hear him at the North Pole. "Dead!" he roared, his voice rising to a savage crescendo.

"Sebastian, please!"

My knees buckled. I was overcome by a sinking sensation, a fainting spell imminent. Sebastian's head snapped in my direction. His gaze slammed into mine, and the color in his face drained.

"Jesus," he mouthed, before he bolted for me, catching me just in time before I collapsed on the floor. Hooking his arm under my legs, he lifted me easily to his chest and held on tightly.

"I got you," he murmured, and placed tender kisses on my forehead, my temple. "I got you."

I could feel the violent beat of his heart as he pressed me closer. Reluctantly, he tore his eyes away from me, and directed a vicious glare at Diana. His anger now locked away behind a wall of ice, he said, "I won't be responsible for what happens if I ever lay eyes on you again."

Diana's face had suddenly aged ten years. Her green eyes were two wide, vacant orbs underscored by tracks of melted mascara that ran down her cheeks. Before she could say another word, he turned and carried me back into the room, the crowd behind us lingering in stunned disbelief.

I couldn't help myself, and I couldn't live with another moment of regret. As he gently tucked me back into bed, I cupped his face in my hands and forced him to meet my eyes. "Sebastian, she's the only family you have left."

His sharp gaze met mine, and I was immediately hit with the intensity of his thoughts, of his convictions. The slashes of his masculine eyebrows pinched together. "She's not my family," he stated unequivocally. "You're my family."

And with that decree, the topic was summarily closed for further discussion.

Chapter Three

AS SOON AS THE CATHETER and IV were removed, I was itching to be released from the hospital. Thankfully, I didn't have long to wait. We never discussed what had happened with his mother and it bothered me. In a way I felt responsible for the rift between them, and something told me I was going to pay the price for it with interest at a later date.

"Why are we going out this way?" I asked over my shoulder while he pushed my wheelchair down a dark, deserted corridor.

"The cock sucking paparazzi are out front," he grumbled. I let that one slide, suddenly too preoccupied to admonish him for the salty language.

Once we reached the underground garage of the hospital, I gazed in astonishment at the convoy of black SUVs idling. "What's all this?"

"This," he said, stabbing his index finger at the SUVs, "is the price we pay for your actions."

He wasn't mincing words. They hit me like a brick and left a bruise. It was a whole new level of control freak, completely out of hand—even for him. But if I was now a prisoner, the cage had been fashioned by my own hands. This was the price for lying to him. And I couldn't make a stink about it when he was in such a state. I knew him too well for that. It would only cause him to entrench more firmly. All I could do was be patient and pray he would come to his senses as soon as possible. Blindly, I reached up in an instinctive move to rub my gold cross and remembered it had been lost. My mother's cross...another piece of her gone.

"Stay," he ordered, and walked away to discuss something with Gideon.

As we pulled out of the underground lot, insect-like creatures swarmed the SUVs, snapping pictures and hurling inaudible questions at us. My careful house of cards was quickly collapsing. Sooner or later the paparazzi would get what they wanted and my face would be plastered on every Internet site and tabloid newspaper in the world. The Albanian authorities wouldn't have to look too hard to find me.

The drive back to the estate was tense, the silence in the car suffocating, an unquantifiable distance separating us. I noticed that he'd shaved. His hair was once again perfect, his clothing immaculate. His literal and metaphorical armor was back on. Remote, unreachable, this was the same man I'd met all those months ago. A part he played a little too well.

He stared out the window without making any contact, eye or otherwise. If it was meant to be a punishment, then he succeeded spectacularly. I'd never felt more alone. My muscles, what was left of them that is, trembled uncontrollably even though it was the middle of August and well in the eighties.

"What happened to Sergio and Etienne?"

Sebastian's gaze flickered over me in an impersonal study before it swung back out to the passing scenery. "Arrested on drug trafficking charges. The boy pled down. It was his first offense. The older one is going away for a long time." I was glad to hear that Sergio had been spared, and prayed he would use it as an opportunity to take a different path in life. He wasn't cut out for a life of crime.

"Do you have any idea how lucky you are that I found

you." It was pretty clear it was a rhetorical question. "You could've spent the rest of your natural life as someone's personal fuckpet."

His crudeness achieved the desired effect. I cringed, cowed by the truth of his words. Human trafficking had risen exponentially in recent years. I wouldn't have been surprised to hear that Yuri had a hand in that as well.

"You said not to worry about Paisley, but you never explained why."

A slight smile lifted one corner of his mouth while his gaze remained out the window. "She's busy putting out her own dumpster fire. She doesn't have time to fuck with my life anymore."

He sounded bored, his bloodlust quenched. I didn't like it one bit. There was an undercurrent of maliciousness I'd never sensed in him before. Then again, I'd never seen anyone threaten him, either.

"You're being purposely vague."

He reached into his computer bag and pulled out a tabloid magazine, the last thing on earth I would ever have expected Sebastian to be carrying around. I was about to tease him when his expression checked me. He handed me the magazine and steered his gaze out the window again.

On the front cover was a picture of Sebastian. The caption over his head kicked me in the stomach. **In Love With His Very Own Cinderella**. *Good Lord, how ridiculous*. I quickly flipped to the article and devoured every word. The story was completely airbrushed, Photoshopped until only the barest resemblance to the real story remained. How we'd fallen in love when I was working for him as a lowly housekeeper. How we were getting married in some exotic location like Fiji.

"Where did they get this nonsense?"

"From me," he calmly admitted. His eyes connected with mine, which were bright with shock. "Let's just say the best defense is a good offense. That reminds me, I don't want you seeing your friend anymore. It's too dangerous. She's living with a hardened criminal."

My gaze swung back to him. The casual tone he used did nothing to diminish the significance of what he had just demanded of me. Because it was abundantly clear there was no room for discussion on it.

"What?" I blurted out.

"You heard me," he warned, aiming a heated glare in my direction. I searched his face for a sign of weakness, something that told me that there was a way to reason with him, but there was none. His Highness was back, firmly standing on the other side of the fortress walls.

There was once a time when I would've laughed in his face at merely suggesting such a thing, much less commanding me. I'd prided myself on my independence, on the power I possessed to walk away from anything and anyone at will. Self-preservation had trumped everything else. But the ugly truth was that with him, I had failed miserably. I knew that I could never leave him again. Walking away from him had taught me a harsh lesson, that my love for him was my greatest weakness—and that he knew it terrified me.

✱✱✱

Steeped in silence, the rest of the car ride was excruciating, my nerves pulled tight. I only began to relax when the driveway came into view. Sebastian ignored every attempt I made to assure him that I *indeed* still possessed the ability to walk. Without a word, he lifted me out of the car and carried me into the house.

The staff congregated in the foyer as if they were expecting the arrival of the Duchess of Cambridge. Mortified, all the attention made me shrink and press myself closer to Sebastian's chest, wishing I could melt into him and fade away. With an entourage of the staff trailing after us, I was shuttled to his bedroom. Mrs. Arnaud caught my expression and, to my great relief, rounded everyone up and ushered them down the hall.

"I have a wonderful consommé with vegetables and rice if you're hungry," Mrs. Arnaud suggested with a sweet smile.

"Can you throw in a cow as well?" I joked because I *could* have eaten a cow. My appetite came storming back with a vengeance.

Her deep blue eyes instantly lit up. "*Bien sûr*! I'll bring up lunch for two," she exclaimed. Then she fired off a list of dishes that made my stomach gurgle in anticipation.

"Not for me."

"Yes—you must eat. You've lost too much weight," Mrs. Arnaud insisted gently.

"At least a stone," I added. When Sebastian stared back blankly, I clarified, "Over fifteen pounds."

He didn't argue. His gaze fell on the counterpane, glaring at it as if it had offended him in some way. Mrs. Arnaud hurried out of the bedroom before she gave Sebastian the opportunity to change his mind. As soon as we were alone, he began tucking the sheets around me.

"Sebastian…" Nothing. He didn't spare me a glance as he worked with single-minded focus usually reserved for balancing the national budget and performing brain surgery. "Darling, I'm not an infant, stop swaddling me."

He stood straight, his hands on his hips and those once imposing swimmer's shoulders curving in exhaustion. A loud sigh slipped out of him. Though the tension left him, the sadness remained. He raked his fingers through his hair. He brushed his palm roughly over his face before his amber eyes met mine again.

"I'd like to bubble wrap you and lock you away." His lips pressed together in a sullen pout.

"But you can't. So instead you will crawl into bed next to me and let me hold you." I knew that if I showed any sign of relenting, it would only embolden him. This need to hoard and protect me could easily consume him if I allowed it.

Holding my gaze, he slowly lifted his hand to cup my face, ran his thumb over my jaw and bottom lip before he kissed me tenderly. "I have work to do." His eyes moved away in a guilty expression. I reached out for him but he caught my wrist and held it between us.

"Sebastian, please." I couldn't hide the ache in my voice.

Without glancing my way again, he said, "I'll come up later to check on you. Try to get some rest," and walked out.

He wasn't simply leaving. He was walking away from me.

***

In spite of my vehement avowal that I was feeling much stronger, after a fortifying meal I passed out early and slept like the dead through the night. The following morning, I awoke to the sound of the shower running.

Next to me, the pillow was perfectly smooth. My breath caught and a sharp pain suddenly gripped my chest, the first crack in the bubble of numbness surrounding me. He was pulling away from me. And if I let him, how long would it take before there was nothing left to salvage?

If he wasn't going to talk to me willingly, I figured an ambush was the best course of action. I walked into the bathroom and sat on the edge of the tub, next to the shower. Then I waited, watching quietly, riveted on the naked standard of masculine perfection behind the glass door. He hadn't noticed me sitting there.

He was a vision, a dream I once had of an archangel falling to earth to seduce me. Steam clung to the glass, condensing into a halo around him. His head was tipped down, his eyes closed as the water poured down his neck and followed the long curve of his elegant back, over and in between his rear end. Quintessentially male. There wasn't a bit of softness anywhere on him. Including his expression.

He squirted shower gel in his palm and ran his hands across his chest, up and down his arms, in between his legs. Eyelids heavy, water drops clinging to his long lashes like rain on a spider's web—his eyes fluttered closed. Enthralled, I lost track of time and place as all my senses converged onto him, mesmerized by the utterly sensual picture he painted.

That's when a pang of shame hit me. I was about to leave, to give him some privacy, when he grabbed his penis and exhaled harshly. He stroked himself from root to tip and his body hardened instantly. Prickling heat blazed up my neck. My heart was a percussion instrument pounding inside my chest. Below my waist everything came back to life, an aching emptiness I hadn't felt in ages growing stronger by the second. He tugged on his erection roughly and cupped his sac. Moaning, his head fell forward. I was paralyzed by the sight of him pleasuring himself, torn between announcing my presence and watching.

His hand kept pumping faster and faster. He was getting close, his breathing harsh. Primal sounds erupted out of him. He let go of his sac, slapped the hand onto the shower wall. The muscles of his back and arms were bulging and rigid, in the way that comes right before release. A loud, almost pained groan broke loose. Head thrown back, eyes squeezed shut. He exhaled harshly as he climaxed, the evidence of his orgasm splashing onto the marble wall. So beautiful lost in passion.

Seconds later, his eyes blinked open and instantly connected with my wide-open stare. His gaze fathomless. His thoughts inaccessible. There wasn't a bit of surprise, joy, or mischief to be found anywhere. His expression gave nothing away.

Mine, on the other hand, gave everything away. I could feel

two hot circles burning on my cheeks. Never breaking eye contact, he turned the water off and grabbed the towel I held out for him.

"Thanks," is all he said as he stepped out of the shower and wrapped it around his waist.

"That's it?"

"What do you want me to say?"

"Where did you sleep last night?"

Walking past me, he headed for the closet. "Library…I was up late and fell asleep on the couch."

"Sebastian—"

"I'm late for a meeting." His tone made it abundantly clear that the discussion was over. I knew it was my turn to practice patience—he deserved a hell of a lot more than that from me—but his cool demeanor was really starting to get on my nerves.

I followed him into the closet where he walked around naked without an ounce of self-consciousness. He took his sweet time picking out a shirt and suit while I waited for him to deign me with a moment of his attention, my irritation growing with every second that ticked by. If this was a battle of wills, he was winning. He looked cool and composed. I, on the other hand, was a hair's breadth from losing it completely. So I did the only thing I could—I distracted myself. I was busy doing just that, studying the muscular globes of his gorgeous backside, when he glanced over his shoulder and caught me.

"Do you need anything?"

Do I need anything? Hmmm, let me think…

I needed to conk some sense into him. His indifference kindled my anger. "As a matter of fact, Your Highness, I do. I need you to talk to me. You always do this when you're stewing."

"I told you, I'm late for a meeting."

Right.

He yanked on his boxer briefs, snapping the elastic of the waistband forcefully.

"What time will you be home tonight?"

He pulled on his trousers and tucked his shirt in. "Late. Don't wait up for me."

I breathed out a heavy sigh. It was impossible to get through to him when he was like this. He draped a tie around his neck and grabbed a pair of handmade Stefano Bemer shoes from a collection of hundreds, purposely avoiding my pointed gaze.

As he walked past me, I laid my hand on his forearm. "Darling," I pleaded. Before I could get another word in he pried my hand off his arm, placed a kiss on it, and dropped it, walking out without another glance in my direction.

The sting of his brush-off quickly morphed into something darker. An indescribable rage began to fester, an abscess deep within me waiting to explode and spew its venom. I stood there for a full hour calming myself down. I'd prayed for the numbness plaguing me since I'd learned about the miscarriage to lift. What I couldn't have foreseen was that it had been replaced by a deep-seated anger that I didn't know how to handle. And I wasn't certain if it was directed at him, or at myself.

Chapter Four

BY EARLY AFTERNOON I WAS desperate for a distraction. Had I read every book in the library? It certainly felt that way. Bored to tears, I couldn't sit in bed for one more Godforsaken minute. A collection of clothing had magically found their way into the master closet in my absence. Boxes and bags from every store imaginable—from Galerie Lafayette to Valentino—were stacked to the roof. When I mentioned it to Sebastian, he dismissed it with a wave of his hand and said, "Send it back and get what you want." I had to admit that I loved every single thing he chose. The man had taste.

Grabbing a pair of black leggings and one of Sebastian's white oxfords, I dressed quickly and headed down to the kitchen to see if I could help Mrs. Arnaud with any of the chores.

"What are you doing out of bed?" Mrs. Arnaud asked, her expression a combination of concern and understanding. Whisk in hand, mixing bowl cradled against her body, she beat the batter for the madeleines with brisk, efficient strokes.

"If I have to stay there another minute, I will need to be committed to an insane asylum. I beg you, give me something to do." Slipping onto a stool, I placed my elbows on the counter and my head in my hands.

"I'll do the toilettes for God's sake, anything," I whined, gripping the roots of my short hair.

A wide smile swept across her face. Then she handed me

the mixing bowl and let me pour the batter into the madeleine shell forms while she began to dress the chicken she was preparing for dinner. Her eyes were still trained on the task at hand when she spoke. "How do you feel?"

"Depends on what you're referring to. Physically, I feel fine, getting stronger every day. Mentally, I'm not certain."

A meaningful silence unfurled between us.

"I had an abortion when I was twenty-five," she announced in her usual blunt, no-nonsense fashion. I sat up straighter, my attention captivated. "I told myself it was an act of mercy. Xavier would get violent when he drank..." Her voice faded while a shade of sadness remained on her face. "The doctor was young, inexperienced. I almost bled out after he...a vein ruptured." I was on the edge on my seat, my attention glued to her, while she continued to baste the chicken with olive oil and rosemary as if she hadn't just dropped a bomb on me. "I never conceived after that."

Her casual admission was all the permission I needed to unburden my soul. "I wasn't happy about the pregnancy," I blurted out, hiding my mouth behind my steepled fingers, as if the confession could somehow absolve me of the responsibility of what had happened, wipe away the shame and guilt I was drowning in. She glanced up then, and what I found in her warm blue eyes was a bottomless supply of understanding. "Not at first," I added quietly.

"You think that has something to do with the miscarriage?"

Instinctively, I reached up to rub my cross, a phantom limb I desperately missed. It took me a moment to remember it had been lost. "I don't know...it feels that way." Tears collected in the corners of my eyes. Fighting them, I bit the inside of my cheek hard enough to taste blood.

"Because you are grieving, and you want to find a reason for why it happened where there is none."

Those words hit home. Was I looking for reason in it? I

guess I was. My analytical self needed a reason. If I could take the blame for losing the baby, then maybe somehow I had control over what happened next. "How did you deal with it?"

She shrugged. "I lived my life one day at a time. Some were better than others. Then I met Olivier. Did you know he has a son?" The love and pride living on her face told me everything I needed to know. The surprise was plain on mine. Shame followed in its wake. I'd been so wrapped up in my own misery that I hadn't even known Olivier had a son.

"Jean Pierre was twelve when we met." Marianne spoke over her shoulder while she placed the chicken inside the oven.

"Does he not live in Switzerland? He's never been over."

"He's a journalist. A decorated war correspondent. Travels constantly. A week ago he was at the India/ Kashmir border. Next week, who knows," she said with a smile.

"You must be very proud. Does it worry you, that he's always in danger?"

"Yes. But he's a grown man. I haven't been able to protect him since he was a teenager."

"And his mother?" I asked, consumed with curiosity.

Marianne's face fell, her expression pained as her gaze steered back to me. "Murdered when they were still living in Algeria, walking home from grocery shopping late one evening."

Tragedy and heartbreak, the two equalizers. Young, old, rich, poor—no one was safe.

"Do you want a child? I know you have ambitions for your career." The magnitude of that question caused my breath to stall, the panic it evoked mitigated only by the gentle tone of her voice. There was no judgment in her expression while she waited patiently for my answer. My heart began to beat wildly as the truth came to light.

"Yes," I said, nodding. "With him."

A knowing smile tipped up the corners of Marianne's lips. "All is not lost—*oui*?"

"*Oui*."

***

As much as I wanted to believe my full strength had returned, it hadn't. After helping Marianne prepare the side dishes for dinner and cleaning up the kitchen, I was ready for another nap. I hadn't heard from Sebastian all day. The screaming silence had given me a tension headache. This chasm between us seemed to be growing wider by the minute.

It was early evening when I saw him again, right after my shower, as I entered the bedroom finger combing my short, wet hair and wearing one of his t-shirts with the Stanford logo on it. In some strange way it made me feel closer to him. The French doors that led to the balcony were open. He stood with his back to me, the heels of his hands resting on the wrought iron railing and his gaze fixed on the red slash that marked the horizon. We both watched the remains of the day faded away in a final blaze of glory.

The intensity of my feelings for this man still took me by surprise at times, making my heart race and my stomach drop as if I was dangling fifty stories high with no parachute and no voice to scream for help. He looked so alone, remote, holding himself apart from anything and anyone that could hurt him—including me. The urgency to wrap my arms around him and ruffle up some feeling was irresistible. I was about to do just that when his words checked me.

"I don't recognize what I feel for you. And it's not because I've never been in love before." The words seemed to flow out of him on a deep, exhausted exhale. "Calling it love doesn't seem enough." When he turned around, his face was absent of emotion. That concerned me more than his anger, or disapproval. He looked like the man I had met all those months ago, locked behind the impenetrable walls of his fortress. His eyes roamed over the t-shirt I wore. "I've never asked you...have you?"

This was a conversation I was not prepared to have. We had always tiptoed around the subject. He had never come right out and asked, and I'd never felt the need to pick at that scab.

"Have I what?"

"Been in love before?"

I chose my words carefully. "Once—a long time ago. But it's not the same thing. No two loves are alike. I was young and impressionable back then. I'm different now. I...I know better." My eyes dropped when it dawned on me that my behavior clearly illustrated otherwise. I had never thought of myself as a hypocrite, and yet, apparently I was.

"Who was he?"

"Someone from home," I said in a knee-jerk reaction. It wasn't home. It hadn't been home in a long time. "I mean, from Tirana...we were engaged."

Not only had Sebastian been married before, but almost a father. And yet, for some odd reason, the look of shock on his face made me feel guilty, as if I had somehow betrayed him.

"Engaged?" he repeated absently. I could see him digesting this new piece of information and trying to make sense of it, trying to rationalize his feelings. His face told me everything I needed to know. It didn't take long for curiosity to replace surprise. "Why did you break up?"

My focus shifted to the hem of the t-shirt I was busy fiddling with. "He wanted to move away and I didn't want to go with him." My eyes lifted to find his still glued on me, assessing me shrewdly. The silence grew heavy. Then, after what felt like an eternity, he nodded.

"I have a theory that the more you suffer, the more deeply

you love." I surprised even myself with that admission. No doubt it had something to do with a driving need to earn his forgiveness.

"That explains what I feel for you."

"Sebastian, I—" I wanted to tell him how sorry I was, but the words rang hollow in my mind. He was right. I didn't recognize the feeling. Calling it regret didn't do it justice.

"You won't even give me a chance to disappoint you," he said in a low voice, a frustrated sigh tacked on the end. Facing me, he squared his shoulders and crossed his arms. "You don't trust me and I don't know how to change that."

"That's not true. I do trust you."

His demeanor transformed instantly, his eyes narrowed and his chin tilted down. "Don't lie to me—ever." The glare he followed that up with was lethal. The discussion I had with Marianne months ago, in which she warned me of Sebastian's inability to forgive any form of duplicity, came back to me in a sudden rush. All I could do was lay my cards out on the table and hope he accepted the offering.

"Before you, I loved two men my entire life. My father and the man I was engaged to. I was betrayed by both of them… you're the first person I've loved that hasn't let me down. I *do* trust you."

"Then who the fuck is Veronica Savarini?" He was battling to contain his anger. As clear as day, it was in his voice, in the taut lines of his muscles. He pulled something out of his back pocket and held it up. My Italian passport. He must've found it when they searched my apartment in Pâquis. On his face was the verdict. In the court of his opinion I had been tried and convicted as a liar.

A beat later he walked past me, into the bedroom, where he began undressing. Yanking off his tie. Unbuttoning his French blue shirt with quick, jerky movements of his hands. It gaped open. He hadn't worn an undershirt that day and the lines of his cobbled abdomen stole my attention. I watched his fingers unsnap his pants and slide the zipper down, exposing a trail of fuzzy dark hair and his black boxer briefs slung low on his lean hips. Almost instantly my entire body heated. When my gaze climbed back up to his face, I found him staring at me with a mix of lust and fury in his eyes.

"I did what I had to to survive."

"You didn't answer my question!" he shouted. It startled me. But the anger festering inside of me began churning like a cyclone, gathering power and momentum. I snapped, accusations and blame springing out of me.

"How dare you stand there and judge me! When have you ever missed a meal or lost sleep because you didn't feel safe? I've spent the last six years looking over my shoulder, in a state of high anxiety over something I had *nothing* to do with and no way to prove it! I'm not *lord* of any manor. I can't just throw money at a problem and it disappears! Yes—I bought the passport because it made me feel just a little bit better to know that I had something to fall back on—a way to hide. And this wouldn't even be an issue if I hadn't met you. If I'd never fallen in love!"

The silence that followed stretched for miles. We both stood there staring each other down, measuring each other up. He was the one to break the stalemate.

"Who is she?" he asked quietly, his anger conspicuously absent.

The fight left me all at once, the aftertaste of adrenaline making me weak. I walked over to the chaise lounge, near the fireplace, and slumped down on the armrest. "A dead girl." My gaze fell to my hands, palm to palm, fingers laced together neatly. "She looked like me. That's what the guy I bought it from said anyway."

Slowly, he walked over and cupped my face, tilting it up to search my eyes. "Do you ever regret—us?"

I'd never seen such stark vulnerability on his face before, as if the fate of his life hinged upon my answer. I clasped his wrists, could feel the anxious beat of his heart under the pads of my fingers.

"When I was on the run, when things seemed completely hopeless and I was certain I would be caught and sent back to Albania, the one thing that gave me peace was you. I could never regret loving you…you're the best thing that's ever happened to me."

Leaning in, he kissed me with such passion I fell off the armrest. Then he sat in the chaise, and pulled me onto his lap. I wrapped my arms around his neck and pressed my face between his throat and collarbone. The spot that belonged to me, in the place where I belonged. I pressed my nose against his skin, and breathed in his comforting scent.

"We're meeting with an attaché from the Albanian government in a few days." His casual announced wreaked havoc on me.

"What am I going to do?" I mumbled.

"You mean what are *we* going to do?"

I pulled away far enough to examine his face and nodded, because in reality I was powerless to do anything except admit defeat. A predatory glint sparked in his eyes. His lips curved up slightly.

"We're going to throw money at the problem." Then, before I could utter another word of objection, he kissed me.

Chapter Five

ALTHOUGH THE STAFF WENT ABOUT their business as if nothing of great consequence had occurred, smiles were tight and eye contact rare and shifty. Even François avoided talking to me, unsure how to approach the subject no doubt. An invisible line now existed between us that never did before and the awkwardness marked the boundary. I'm ashamed to admit I did my best to avoid them, too.

There was no avoiding the two heavily armed men who trailed after me everywhere I went though. The loss of privacy was a serious annoyance. Like when I had to pick up tampons at the pharmacy only to have them standing right behind me, an arm's length away. I was so irritated I turned and asked Justin what brand he used. The one time I attempted to discuss it with Sebastian I was leveled with a searing gaze that could've turned me into a pillar of salt.

My strength had almost fully returned. Less than a week had passed since I'd been out of the hospital, and already I'd stopped needing to take breaks, or naps. That's why when Mrs. Arnaud informed me that Sebastian's beloved hawks needed to be fed their lunch, I volunteered.

My head plagued with heavy thoughts, I decided that fresh air was exactly what the doctor ordered. *Doctor?* I hadn't given thought to my career once since waking up in the hospital. Strange how losing something I never knew I wanted had reprioritized my entire life.

The pale blue sky was cobbled with white cumulus clouds, the humidity thick. I wandered aimlessly through the manicured gardens shielding my eyes under the roof of my fingers from the summer sun. The flowerbeds were in full bloom. A sight for sore eyes. The irises a shock of ultraviolet so intense it was impossible to ignore them. The rosebushes hadn't been pruned yet. A tumble of flashy pink spilled over the boxwood hedge that did a poor job of containing their glory.

"How do you feel?" Charlotte stood a few paces behind me. The joy of seeing her put a huge grin on my face. I gave her a wry glance, my eyebrow hitching up. "Many things, but above all, tired of everyone asking me that. I'm fine—where have you been by the way? Hiding from me?"

That elicited a hesitant smile out of her. "I wanted to give you two some time." That made me think about how little time Sebastian and I had spent together.

"I'm going to feed the falcons. Want to join me?" I said, before my mood turned sour.

Nodding quickly, she jogged to close the distance between us. The silence seemed to mark the boundary of an important conversation we both didn't know how to begin. She blew out a deep breath. "You can't imagine what it was like around here when...when Gideon told him what had happened."

I *could* imagine. That's what bothered me most. I noticed her examining my head and automatically ran a hand over my short hair. Our eyes met. "What?" I asked when she rolled hers.

A wide smile broke across her face. "Only you could make a shaved head look chic. Being your friend is kind of annoying at times." I couldn't help but chuckle at her dramatic delivery.

"Hardly, although it seems to be growing in quickly. At least, I can't see my scalp, or the stitches anymore." An awkward silence followed. "Charlotte, you understand why I did it?" Her blank stare induced me to explain. "Paisley found out and threatened to ruin him, to go to the tabloids and make it sound like I was after his money, that his judgment had been compromised. I'm an illegal...I was pregnant—not to mention the trouble I'm already in."

"What trouble?"

"Remember the scandal I told you about? The one that involved my father?" She responded with a quick nod.

"He..." I swallowed the bitter taste of shame. "I'm... suspected of embezzling money from the university where my father was the president." At her wide-eyed stare, I rushed to defend myself. "Which I had nothing to do with of course—proving it is a different matter though."

"*Shite.*"

"Exactly. It could destroy Sebastian's reputation. It still might. I haven't been able to speak to him about it, and I'm really worried."

"She found out you were pregnant?" she asked, her tone overly careful.

I looked out over the meadow as I spoke. "Yes." The silence caused my gaze to return to hers. "Are you mad that I didn't tell you?"

"Not mad," she replied, shaking her head. "Maybe a little disappointed—I wish you would've let me help."

Sweet Charlotte. I was so grateful for her friendship. "You couldn't have helped. Nobody could have."

Her face lit up. "I thought he was going to tear Isabelle limb from limb. Mrs. Arnaud is the only thing that checked him."

"Why are you smiling? I don't particularly care what happens to her, but she must've been scared out of her mind."

"Oh she was, trust me."

"Where is she now?"

"I don't know. Bear gave her a ride into town." I made a

mental note to talk to Sebastian about it later. I didn't want to see anyone wind up destitute and homeless on my account. After all, she was only the messenger.

When the mews came into view, a strange sinking sensation took hold of me. Something didn't feel right. My pulse quickened. Instinctively, I began scanning the area. Whatever Charlotte was saying faded away as the rustle of the oaks and the singing of birds drowned out her voice.

"Wait," I said, placing a hand on her arm to stop her.

"What is it?"

"I don't know yet."

When nothing in particular caught my attention, we continued on. The feeling refused to go away, however. Only when we got closer did I realize how right I was. The bloodcurdling scream Charlotte let out mirrored the one I heard in my head. Except I couldn't speak—I couldn't make a sound if I tried.

There was blood everywhere. Stained crimson, downy white feathers lay scattered around the yard, some tumbling away with the wind. Soft footsteps approached. The snapping of a tree branch startled me. I whipped around and found Bear and Justin standing right behind me; I was completely unaware that they had been following us the whole time.

"Fuck," one of them quietly swore.

Sebastian's hawks were dead. Those beautiful, noble creatures had been heinously butchered. The birds had been skinned and beheaded. The evidence nailed to the posts the birds once used as a perch, attached to the wood with a large hunting knife. Behind me one of the men murmured something on the phone. His words lost their shape, the sound of my heart breaking blotting everything else out.

"Did you speak to him?"

"To Ben—they're both on their way," Bear answered while he inspected the crime scene. In the distance, I noticed some of

Ben's other men walking through the forest surrounding the estate, heavily armed and on a mission.

"Who would have done this?" Charlotte sobbed, her fingers resting over her mouth. Tears caught on her lashes. She wiped at them furiously before they could run down her cheeks. I rubbed her arm in comfort.

"Whoever tried to kill Sebastian did," I answered, the evidence plain to see. Like the bullet he took months ago, this was another warning.

Justin touched the carcass nailed to the post. "Cold."

"Vera, I have to get you to cover. Let's go." Bear's voice, however forceful, held a hint of fear in it as well. Moving into position, Bear and Justin's extra-large bodies flanked Charlotte and me. They scanned the area furtively as we walked at a brisk pace until we reached the safety of the house.

Twenty minutes later I heard gravel firing off under the tires of the Mercedes 550—a trip that should've taken at least forty-five minutes. It skidded to a stop in front of the manor. The front doors banged open and loud voices followed.

I hurried out of the kitchen to find Sebastian eating up ground in my direction, Ben right behind him. His fiery gaze was pinned on the man standing next to me.

Poor Bear. I knew what was coming.

"How the fuck could you have let this happen!"

More men I didn't recognized poured in through the front door. At least twenty and all of them heavily armed. The air was suddenly thick with too much testosterone. It would've taken garden shears to cut the tension. Sebastian hadn't yet spared me a glance. Instinctively, I reached out and placed a quelling hand on his forearm. He jerked, as if only now realizing that I stood a foot away. His eyes slid to me, traveled over every salient point on my face and body. His lips tightened, anger emanating from every fiber of his being. Standing this close, I'm surprised I didn't get a third degree burn from it.

"We've been running perimeter checks every thirty minutes—" Justin said in his defense. He should've known better. The rest of his sentence was silenced by Sebastian's withering glare.

"Vera was in the house."

A sudden stillness fell upon the crowd of men. The low, gravelly murmur, the opaque, lifeless look in Sebastian's eyes raised the menace to a whole other level. He didn't look like the man I loved. I didn't know *this* man.

"I know," Bear murmured, guilt coloring his voice.

Justin interrupted with, "The men combed the property." Sebastian's glare slid over to him again. "Nothing yet," Justin added, "and the birds were cold."

But Sebastian had already stopped listening. He was halfway down the hall, walking towards the back of the manor, taking longer steps than was wise and stressing the injured leg. Knowing where he was headed, I hurried after him, because in no way did I want him facing it alone.

✱✱✱

Ten of us stood behind him without making a sound. He stared at the carnage for what seemed like forever. His broad back was stiff, his shoulders tight under the close cut of his handmade suit. He looked ready to shatter from all the tension. His fingers, poking through the chicken wire, closed around it so tightly I'm surprised the metal didn't slice them open. A long tail feather was stuck on the fencing. I watched him pluck it off and twirl it between his thumb and index finger, wincing when I realized that the tip, soaked in blood, had stained his fingers.

I couldn't see his expression. And yet I didn't have to. His posture told me of the sorrow, the sense of loss. Pain—the common denominator of the human race. Ask people what love is and you'll get a different answer every time. But pain... pain we can pretty much agree on.

I couldn't stand idly by a second longer. Afraid to startle him, I walked slowly, very gently encircled my arms around his waist, and placed my cheek on his back. "I'm so sorry," I murmured, my voice cracking.

He lifted one arm high, giving me the chance to come around and bury my face—and my anguish—in his chest. Both his arms wrapped around me tightly, pulling me flush against him, offering me comfort when he needed it most. Sweet, selfless man. He kissed the top of my head, and in return I kissed the place over his heart.

"Don't touch anything. We'll send the knife to the lab." It was Ben's voice that abruptly ended the silence.

"You won't find any prints," Sebastian flatly stated.

"No...I don't think so."

Prying me off of him, Sebastian turned his attention on Bear and Justin. "I want every inch of this place locked tighter than a nun's cunt. Get a hundred more men if you have to. I don't want a fucking breeze to get in—am I making myself clear?" A chastened look on both their faces, the two men nodded.

"When are you leaving for Paris?" he asked Ben.

"Couple of days."

"Is this about the man they arrested? That has information on your car accident?"

"Yes." Sebastian's expression was as cold as the tone of his reply.

"The bullet wound—they meant to miss, didn't they?"

"Yes."

After that we all walked silently back to the house. I laced my fingers through his, holding onto his hand with a death grip while his attention wandered far away from me. Once we got back to the house, he disappeared while the rest of us loitered in the kitchen. I figured he went in search of a dark place to brood, and I didn't want to push him if that's what he needed. I certainly could relate.

"I can't get the scent of blood out of my nose." Charlotte brushed away the tears still quietly falling down her cheeks. She sat at the counter while I stood across from her near the stove, waiting for the kettle of water to boil.

"Cut the shit, Beckwith. Now's not the time for your drama." Ben's voice was so caustic it could've stripped paint off a car.

Slack-jawed, I turned to find his expression impassive. Leaning his shoulder against the window with arms crossed in front, his tattooed biceps, shockingly large, stretched the sleeves of the white t-shirt he wore to within an inch of its life.

Charlotte's rage was as clear as daylight. Brown eyes narrowed, red faced, the vein on her forehead ready to burst. I braced for what was coming. "Winters." Her voice was eerily calm. Ben glanced at her, his eyes as cool as peppermint. "Anybody ever tell you what a FUCKING ARSEHOLE you are?" She stalked out of the kitchen after that.

"Ben?"

Those pale, green gray eyes met mine. "Why do you have to be like that with her?" Whatever was going on—this was out of character for him. If anything, Ben was always the one cracking jokes when things got tense.

"What can I say? She brings out the best in me."

I was already running on fumes and dealing with whatever was going on between these two was not at the top of my list, only the wellbeing of one tall blonde was. That's why I turned my attention to the shrill of the boiling kettle, triple bagged my chamomile tea, and kept my mouth shut.

✸✸✸

Night fell as abruptly as a heavy drape of inky velvet. By

eight, concern surpassed patience. I went in search of him, certain that he was industriously adding more bricks to the wall he had already built up around himself. I couldn't just stand by and let it happen.

I found him in his office with the lights off, only a shaft of moonlight as respite from total darkness. Sitting behind his desk, the chair was tilted back and his gaze fixed on the ceiling. Even in the dark there was no mistaking the anguish etched into his profile.

"Do you want to be alone?" I asked as I stood in the doorway.

His eyes ran up and down the length of my body as sensually as a mink glove caressing my skin. "No," he said in a quiet voice. "Come here."

He didn't have to ask twice. I ran into his open arms and curled up on his lap. Drawing me closer, he kissed me softly. Two dry brushes of his firm lips on my temple. Then he pulled a small, leather box out of a desk drawer and turned on the lights with a remote.

"I meant to give this to you sooner."

I stared at the leather box with the word Cartier stamped on it. When I didn't take it, he opened it and held it up for me. Inside, on a leather pillow, sat a small cross made entirely of diamonds. The stones caught the soft, overhead light and turned it into fire.

"I know it's not the same thing—it's not your mother's. But I thought...you might like this." His voice faded away as I continued to stare at it. "If you don't like it, I'll return it."

At the disappointment in his voice my eyes snapped up to his. The light had revealed all his heavy thoughts, his burdens and sorrow. He wore them all on his face. "I love it," I said emphatically. "I love it because it's from you. If you gave me sticks and stones I would love them just as much."

He managed to muster up a smile for me, though it didn't

reach his eyes. He removed the cross from the box and nimbly fastened the chain around my neck. Gingerly, I touched the stones, the platinum backing cool against my skin. Resting on my sternum, his gift lay over my heart, protecting what belonged to him. And always would.

Chapter Six

I WOKE UP SUDDENLY, GASPING for air. Dazed and confused, I searched the dark bedroom for whatever it was that had roused me from deep sleep. Only when I glanced at the spot next to me did I realize what it was. The bed was empty, the sheets pristine where he should've been.

A cold hand slid up my spine and a profound sense of loneliness swept through me. He was deserting me a little at a time, shutting down, even though he had me trapped in this fortress with him. Instinctively, I knew that if I sat back and did nothing, he would disappear on me forever. I'd be damned if I'd let him go without a fight, however.

I jumped out of bed and padded down the hallway to where a number of the guest bedrooms were located. One by one I found them empty. Except for the last. I stood in the open doorway fidgeting nervously, a million dreadful scenarios suddenly running through my mind.

What if he turned me away? What if he didn't want me anymore? What if he didn't love me anymore?

The curtains were drawn open. He was on his back with his hands tucked behind his head, his chest bare and the sheet covering his lower body. Moonlight, spilling in, painted him in silver while everything else in the room receded into the darkness. It was as if the moon had eyes only for him. Not a man. An ethereal creature with the moon as a lover. Stoic. Resolute. Alone. Out of reach for the rest of us mere mortals.

"What is it?" His raspy voice jerked me out of my reverie.
"I couldn't sleep."
More silence.
"Me neither."
"I'm so sorry about the hawks." My voice trembled as the last words left my lips. I ached for him, the sweet boy who rescued injured animals and nursed them back to health, the one who loved deeply and completely. What had love ever taught him other than loss and pain? And I was guilty of perpetuating it.

I stood rooted to the spot, waiting for him to make a move, to give me some sign of what he was thinking. When he propped himself up on an elbow and lifted the counterpane, I didn't waste a second jumping into bed with him. The urge to touch him, to close the literal and figurative distance between us was overwhelming. Pressing myself against his hard body, I burrowed as close as I could possibly get and soaked up his heat. I caressed his cheek and his eyelids became heavy, fluttering. When they blinked open again, what I saw staring back at me broke my heart. So much sorrow.

"What are you doing in this bedroom?"

"I didn't want to keep you up. I haven't been sleeping lately."

"Keep me up? I can't sleep without you beside me anymore...we need to talk."

Grabbing my hand off his cheek, he kissed the palm and held it between us. "Can we do this some other time?"

"No, I'm afraid we can't. I'm afraid that if another second goes by and we don't talk about this I may lose you forever."

Rolling onto his back, eyes fixed on the ceiling, he said, "You'll never lose me."

"I feel like I already have." When he didn't respond, the fear gained momentum. "I know you blame me for losing the baby." My voice disappeared on me as I forced the last word out. "No, don't," I pleaded when he tried to interrupt. "You have no idea how sorry I am. I'm so damn sorry. But there was no other way. None that would keep you safe, keep the bank safe." My voice broke, my panic spinning out of control.

He pushed me down onto my back and hovered, careful to keep his weight on his elbows. His eyes, liquid soft and full of empathy, searched my face. His fingers raked through the short crop of dark hair that was now long enough to fall over my forehead. Touching his lips to mine, he brushed his back and forth.

"I don't blame you," he said quietly.

"Then why are you pushing me away?"

Exhaling a sharp breath, he shook his head. "I..." He became agitated, inhaling and exhaling sharply.

"What is it, my love?" I asked, cradling his face between my cupped hands. Another interminable silence followed.

"I failed you...I failed, again." His voice was barely above a whisper. Moving down my body, he placed a kiss between my breasts, over my heart. Then he wrapped his arms around my waist and held on as if he faced an eternity in purgatory and I was his only chance at salvation. I soothed him the only way I could, stroking his head and whispering words of love and encouragement.

"I'll be damned if I let you take the blame—if it's anyone's fault it's mine. Stop punishing yourself. You've done enough of that to last ten lifetimes."

Words can be misconstrued, manipulated, measured. But a touch...a touch never lies. He began to stroke my body over the thin cotton of my nightgown. The love was there, his touch worshipful. His large hands cupped my breasts, his fingers drawing circles around my nipples. Tender, light touches that drove me crazy. He teased them until they stood at attention, begging for him. I felt the suction of his mouth and my body bowed off the bed.

A wave of lust so intense broke over me that I gripped the sheets tight enough to pull them off the mattress. I pushed him onto his back and straddled his lean hips. Underneath me he was rock hard, his erection peeking out over the top of his boxers. Instinct took over. I ground my pelvis against him, and he sucked in a harsh breath.

"I miss you," I whispered, the words backed by the longing in my eyes and voice.

His attention on me was absolute. The importance of the moment not lost on either one of us. When he didn't make a move, I impatiently ripped the nightgown over my head and flung it off, the drive to get closer, to be skin to skin relentless. More than ever I wanted him inside of me. As if that sacred connection could cement that we were still us, that my actions hadn't damaged us beyond repair.

Leaning forward, I planted my hands next to his head. He reached for me then, his hands skating from my waist to my shoulder blades, and pulled me down closer, kissed me. That's when I felt it, the slight tremble of the hands that held me in place.

"I need you," I murmured, my voice quivering from the struggle to contain a surfeit of emotion. "Please." Begging was not beneath me. I would've crawled over hot coals for him.

His hands slowed down, his muscles stilled, every slight nuance of his body language so clear to me, so dear to me. He was withdrawing in flesh and mind. A bolt of fear raced up my backbone. It conjured awful images of him with other women, of me without him. Panic set in. I kissed him roughly.

"Hey," he crooned as his thumbs caressed my cheeks. "Easy." His lips gently brushed mine.

"Make love to me." I sounded desperate and needy. Not my best moment, but I was too far gone to care.

"Not yet. Don't worry, I'll take care of you."

"No," I practically shouted. "I need you—*you*." And then it hit me. "You're not attracted to me anymore? Is that it?"

I slid off his body, onto my back, and covered my face with my hands, my fingers rubbing my brow as mortification turned my skin a deep shade of scarlet. One finger at a time he peeled my hand away from my face and placed it on his impossibly hard erection, pushing it up and down its swollen length. A guttural moan rattled in his chest and surged up his throat.

"I could drill through granite with this. Does that answer your question?"

His tone, sharp and angry, took me by surprise. A most juvenile, insecure part of me felt vindicated, and yet the part that could still reason knew that men could get hard by physical stimulation.

"Then why won't you make love to me?"

"It's too soon. I want to speak to the doctor first."

"I'm fine," I disputed, though I didn't get to finish. My words were swallowed up by a deep kiss. His skilled fingers slipped under my panties and slid between my thighs.

My train of thought lost. My will to argue faded away. Fire shot over my skin, radiating from where he touched me to everywhere else. My knees fell open. My hips lifted off the bed when the pressure of his fingers eased off. I whined for him not to leave me. Gripping his wrist, I dug my short fingernails into his skin, only stopping when he resumed the sweet torture.

His fingers teased me into a frenzy while he nipped my nipple, licked and sucked. Three fingers caressed my clit. Down they traveled and slipped inside, over and over, giving me just enough to leave me wanting more. Between the temptation of his hard body thrusting against my hip and the sensation between my thighs, I was pulled tighter than Artemis' bow. His mouth fastened onto my nipple and tugged in rhythm with the push and stroke of his hand. And I was lost…and lost…and lost.

Slow to build, once the climax broke over me I was shaking from the force of it, a burst that spread as quick as wildfire. I cried out his name and clawed his back, his shoulder, any part of him I could reach. He eased me down gently. So much reverence in the way he touched me it brought tears to my eyes.

When semi-coherent thought returned, I turned my head on the pillow and watched him. Propped up on an elbow, his hand gently stroked up and down my body. He was still hard. I reached over to touch him over his boxers, but he grabbed my wrist and stopped me.

Being denied brought out every puerile insecurity I ever had. I felt vulnerable, unsure of myself. "Let me do something for you," I murmured.

"Not tonight. I just want to hold you and sleep."

"But—"

Interrupting, he reiterated, "That's all I need right now." Whatever was going on in his head, his eyes kept hidden. He brushed his thumb on the delicate skin inside my wrist, soothing me into compliance.

"All right." Wounded, I turned away. He didn't let me get far though. He pulled me back into him, his large body cupping mine. A heavy muscular arm wrapped snuggly around my waist. I exhaled the breath I didn't know I was holding.

For hours I stayed awake listening to the comforting sound of his breathing. I knew exactly when he let go and fell asleep. After an epic orgasm that at the very least should've helped me relax, I couldn't shake the feeling of unease. Regardless of what he'd said, he was quietly slipping away. And I had no idea how to stop it from happening.

Chapter Seven

THE FOLLOWING MORNING I FOUND my entourage in the kitchen. Bear and Justin were seated at the oak table, cleaning their handguns, leaning back with their legs spread apart. Their oversized bodies dwarfed the wooden chairs they occupied. The sight of all those weapons scattered on the table made my skin crawl. After what had happened with the red-tailed hawks however, I didn't need to be reminded that the threat on Sebastian's life was very real.

"Marianne?"

"In the garden," Bear answered.

I found her fondling the tomatoes, fat, ruby red ones hanging low on the delicate green stalks which sagged under their weight. She heard me approaching and an affectionate smile spread across her face. Seeing that gap between her front teeth lifted my spirits.

"Do you have a moment?" I asked, my eyes falling on the bounty of vegetables overgrowing the fencing.

"Anything for you."

I truly love this woman. The words rang loudly not just in my mind, but also my heart. My eyes timidly met hers. I didn't know how to begin. Marianne was as close to a mother as Sebastian had—if anyone knew how to get through to him it was she—though discussing your lover with the person who raised him was awkward business.

"I don't know what to do with him," I announced, shifting

nervously from foot to foot. "He's keeping me at arm's length."

Plucking one by one off the vine, she placed the last of the ripened tomatoes in a basket. "He was beside himself when you went missing. And when you were in a coma..." Her words faded away, her lips pursed tightly. After a headshake, she continued. "God knows what would've happened if you didn't come out of it."

My knees weakened under the weight of all the guilt I carried around. I knew the burden of responsibility for his mental state shouldn't have been mine, and yet wasn't the most important rule of loving someone as thoroughly as I loved this man, *"first do no harm"*?

"I'm not telling you to make you feel worse, *chérie*. Give him time to sort out his feelings. Just don't let him push you away. He's very good at that—shutting people out. It will only get harder if you let him."

I had a pretty good idea of what that looked like.

"He didn't speak to me for three months after his wife died. Did I ever tell you that?" All I could manage was a head shake. "I was beside myself. I was terrified of leaving him alone." With a sideways glance, she said, "He did eventually hurt himself, he just did it slowly." I thought of the state I found him in when we met. The drinking, the oxycodone—he had been killing himself slowly.

The gravity of her confession hit me hard, my concern growing by the minute. Because I was armed with the knowledge that he had never been in love before. And if guilt could drive him over the edge of sanity and put his life at risk for India and the child he lost, what would the near loss of the person he was in love with do to him?

"Diana came to the hospital," I announced.

"He told me." Grabbing a cotton towel, she wiped her dirt covered hands. "That woman leaves a wake of destruction everywhere she goes. I'm afraid none of this will ever be resolved until he makes peace with it."

I nodded in agreement as I stared out at the horizon where perfectly sheared grass met the quilted, dove gray sky. That truth had been needling my conscience since the scene at the hospital.

"I don't think she sets out to harm him. She's just selfish, and self-absorbed. She's never been there for him. Not once that I can recall." The more Marianne spoke the more powerless I felt in the face of this seemingly insurmountable task. I was losing hope.

"How do I get him back?" I asked, sheer desperation in my voice.

Marianne glanced up from the basket she was arranging. "Do what no other woman has ever done for him, *chérie*. Be there for him no matter how hard he tries to push you away, no matter what."

***

"I need a haircut," I announced as I entered the kitchen some time later. What is it they say about idle hands being the devil's plaything? Well, the more free time I had, the more I fretted about Sebastian. I needed to keep busy. One way, or another.

Bear and Justin stared back at me with matching blank expressions, the guns they were busy cleaning all but forgotten in their hands. Justin's hand crept up and rubbed his scruff covered chin, all that chiseled handsomeness looking very thoughtful.

"I've never done it before, but I'm willing to try," he offered, to my everlasting amusement. I couldn't keep the corners of my mouth from lifting.

"I *meant* I need a ride into town so I can look for a hairdresser."

Bear nodded his big, bald head and breathed out a sigh of relief. "Sure thing. I'll get the car."

The silence in the car wasn't exactly comfortable. Every time we set foot off the property the risk increased. It had everyone's nerves balancing on the edge of a razor blade. But what was the alternative, become a shut-in?

Two black SUVs shadowed us. No doubt the people who dwelled in the tiny village would find it interesting. Bear had made some phone calls and found a tiny shop that agreed to do the deed. My head was a misshapen mess. No amount of hair product could mold it into something presentable. Therefore, the choice was either a pixie cut or—a pixie cut. The hairdresser was a snobby Parisian that feigned speaking no English rather poorly. Frankly, I didn't care. It wasn't his language skills or his manners I was interested in, and I was pleased to find his haircutting skill were impeccable. With the little he had to work with, he worked wonders.

While I was thanking him profusely in French, the door chimed and Isabelle entered the shop. Her eyes, chastened and submissive, immediately met mine in the mirror. Her attention shifted to Bear, who quietly murmured something in her ear. Then Bear walked over to where I sat. "She wants to apologize," Bear said in a low voice, his expression uncomfortable. My gaze slid to Isabelle once again. She wore an anxious look on her face and clutched her purse with both hands, strangling it to death.

"Okay," I replied because after everything that had transpired, I couldn't muster up the energy to stay mad anymore.

Right after Bear gave her the nod, she approached slowly while he took a step back and hovered. Her gray eyes darted around, looking for courage. Her lips suffered from repeated bites before she opened them to speak. "I know nothing I say can undo what's been done," she mumbled quietly. A pause followed. Maybe she was waiting for me to assuage her guilt. But I wasn't about to make it that easy for her. "You must really hate me," she continued, shifting from foot to foot. Again I remained silent. "I just want to say that I am *very* sorry. I never meant for things to get out of hand like they did...and...well, Mrs. Redman, Paisley not Diana, she frightens me."

That piqued my interest. "How?"

"At first, she was all friendly like. And then, when I had nothing else to tell her, she started threatening me, telling me she would have me arrested for stealing." Isabelle's voice gained volume. "I never stole anything in my life!"

"Isabelle, slow down."

"She is a fucking *putain*!"

"Okay, easy," I said, putting the breaks on where that train was headed.

"She got what she deserved," she said, finishing in a huff. Then she crossed her arms under her ample breasts.

Got what she deserved? Glancing sideways at Bear, I found him suddenly inspecting his shoes in total fascination. "What do you mean by *got what she deserved*?"

The handwringing started all over again. Isabelle's gray eyes went wide, darting back to Bear, who gave his consent with a slight nod. It seemed I was the only one out of the loop.

"She was arrested."

"For what?" I unintentionally shouted, shock getting the better of me.

This time it was Bear that answered in that deep voice of his. "Possession of a controlled substance and driving under the influence." There was more to this story. Call it intuition. The implied question was in my eyes. After a roll of his, he added, "Substantial quantities of cocaine and ecstasy were found in her car while she was on her way home from a party."

"Is that the script all of you are following?"

While he considered my claim, Bear scratched his goatee, the letters r-e-l-a-x tattooed on the back of his fingers taunting me. It would've been ridiculously funny if it weren't for the fact that I suspected the man I loved sought his vengeance by planting evidence.

"No. But if you have any more questions, you should speak to him about it."

***

Whatever had happened to Paisley would have to wait. At present I had more important issues to deal with, first and foremost to close the ever widening gap between Sebastian and me. I was anxious to see him. All day I had been glancing at the clock, counting the minutes until he came home. It was already late when he texted that he wouldn't make it in time for dinner. After that, I lost my appetite completely. With my nerves on edge reading was out of the question. It was impossible to concentrate. So, in a desperate effort to relax, I decided on a bath.

The tub in the master bathroom was so big it took an eternity to fill. After dimming the lights, I turned on the sound system that was wired throughout most of the house and slid into the water up to my chin. *Gnossiennes No. 1 Lent*, the sweet sound of Satie, filtered through the air, dominating my attention and easing my worries for the moment. My head fell back on the beveled edge and my eyes fluttered shut as the music cast its spell on me.

Slowly but surely the heat leeched away the stiffness in my muscles. It also loosened the steel grip I had on my emotions. All alone, with only the sound of my thoughts to keep me company, everything I was trying to keep at bay surged forward. The pain it evoked seared my throat and stung my eyes.

"Hey," a sexy, gravelly voice called out.

My eyes popped open to find him standing next to the tub, yanking on his tie. The expression on his face was unguarded. It felt as if he was reaching out to me. For the first time since I'd left the hospital hope blossomed in my heart that he was ready to let me behind the walls of his fortress again.

He stepped closer, and ran his fingers through my hair. "You got a haircut?"

All I could do was nod, rendered mute by the feel of him. The power he had over me was frightening. He could enslave me with a mere touch. My eyelids grew heavy as he ran his fingers along my jawline and down my neck. When he stepped away to undress, my skin turned cold and hypersensitive where his warmth had been.

One piece at a time, he discarded his clothing carelessly. His cufflinks clinked on the marble floor. His shirt and trousers pooled at his feet. His boxers were next. My hungry eyes drank in every square inch of tan skin he revealed, the long, graceful lines of his body—the scars. A reminder of all he'd suffered and overcome...a reminder of what an amazing man he was. Every time I saw him it felt like the first time. It also felt as if it could be the last. I tucked the image away to treasure forever.

He stepped into the water and sat down facing me. His long legs stretched out, surrounding my body. My knees came up to give him more room. I reached for him without thought, my hand idly stroking his injured knee. If he was within reach it was imperative that I touch him, compelled by some magnetic force I was powerless to resist. I drew circles around the kneecap and watched the tight line of his full mouth go slack at the sensation.

The air between us felt pregnant with truths and omissions that hadn't been revealed yet, with words that hadn't been spoken. I didn't know how to begin. I was a coward, a fraud.

My entire life I'd prided myself on my strength of will, and yet when I needed it most, it had deserted me.

Paralyzed by indecision, I placed my chin on top of my knees and watched him slowly sink below the water. A beat later, like some mythical sea creature, he broke the surface for air and slicked his wet hair back. Sometimes I wondered if he understood the measure of his appeal. It certainly didn't seem so. Droplets of water collected on his long lashes. The path they took as they slid down his cheeks and caught on his sensual lips held me captive.

An urge to lick them away came over me. Leaning in, I traced his lips with my tongue, nibbled on his full bottom one, and kissed him gently. When I pulled back there was no doubt, no question of what he was thinking. It was all there in those bottomless pools of amber. So expressive…those eyes. I wanted to dive in and lose myself in them, disappear altogether to a place where I wasn't haunted by the mistakes I'd made.

"It's my fault," I whispered, my lips barely moving, my jaw quivering from the pressure. Everything I was fighting to keep tightly locked down had finally broken loose. "I didn't want the baby…not at first." I began regurgitating words like sour milk. They couldn't stay down a second longer; they were making me ill. More than anything, I needed him to assuage my battered soul. I needed his absolution.

He moved first. Closing the distance between us, he pulled me onto his lap and crushed me to him. I threw my legs over his, straddling him. Only then did I realize how violently I was shaking. As always Sebastian knew what I needed before I did. He cocooned me in comfort, curving his much larger body around my lesser one. I pressed my face into his throat, and buried my shame along with it. A river of tears slid down my temple, blending with the drops of water on his damp skin.

"What if...my body rejected the baby because I didn't want him?" I forced out between hiccups and sobs.

"You know better than to say stupid shit like that." A large hand rubbed slowly up and down my back, lending me the strength to confess everything.

"And now I do want him...I did this. I did this to us," I spewed, my voice breaking as the emotion wrapped its fingers around my throat and squeezed.

"Shhhhh. It's not your fault." Holding me even closer, he murmured words of love and encouragement in my ear. "We can try again as soon as you're ready," he added in the end, making me cry even harder.

"I need you to forgive me—I can't lose you. I *can't.*"

"There's nothing to forgive," he practically growled. "It pisses me off that you..." His words stopped short, his frustration palpable. Grabbing my shoulders, he shook me. "Fuck, Vera, you're everything to me. I'm in it for the long haul and you as sure as fuck better be, too."

In the midst of all the pain and suffering, he made me laugh, this complicated, wonderful man who gave everything and asked for nothing in return. He wiped my reddened, swollen face of the leftover tears running down my cheeks.

"Don't I get a choice?" I said, smiling.

His head cocked slightly. He studied me thoughtfully. "From the moment we met, neither one of us had a choice."

My expression sobered. "You really believe that?"

"No," he answered. *How could one small word hurt so much?* Until he added, "I know it. You're mine forever and that's the end of it."

His unabashed honesty impelled me to ask the question that was burning a hole in my gut. "Do you want children?"

I didn't think his eyes could get any softer, but he proved me wrong. "I want us. I want them with you." His arms tightened around me until there was less than zero space between us. Chest to chest, I felt the heavy thumping of his heart next to mine. I knew then that together we would get through this. We would be okay. No matter what.

***

The din woke me. Drifting up from the ground floor, a collection of voices entered through the front door, the ancient stone walls amplifying every sound. "What time is it?" I groggily asked as I rubbed my eyes. Sebastian was already shoving on a pair of sweatpants by the time I glanced up. He planted a tender kiss on my lips, and was halfway to the door when he answered, "Four. Go back to sleep."

There was no way that was happening. I grabbed a pair of leggings, a long-sleeved top, and dressed in a hurry. Down the marble steps, I followed the breadcrumb trail of voices into the den, a room seldom used. It had a decadent, masculine feel to it. Large, comfortable couches in midnight blue velvet and heavy silk drapes with a faint *fleur-de-lis* pattern complemented the ornate, antique billiard table that sat in the middle. The vaulted ceiling was decorated with plasterwork worthy of a fourteenth century church. It was definitely one of the more grand rooms in the house, and I suspected that had something to do with Sebastian's father.

I pushed open the walnut double doors and scanned the area, taking note of who was present. Everyone fell silent as I entered. Ben and his men—Justin, Bear, and two others whose names escaped me—lounged back on the couches. Some with beers in hand, some loading bullets into the clips of their guns.

Interesting combination, that.

Gideon and Sebastian studied the screen of an open laptop resting on the pool table. Dressed casually—casual for her that is—in dark designer jeans and a deep purple silk shirt, Shay stood at the bar with her back to me. She was busy filling a cut crystal tumbler with liquor. At the silence, she glanced over her shoulder and our eyes met, hers widening. That's when I noticed the worn-out look on her face, and the disheveled state of her shoulder-length auburn hair.

"Vera—shit, it's so good to see you!" She covered the ground between us in a couple of long-legged strides and engulfed me in a tight, almost suffocating hug. "We just got back from Panama and had to see Bash."

Bash?

"I'm so sorry if we woke you."

"No, no. Don't worry. This is important," I rushed to reassure her.

"Yes, unfortunately," she agreed, her expression troubled. My gaze slid to Sebastian and Gideon, who were following the conversation. Gideon's dark, exotic eyes met mine briefly. He greeted me with a short nod.

"Did you get any answers?" The eagerness in my voice rang loud and clear. I was anxious for this to be over, for Sebastian to be safe.

With the audit by the American Department of Justice hanging overhead, Gideon and Shay had flown down to Panama to see if they could get any information about a bank account that had been wiring large sums of cash to Horn & Cie. Everyone agreed that something nefarious was in play. After repeated attempts to reach them by phone, to no avail, Shay had decided to take matters in hand.

"We sure did," Shay said with pride in her voice.

"By placing yourself at undue risk," Gideon chimed in, his tone sharpened by irritation. Shay's large, dark eyes narrowed. Sifting her long, tapered fingers through her hair, she scratched with her short red nails, ratting it up. I was getting a clear picture of why it looked like that now.

"It wasn't unnecessary. As a matter of fact, it was extremely necessary. And I wasn't *at risk*. Why the hell am I even trying to reason with you when I know it's easier to turn water into wine!"

"Playing strip poker with the bank manager is no way to gather intel," Gideon fired back.

"I got the malware in his laptop didn't I!"

"Can we stay on point?" Sebastian bit out, a frown on his face.

Taking a deep breath, Shay continued. "We weren't having any luck going the conventional route, and tracing the money wire proved fruitless. Whoever's doing this is using Russian proxy servers. In other words, we can't follow the signal to the point of origin. We have no way to trace where the money originated. Obviously, it wasn't clean—no one goes through this much trouble to hide clean money."

"What does that even mean?" I mumbled.

Shay tried to smooth her hair with no success. "That they purposely sent the money from an untraceable location. The Panamanian bank account it was wired into is assigned to a shell company, adding another bag of dicks to this clusterf—"

"Shay," Sebastian interrupted.

"Sorry," she grumbled. Taking a deep breath she continued. "We have no idea who owns the account. Panama is notorious for this. And here's the kicker—they've wired over three hundred twenty-five million dollars in the last ten years into an account undersigned by Charles Hightower." The room went dead silent. I didn't know what to say. And I didn't have to understand all the intricate ins and outs of this deal to know that something highly unethical was happening.

I found Sebastian leaning against the pool table with his hands planted on the burgundy felt, his head hanging low. More than anything I wanted to comfort him. This was not the time, nor the place, however.

"Is there any way that this can end well for Charles?" I asked, still holding onto a sliver of hope. I knew how much

Sebastian cared for the man, and it killed me to even consider what he must've been feeling. What would one more betrayal do to him?

"We thought he was providing tax shelter for another party. That might still be the case...or it could be far worse," Sebastian admitted, his eyes bleak. "He made trades with that money, held onto it for six months, then wired half the amount he initially received to a non-profit organization based in Beirut."

"You've lost me again."

"He's washing money. Could be drugs, could be any number of illegal enterprises. And then he's sending it to a nonprofit, a charity we know nothing about." He pinched the bridge of his nose, squinting in discomfort.

"Ten years..." The thought slipped out of my mouth. "Did your father know?"

Sebastian's eyes met mine, his face a beautiful ruse of tranquility. And yet, the turmoil beneath the surface was plain to me. "I don't know," he answered softly, his expression indicating that he'd already formed an opinion. "But I'm gonna find out."

Chapter Eight

THE FOLLOWING DAY, FEDPOL, THE Federal Department of Police, the Swiss agency that handles money laundering cases, agreed to meet with Sebastian at Horn & Cie. I refused to be left behind. The man I loved was in danger—whoever was responsible had already come dangerously close to succeeding—and I wanted to know exactly what we were dealing with. Needless to say, I pestered him until he agreed to let me sit in on the meeting.

Two agents from the American FBI, who were apparently taking the lead in the case, accompanied the Fedpol and Interpol agents also present. I hid behind Sebastian, out of the way of everyone's curious glances. Leaning up against the bookcase in his office, I stood with my arms wrapped around my middle while Sebastian half sat on the corner of his massive desk. He raked his fingers through his hair in a gesture I knew meant he was stressed.

"We've intercepted a number of calls between an Iranian national living in Beirut, and Mr. Charles Hightower—one of your clients," said one of the American agents, a heavy-set woman in her mid-fifties. She introduced herself by last name only, Vasquez. Her partner, a much younger woman, a tall blonde that seemed to take her fitness training very seriously, introduced herself as Lewis. Agent Vasquez's astute, green eyes contradicted the bored expression she wore. Sebastian offered them a seat but neither of them took one. Lewis stood by the door while Vasquez paced.

"This is not about tax evasion, is it?" asked Sebastian, a resigned note in his voice.

"Afraid not," Agent Lewis answered.

Sebastian's barrister, David Bernard, turned away from the wall of windows he'd been gazing out of. There was a cool, confident air about him that reassured me. As if he'd popped out of the womb wearing the impeccably sharp navy suit he had on and a briefcase in hand.

"Mr. Horn wishes to help in any way he can of course. However, as you already know the bank thrives on discretion." The implication hung in the pause. He locked his arms behind his back and waited.

Placing her hands on her hips, Agent Vasquez's expression hardened. "This isn't a simple case of money laundering." Another pause. Mr. Bernard was a sphinx. Vasquez's eyes met his squarely. "We have reason to believe the money is being funneled to multiple terror organization."

The silence in the room was suddenly as dense as mud, the gravity of the situation descending heavily upon the three of us that weren't privy to what the FBI and Interpol had uncovered.

David didn't miss a beat. "If word gets out that we let you rummage through the books there will be hell to pay, a mass exodus of every high net worth client the bank services."

Unaffected, Agent Vasquez barreled full steam ahead. "We can do this the hard way."

"Agent Vasquez, is it?" At her brief nod, David continued. "I relish the opportunity to flex my legal muscles in court. In which case precious time will be wasted, and in the process, your investigation severely compromised." Agent Vasquez was about to interrupt when David continued, speaking over her. "However, this is not what my client wishes to do. He has gone to great lengths to investigate this matter, and is prepared to hand over all the evidence he has obtained with only a few minor stipulations."

"Which are?" Lewis chimed in.

"We expect you to freeze and confiscate only Mr. Hightower's accounts and any associates directly involved in the case. All else will fall under an immunity deal. Any evidence naming the bank remains sealed. And in the event that it becomes public, a statement will be issued clarifying that Horn & Cie. was instrumental in alerting the authorities."

Vasquez's glare turned languid, held steady for a beat. "I'd have to check with Washington, but I don't anticipate it being a problem."

"As soon as I we have that in writing, we will be happy to hand over all of Mr. Hightower's transactions with the bank, along with other material Mr. Horn's private security team has uncovered. There's also the small matter of the repeated attempts on Mr. Horn's life."

Lewis and Vasquez exchanged knowing glances. "Yes. We've picked up the driver of the truck. He's in our custody."

"My wife was killed," Sebastian served this up quietly, gaining everyone's attention. Although his tone was vacant, his eyes weren't. Aimed at a spot on the floor, they were haunted, the ghosts of his past resurrecting all the guilt we'd worked hard to bury. The helplessness I felt at the moment nearly brought me to my knees. Because there was nothing I could do to comfort him, nothing I could say that wouldn't ring false. India had been killed because someone wanted Sebastian dead. In his mind, he might as well have held a gun to her head.

"When you took over stewardship of the bank, you made someone very nervous."

His eyes climbed back up. I could see his mind working backwards, chasing leads down dead ends, pivoting in another direction until he finally hit on something. A deep v carved itself on his brow as the memory came rushing back. His eyes slamming shut for a brief moment, he said, "I requested an audit by an independent accounting firm shortly after I took over the bank."

"Add probable murder, and conspiracy to commit murder to a long list of potential charges then," Vasquez said to no one in particular. "We suggest you keep your security team in place until this case is closed, Mr. Horn."

"What next?" David said, pushing the conversation onto less sensitive territory.

"All trades placed through Charles Hightower's account are to proceed as usual," Vasquez ordered. "We'll be in touch once we question the truck driver."

All the pieces of the puzzle were starting to come together. The crime, according to the American authorities, was much more nefarious than we had initially thought, the stakes exponentially higher. Every time Sebastian tried to take inventory of all the accounts at the bank, his life had been in danger. If what the agents were speculating about was true, there was no doubt that whoever was responsible wouldn't stop until he achieved his goal.

***

Shortly after the meeting with the FBI—and with a lot of legal arm twisting from David Bernard—the Swiss agreed to stay my deportation and extend my visa until my case with the Albanians was resolved. I may have been momentarily free from the law, however, the choke collar around my neck only grew tighter and tighter in Sebastian's hand. I couldn't even make a trip to the toilet without him asking where I was headed. I did my best to be patient with him, considering the circumstances. Essentially, I had traded one prison for another.

Everyone had fallen eerily silent over breakfast when I

walked into the kitchen and announced that I wanted Gideon to drive me to church. Sebastian arched an eyebrow. To give him credit, he didn't argue. I didn't know if it meant he was beginning to trust me again, or he was certain that under no circumstance, not even death, would Gideon allow me out of his sight ever again—probably the latter. Though that was hardly an issue when we now had not only one SUV full of armed men trailing, but another leading.

Surprisingly, Gideon was the only one that treated me no differently. A few times I caught him studying me, gathering his thoughts as if to say something, but he never did. Other than that, his demeanor was the same one he'd always adopted around me. One of careful casualness.

"Are you mad at me?" I asked as I examined him in the rearview mirror.

Sitting in the back seat of the bulletproof Mercedes 550, one of the additions to the new security measures, I waited patiently for his answer, uncertain whether I would get one.

"No...I'm mad at myself. I should've been paying closer attention."

"Don't blame yourself, Gideon. Ever hear the expression *'where there's a will there's a way'*?" Regret was thick in my voice. I turned to look out the window. As far as the eye could see flowering thyme was in full bloom. Every square inch of hillside was covered with it. On its own, the tiny purple flower isn't much to look at, but in abundance it was breathtaking.

"Had I done my job, you wouldn't have lost the baby. I'm sorry about that."

His words pulled me out of my silent admiration of the flowers. *The baby.* It was a relief to hear it said out loud.

"Thank you for being frank. I'm so tired of everyone walking on eggshells around me." His quick nod reached inside of me, unlocking some of the stiffness, some of the frigid cold near my heart that had set up permanent residence.

"What happened to you, Gideon?"

His black as pitch eyes, with those spiky lashes accenting them, grew even more piercing. "What do you mean?" he asked softly, his words in direct contrast with his expression.

"You know what I mean. You weren't born a cynic."

A challenge hung in the air, loaded and charged. His eyes narrowed and left mine. His lips moved, forming words as if he was testing them. No sound came out.

"My mother was killed in an open-air market two blocks from my house in Tel Aviv. It was a suicide bombing."

I felt the impact of his words instantly, his pain as acutely as my own. "I'm so sorry. I know what it feels like—to lose a parent unexpectedly."

My mind drifted from the man driving, to the man who raised me. For so long, thoughts of my father had been tainted by a combination of shame and scorn. Time and distance had finally softened those feelings. His betrayal had taken a back seat to the memories of the good times we shared. Now it was those I remembered first. And how much I missed him.

"My six-year-old daughter was with her."

His words were razorblades. The wound in my soul that had been slowly knitting back together split open again. My eyes snapped to his in the reflection of the mirror, but his had already moved away, returning to the road ahead. The tremor started in my jaw, and traveled to my bottom lip until my teeth were chattering as if an arctic chill had invaded the space inside the car.

In an effort to get a handle on it, I bit my lip hard enough to break skin. The smack of metal and salt hit my tongue. A lifetime of swallowing wouldn't erase the taste of it. Nor the sorrow.

"I don't know what to say," I mumbled and quickly licked away the tears coating my lips, tears I hadn't even noticed leaking from my eyes.

"There's nothing to say," he replied in a tired voice. "This is just a bus stop. Some waiting to get on, some to get off. We attribute meaning to it because the truth is too frightening to contemplate."

"And what truth is that?" My anger boiled up at the apathy I heard in his voice. Was this what losing everything sounded like? Was this what hopelessness looked like?

"That it's all meaningless. There's nothing other than what we see."

We pulled up to the little church as the doors were closing. Gideon took a good hard look at it. "You still hang onto this— illusion? After everything you've been through?" His troubled eyes held mine. Pleading? Looking for answers? Or was I ascribing meaning where there was none?

I didn't have to consider my answer. "With both hands."

As I opened the car door, he turned and pinned me in place with his dark, hypnotic eyes. "Do I have to come inside with you, or can I trust you to come out in an hour?"

I had quite a bit of wrongs to account for. Sheepishly, I answered, "You can trust me. I'll give you my promise, but I'd rather prove it to you."

He gave me a quick nod in agreement, and just as quickly I was out the door and inside the church, seeking peace and absolution. I thought about Gideon and all he'd suffered. Only later would I come to realize that sometimes, if we're lucky, as the deepest wounds begin to heal, the scar tissue binds us together.

Chapter Nine

ONCE I WAS INSIDE THE church, my first order of business was to find the dear priest whom I had shamefully lied to in my escape and explain everything. After relaying the story from nuts to bolts, I pleaded, "Can you forgive me, Father?"

The priest smiled warmly, mischief lurking in his pale blue eyes. "You are in luck, *madame*. We specialize in forgiveness here." Then he held up his hands, indicating our surroundings. The wide smile that spread across his face sent relief and gratitude sweeping through me.

The service started shortly afterwards. Even though the church was mostly empty, I sat in the back pew, an old, hard-to-break habit from all those years of being on the run. I also learned never to go to the same church too often or people would start to recognize my face and get nosy. The sound of the priest's voice speaking in French lulled me into deep contemplation, my eyelids floating shut.

"Praying won't help, you filthy bitch. Neither will the man you're fucking for protection." There was profound hate in that quiet voice. Not even the lilt of a French accent could soften the vileness of those words. My eyes slammed open.

Sitting to my left, I looked into the cold, hard face of Inspector Tribolet. A hand wrapped around my upper arm, meaty fingers digging into my flesh. Tightening his powerful grip, he yanked me closer to him.

"I knew you'd be back. You people are like cockroaches."

Calling me shocked would be putting it mildly. While my mind threw up question after question, my voice was lost somewhere between disbelief and naked fear. He made absolutely no attempt to hide the intense passion with which he hated me. That fact alone made my pulse gallop. The contempt on his face was only slightly offset by the lust lurking there as well—I didn't know which was worse.

"It's almost impossible to get rid of you. But I will—I will send each and every one of you back to the shithole countries you come from one by one."

I was in the midst of a waking nightmare. He jerked me painfully to the end of the pew until I had no choice but to get up. The service continued. Nobody noticed anything out of the ordinary. He tugged me to the side door. The priest, in the middle of the service, caught the scene and frowned at us. In total bewilderment, I stared back at him with my mouth gapping open. Still in shock, no sound came out.

Tribolet shoved the door open with his shoulder. I made a last-ditch attempt to stop him by holding onto the frame of the door. This too ended in vain. A second later, we were standing on the street, on the side of the building, and cold metal cuffs were snapped onto my wrists and secured behind my back.

"What the hell are you doing? Are you insane?" I finally croaked.

His face froze—except for a nervous twitch under his eye. I didn't think the situation could get any scarier, but I was wrong. He began dragging me up the cobblestone street.

"Listen up, dirty cockroach. You aren't going to fuck your way out of this. I'm taking you to the station, and then we are shipping you out of here. Maybe I'll get a taste of you before I do that, see for myself what that rich piece of shit thought was so special about you."

I sat down on the road. I wasn't about to help him lead me to my own demise. He kicked me in the hip, and pulled on my arm so hard I was certain he dislocated my shoulder. I screamed in pain. It did nothing to slow him down. Then he yanked me up by the hair. I stood up as if I was shot out of a cannon. A woman carrying grocery bags stared at us suspiciously. He glowered at her, and she walked past us without a second glance.

All the struggling had us both sweating profusely. With his free hand, he hooked two fingers into his collar and tugged, and in the process exposed a portion of a tattoo on his neck...a tattoo anyone would've recognized.

"You're a hammer skin," I scoffed. Schweizer hammer skin, to be precise, a branch of the Swiss skinhead movement. He skewered me with a vicious glare. Almost immediately, he realized what he'd done and smoothed the collar of his shirt back into place, hiding the visual evidence of his hate.

"Stop right there."

Both our heads swiveled in the direction of the voice with the rolled Rs. Behind us stood Gideon and five of his men. All of them with guns pointed at Inspector Tribolet. In an extremely tense moment of silence, Tribolet placed his hand on his holstered gun.

"I am an officer of the law, you piece of shit. Tell your men to lay down their weapons immediately."

Nobody moved, the tension escalating by the second. Armed with the knowledge I had about the inspector, I knew how volatile the situation was. "Gideon, he's taking me to the station. Meet us there. Please do as he says. And bring the papers the Swiss issued—ask Sebastian." My words were cut short when Tribolet yanked on my cuffs.

Gideon snapped out of the trance he was in and his remote black gaze met mine. The supplicating look I gave him worked. He slowly lowered his weapon and commanded the other men to do the same.

It didn't take long for us to reach the police station; the

town was the size of a postcard. The minute I was dragged inside, my worried eyes collided with Inspector Deubel's. He stopped midstride and cocked his head, his cheeks stuffed with food. His expression of total confusion turned scalding with anger when he saw Gideon and his men standing ten paces behind us. His attention shifted back to Tribolet, who still had a death grip on my arm. Swallowing down the lump of food, Deubel marched over to us.

"What do you think you're doing?" he said in French.

"Booking an illegal," Tribolet replied casually.

I wanted to punch the smug look off his face, though I had a pretty good idea that Sebastian was going to want that honor. Deubel retrieved a key out of his pocket and unlocked the cuffs. I winced in pain. "I'm sorry, mademoiselle. Are you injured?"

"My shoulder," I explained, groaning as I gently stretched my arms, prodding and the shoulder that hurt, which wasn't as bad as I had initially thought. It didn't feel dislocated.

"Do you have any idea whom you're fucking with?" Deubel seethed, speaking through clenched teeth in French to Tribolet. Did he think I didn't understand French? Apparently, because he continued. "That family built this town. He's a personal friend of three of the seven ministers!" Spittle flew out of a mouth that reminded me of a sea bass.

Red faced, he straightened his tie, smoothed his shirt, and turned to me. "I'll get you an icepack and some aspirin. Please have a seat." Then he guided me to a blue chair pushed up against the glass window of the empty police chief's office. As soon as the two men entered the office, the screaming commenced. Ten minutes later all hell broke loose.

Sebastian came charging into the station like a rampaging bull. You could hear him from a mile away. The bellowing, the stomping around. It put a smile on my face.

"Where is she?" The deep rasp echoed from the front of the

station. A beat later he rushed into the room with a squadron of security personnel trailing closely behind him, Gideon to his right, Bear to his left. There wasn't even a hint of a limp.

Two uniformed police officers immediately jumped in to stop him from coming further into the room. Deubel halted his tirade at Tribolet, and stepped out of the chief's office, straightening his tie and flexing his neck left and right.

"Mr. Horn," he said, his hands up in a supplicating gesture. "There's been a small misunderstanding."

The pause that followed was brutal. Sebastian stared at him as if he was slicing meat off his bones with a dull paring knife. "I'd say so."

Deubel's rotund physique was blocking me from view. He stepped aside, and all the scrutiny in the room shifted to me. Sebastian's glare landed on the icepack and his nostrils flared. Gideon came over at once and helped me up.

"Are you all right?" he murmured quietly, wrapping a supportive arm around me.

"My shoulder's bruised. Otherwise, I'm fine—don't look so worried," I whispered back but it was useless, the concern remained stamped on Gideon's face.

"My colleague tends to be a little overzealous at times. He's young and passionate about his work," Deubel pleaded with a thin, crooked smile. "You understand?" A lot of handwringing ensued. If Deubel thought he could salvage Tribolet's career, he was seriously mistaken. He was lucky to salvage his life.

"Understand?" Sebastian's voice was eerily calm. His gaze shifted to Tribolet, who was still seated in the office with his back to us. Sebastian's countenance may have been carved out of ice, but I knew what was churning beneath the surface. "No, I don't understand."

"Where's the chief?" Gideon chimed in.

"Lunch, I'm afraid."

Shortly afterwards, the chief of police appeared. Looking

extremely embarrassed, he did his best to calm the situation down. Though nothing would have appeased Sebastian short of putting Tribolet down like a mad dog.

Once we were safely ensconced in the back of the car, Sebastian dialed his cell phone. "Yeah, I have her." Glancing sideways at me, his eyes did a cursory check for any more injuries. "I want him banished to fucking Siberia if you can swing it…call Fedpol…yeah, okay." After ending the call, he breathed out a long sigh, his eyes floating shut while his head fell back onto the headrest. I reached out and covered his hand, lying on his thigh, and his eyes opened again, relief reflected brightly in them.

"I feel like all I ever say to you is how sorry I am."

He turned in his seat to face me. His hand slowly came up and raked through my messy hair, brushed along my jaw. "There's nothing for you to be sorry about." Leaning in, he kissed me gently. One meant to comfort and reassure more than anything else.

"I hate being another burden you have to cope with," I anxiously admitted. How many times would this man have to come to my rescue? It was starting to border on ridiculous. He unbuckled my seatbelt and pulled me onto his lap, careful not to bump into my sore shoulder.

"None of this is your fault." And then his gaze turned scalding, directed in the rearview mirror at the man who was driving.

"He's an officer of the law, Sebastian. One we're familiar with. When we watched him enter the church—" Gideon explained.

"It's not his fault either," I exclaimed in Gideon's defense.

"It is my fault," Gideon argued for his guilt in a self-deprecating voice. "I promised myself I wouldn't ever let this happen again."

"Stop it. It's nobody's fault—he's a hammer skin. He has a

thing for immigrants."

The car was suddenly quiet, the atmosphere crackling with an influx of energy. "How do you know?" Matching alert expressions were on both men's faces.

"I saw the tattoo on his neck."

Sebastian's eyes slammed into Gideon's in the rearview mirror again, this time a conspiratorial glint in them. He dialed his phone. "David, the motherfucker's a skinhead. Vera saw a tattoo...I want him to suffer. Family, friends—take them all down."

"Sebastian." No other explanation was necessary—he could see the disapproval on my face.

"Don't," he warned. There was no sign of weakness in his bearing. No indication that he would listen to reason. Vengeance was his and he wouldn't hesitate to act. I stared at the man I loved and saw something I'd seen only once before in his countenance, malice, wrath that reached into my core and turned it to ice. And for the first time, I questioned what he was really capable of.

***

Back at the manor, he forced me up the stairs and into the bedroom. Immediately, he ran the water for a bath, pouring in half a bag of the bath salts. If I hadn't been so drained from the aftermath of the fight and the lingering effects of the adrenaline rush, I could've appreciated how well he played the part of a lady's maid.

Gingerly, I peeled the dirty clothes off my battered body. My silk shirt ripped, a tar stain running down the length of my pants. Now that the rush had worn off, everything ached.

"Motherfucker!" Sebastian shouted. I jerked in surprise, my nerves painfully sensitive. There was a welt on my hip the size of a dinner plate. Grimacing, he sat on the edge of the tub and inspected the wound closer, tracing it with his fingers.

"Does it hurt?" His voice was gentle, comforting, a cashmere blanket, hot chocolate on a cold winter's day…a complete departure from the harbinger of doom I met in the back seat of the car.

God, I loved this man. I still hadn't reached the bottom of that supply. With everything he had endured, he still thought of my welfare first. "It's just tender." I stroked his hair off his face, ribbons of silk gliding through my fingers. "What would I do without you?"

He glanced up then, his eyes capturing mine. "You'll never have to find out." The force of his thoughts, of his adamantine will, was a palpable thing.

Minutes later we were both in the tub, the hot water washing away all the obstacles life kept throwing at us. For the moment I felt born again. I lay back against him, wrapped in the safe harbor of his arms, both of us quiet, lost in contemplation. I was rubbing his injured leg, stiff from overexertion, when an insidious thought entered my mind.

"Darling…"

"Hmm."

"I saw Isabelle in town." Behind me, he shifted, his muscles tightening with a heightened sense of awareness. "She apologized."

"Did she?" he drawled darkly.

"Yes. She was genuinely remorseful." As silent as he was, he may as well have been shouting his judgement at the top of his lungs. I pressed on. "She said Paisley had been arrested."

"Hmm."

"For drugs and drunk driving."

"Yeah."

The question was on my lips, and yet I couldn't force it out of my mouth. Always three chess moves ahead, he beat me to it. "What do you want to know, Vera?"

I hated the note of disappointment in his voice. As if I'd let him down in some way. Holding my breath, I said, "Did you have anything to do with it?"

"Are you asking if I had her arrested for a crime she didn't commit?" Out loud, it did sound absurd. He breathed out and said, "No, I didn't."

The tension in my chest faded away, only to be replaced by more shame. I loved this man. I respected this man. And what had he ever gotten in return from me but a steaming pile of distrust. I was ashamed of myself. But I didn't know how to change it. I'd spent too many years looking over my shoulder, expecting people to disappoint me, and up until he walked into my life, they had.

"I knew she was using. I knew her habits. I just brought it to the attention of the right people."

The silence that followed was not a comfortable one. I turned around to face him, floating above his prone body. On the surface he was a mythical, larger-than-life creature, but on the inside just a man, with all the same needs and wants as any other human being. To be loved, to be understood. It was easy to forget when confronted with all that power and the glossy veneer of his model good looks. He watched me expectantly, his eyes begging for something I didn't know how to give. He didn't need to voice the question, the accusation. It hung between us as clear as a neon sign. *Why won't you trust me?*

Leaning closer, I brushed my lips on his. Once. Twice. "Be patient with me," I murmured, guilt coloring my tone. I wondered if he could hear the desperate longing in my voice. He grabbed my face and kissed me passionately, the answer on his lips

Chapter Ten

IN THE EXAMINATION ROOM, BARE, antiseptic walls glared back at me. The last time I'd sat on this table my world had come undone. All those confused feelings...

There was no longer any confusion. If I could only travel back in time, I'd let myself be happy about it. I'd savor every precious minute.

Stepping into the room, Maria Rossetti pushed her horn-rimmed glasses high up on her head and smiled affectionately. "How have you been?"

"Good. I feel really good—back to normal." She checked my paperwork and put on a pair of rubber gloves.

"Let's see. Open your gown." She listened to my heartbeat, checked my pulse and temperature. "And emotionally?"

"I'm...I'm not sure. Some days I feel like I'm doing better, that I've finally put it in its place, and then something will remind me and I'm in hysterics again. It's driving me crazy."

"Lie back," she instructed. "That's perfectly normal. Have you resumed having sex? I know you stopped by the other day for a Depo shot."

"No," I said tentatively. "I'd like to, but Sebastian..." My voice faded away as I struggled to put my feelings into coherent order. In the meantime, she finished her pelvic exam and peeled off the rubber gloves.

"Give him time. He was quite distraught. I wanted to prescribe him something to help him sleep, but he refused to take anything."

That old friend guilt reared its ugly head.

"Yes. He's incredibly stubborn. The pills—he wouldn't take them because he used to have an addiction to oxycodone. He was keeping a promise he'd made to me."

"Everything looks good. You can get dressed."

After the physical exam, she instructed me to meet her in her office. Sitting behind her desk, Dr. Rossetti watched me fidget with the hem of my skirt, speculation in her hazel gaze.

"Physically, you're completely healed. You can try for another baby as soon as you want." My gaze snapped up to meet hers. The pain and panic must have been shining openly because she didn't pursue that topic any further. "I have an idea—do you have any plans until your interviews for residency?"

"No," I answered, shaking my head. It felt like I was staring into an abyss of boredom. For the first time in my life I had no direction, nothing to work towards. I was rudderless and adrift.

Scribbling on a notepad, she said, "I have a dear friend who runs a free clinic. He's often understaffed, and is in desperate need of volunteers." Her lips curved up faintly and mischief lurked in her tip-tilted eyes. "I'm warning you. The reason he's often understaffed is because he runs them off. He's brilliant—his instincts as a physician are bar none—but what he lacks severely are people skills. And I mean *severely*. I have a knack for these things, and I think you can handle it."

An electric awareness ran through me. This was exactly what I needed—a plan, a job, a way to channel all these muddy feelings into something good and worthwhile. A purpose.

Dr. Rossetti smiled at the excitement on my face. Walking me to the door, she handed me the paper with the information on it. "Don't let the arrogant bastard intimidate you."

I turned and smiled. "I have plenty of experience handling arrogant bastards."

On the way home, Bear in the driver's seat, the Mercedes sandwiched between a convoy of SUVs, I sat in the back of the car and Googled, Dr. Yannick Kama. Dr. Kama, it seemed was something of a celebrity. And younger than I had expected— late thirties. The only son of a Danish supermodel and a famous Senegalese professional soccer player. He attended Oxford and received his medical degree from the Sorbonne. Arrogance stared back at me from the picture accompanying his bio. Though with his pedigree and accomplishments, who could blame him.

***

As soon as I left the doctor's office I checked my phone.

His Highness: On my way home early. Tough day. I'll see you soon. Love you, always.

Love you, always...

He ended every text with those three words. Words that turned me inside out every time I read them. Because he meant it with all his heart. He may not have been Lord Byron, but that's not what I wanted. I wanted honesty and straightforwardness. I wanted white or black. Not gray, not empty, disposable words and broken promises.

We pulled around the side of the manor twenty minutes later. François opened the car door for me looking like he had finally gathered the courage to say something. When his lips parted, I cut him off. "I'm sorry. I'm in a rush." I ran past him like my hair was on fire. In a mad rush to find the man that owned my heart, I stormed into the kitchen and almost crashed right into Olivier.

"Marianne...Olivier," I said in greeting, a huge smile stretching across my face. "Have you seen—"

"The gym," Olivier replied before I could finish.

My stride didn't falter. Turning immediately in the direction of the stairs, I hurried up the steps, taking two at a time. From down the hall I could hear two voices coming from the gym. The raspy one spoke forcefully.

"Get your hands off me. I know what you're doing." That bored, languid voice was laced with contempt. "Yeah, I do—drop the pretense. We're done. I won't be needing your services anymore…you're fired, Yvette. Do I need to say it in French?"

It was moments like these, when he didn't know I was watching and listening, when he was most under duress, that my love for him felt like an unstoppable force of nature, gathering strength and expanding. His moral compass was never in question. It never wavered. He could be counted on to do the right thing without thought, or hesitation.

I stepped into the gym to find Yvette gathering her things and putting them in her gym bag. She wore a cowed look on her face, and shorts so small and tight they were practically nonexistent, barely covering her butt cheeks. Her dark eyes darted from me to Sebastian. *Is she wearing fake eyelashes to work?* Yes, she was. Without a word, she quickly scooted past me and exited.

Sebastian stood across the room with his hands resting on his hips, fingers tapping anxiously. His expression was one of utter exasperation. Our eyes met, and his softened. My admiring stare descended to a naked chest deliciously covered in sweat. He scraped his wet hair back and grabbed a towel. I didn't waste a second running into his arms. My unbridled excitement took him by surprise. He caught me in time, then chuckled while I spread kisses all over his sweaty face. I wanted to lick him like a lemon popsicle on a hot and humid day.

"Babe, I'm covered in sweat," he murmured, sandwiching the words in between kissing me and laughing at my enthusiasm.

"Yes, I know," I purred, and wrapped my legs around his hips to let him know exactly what I thought of that.

The red jersey Max Mara wrap dress I was wearing fell open at the waist. His hands slipped under the edges of my lace boy shorts, gripped my butt cheeks, and squeezed. I broke the kiss for a moment to look into his brandy colored eyes, and found a blaze of lust swirling and burning out of control. Against my intimate parts, I could feel every inch of him, rock hard and ready for me. My pelvis rubbed against his, my calves frantically trying to shove his black track pants down over the pronounce muscles of his beautiful rear end.

"I saw the doctor. We're good to go." I couldn't keep the silly smile off my face. His heavy-lidded gaze descended to my lips in a possessive, predatory stare I was delighted to see. It had been way too long since he'd looked at me that way.

"Birth control?"

"Depo shot five days ago after I finished my monthly."

"Well in that case…"

He walked forward, carrying me over to a machine that had nylon straps hanging from it. "Grab those straps," he ordered. His tone sent a shiver rippling across my skin, putting my senses on high alert. This was the man I fell in love with, before pain and heartbreak came between us, before the seeds of doubt germinated into full-blown distrust.

The craving I had for him was relentless, the anticipation driving me insane. I grabbed the straps over my head and twisted them around my wrists. Secured by the straps, anchored to him, I wanted to be taken, used and abused in every way imaginable. Something I would not have entertained, not even in my worst nightmares, only six months ago felt natural with him. I locked my ankles around his waist and my ballet flats fell one by one with a thud onto the wood floor.

"You have no idea how many times I've dreamed about this," he muttered. I mumbled something about making all his dreams come true, and he chuckled before I shut him up with a kiss. Desire exploded between us, turning amusement into ashes.

Without warning, he grabbed my dress and ripped it apart. It disintegrated in his hands. My poor underwear met the same fate. I gasped. The shock transformed into a huge grin. For once I didn't care who walked in on us. There was no contest and no doubt, desire easily trumped prudence.

Pulling my bra down, under my breasts, he stroked his wide palm over them, then fastened his mouth over my nipples. Drawing on them, teasing them until my eyes slammed shut and my body arched. A thin veil of sweat covered my skin. I could feel his hot tongue on my neck before he scraped the fine skin with his teeth.

"Stop teasing me," I muttered like a lust-starved teenager desperate to feel him take me. My eyes fluttered open to find him staring at my naked body with such fascination that it made me self-conscious. "What is it?"

"Every time I see you..." He shook his head. "It's like the first time." The murmur was barely audible, the vulnerable look on his face said he'd revealed too much. A moment later he grabbed my face and kissed me, devouring my mouth as if he hadn't tasted me in ages, until all thought ceased and passion obliterated everything other than us.

He pushed his pants down his muscular thighs, and his erection sprang free. Surrounded by a patch of dark blond hair, it bobbed up towards me, tempting me, wanting me. He gripped the base, and pumped up and down its entire length. Then he positioned himself, the head rubbing against me, the slickness between us easing the way.

"Wait," I suddenly said. Startled, he pulled back. As he stared into my eyes, I told him what my heart and my body were screaming, "I fucking love you." He blinked, surprise and amusement taking turns flashing in his expressive, amber gaze. "I *fucking love* you," I repeated, my voice full of conviction, encompassing so much more than what those four simple words meant.

His mouth curved up. His eyes overflowed with adoration. He looked happy and unburdened for a moment. I would've done anything to keep that look on his face.

"Language," he said, teasing me.

"You're a very bad influence, Mr. Horn."

"Damn right, I am," he muttered in a tone soaked in lust. "And for your information—I fucking love you, too." With that, he thrust his hips and filled me up. He was home. Where he belonged. And always would.

Chapter Eleven

AFTER WEEKS OF NEGOTIATIONS, THE Albanian Minister of Justice had agreed to hold the meeting at Horn & Cie. At least, that's what David Bernard told me when he prepped us for the meeting.

"Now remember, they will try to goad you into anything that resembles a confession. You *must* let me handle it." His neatly combed, silver head swiveled in the direction of Sebastian who was half sitting on the corner of his desk, his face a study in power and confidence. "That means you, too." Mr. Bernard's sharp, blue glare brooked no argument. With a scowl fixed firmly in place, Sebastian tossed his Hermés tie over his shoulder and crossed his arms, his silver cufflinks clinking as they brushed together. Watching Sebastian back down was a rare sight—one I took secret pleasure in.

At present, we were in the conference room, the three of us on one side of the ten-foot-long conference table, them on the other. The attaché, Mr. Imami, wearing an Italian suit that looked far too expensive for a government official, sat unnaturally still. The two colleagues seated next to him looked bored and useless. It was clear they were only along as a show of force.

"She will have to admit to some degree of responsibility," Mr. Imami stated, his English only slightly colored by an Albanian accent.

I didn't need to see Sebastian to feel him tense. Stealing a sideways glance, I watched his jaw pulse and his nostrils flare, and I knew he was getting ready to strike back. "Not a chance," Sebastian replied in an ominously low voice.

Interjecting before the meeting acrimoniously unraveled, Mr. Bernard clarified, "What my client means to say, Mr. Imami, is that we can all agree that there isn't a shred of evidence to link Miss Sava to the theft."

Mr. Imami's heavy-lidded, dark eyes shifted back and forth between Mr. Bernard and Sebastian. The sharpness of his cheekbones made the heavy, dark bags beneath them more pronounced. But it was the incredible stillness of his body that had my attention. My instincts told me there was cunning behind that stillness, and possibly violence. It had me on edge.

"Are you suggesting that the missing money be explained as an accounting error?" His lips barely moved when he spoke. I understood the subtext all too well. It would have been an egregious mistake to imply that the Minister of Finance could have bungled something so thoroughly. It would've been construed as serious breach of respect, and any negations would have suffered a quick and sudden death.

"We're suggesting that Dr. Sava acted alone. That Miss Sava had no knowledge of the crime until his apparent suicide," Mr. Bernard concluded while stealing a glance in my direction.

My entire body turned to stone. Under the table, Sebastian squeezed my hand. They were going to pin it all on my father based on a slew of assumptions, without any concrete evidence. Mr. Imami showed no outward display of his consent. However, the tension in the room seemed to lessen by a few degrees.

"Furthermore, the five million dollars my client has agreed to donate to the university should go a long way to smooth any ruffled feathers the minister may still have over the details."

Five million dollars... The shame and guilt I felt at the moment was indescribable.

"Have you located the account in her name?" Sebastian inquired. Everyone's attention slid to Mr. Imami who was doing a terrific impression of a statue. Sebastian's expression altered, a sly understanding replacing his curiosity. Deducing the answer, he announced it to the rest of us still in the dark. "It's not offshore."

"Montenegro," offered Mr. Imami.

I stood suddenly, my chair screeching across the marble floor. "My father is innocent!" I heard the words come out of my mouth too late to stop them. "And when I was interrogated the police said it was offshore." All at once I felt the scorching heat of every pair of masculine eyes in the room. I sat down abruptly.

"They were bluffing," Sebastian clarified. Mr. Imami simply stared back, his face a portrait of apathy.

Mr. Bernard didn't miss a beat. "Then we can all agree. Miss Sava has clearly proven she had no knowledge of the whereabouts of the money. Let her give you an official statement indicating as such, and let's have the matter be done with."

"There's still the issue of the money," Mr. Imami added.

"Which we are prepared to wire as soon as the case against Miss Sava is dismissed," David Bernard swiftly countered. "We have no objections if you wish to pursue the case in any other direction."

Time seemed to expand as we waited for Mr. Imami's agreement. Only a little thing such as the course of my life hanging in the balance, but why hurry. And then, there it was, a slow blink signaling Mr. Imami's consent. That's all it took to alter my destiny forever.

David Bernard rose out of his seat and extended a hand across the table to Mr. Imami who also stood. The two men shook hands.

"I'm curious," Sebastian started, surprising everyone, including myself. "What evidence did you have against Dr. Sava?" His voice had adopted a nonchalance I recognized as artifice, though I highly doubted anybody else would. "Other than the circumstantial evidence of his suicide, and the money being wired out of the university bank account to one under Miss Sava's name?"

Dark, fathomless orbs dueled with whiskey colored ones. I could almost see Mr. Imami's mind working quickly, throwing up hypotheticals, measuring cost to reward ratios. He cocked his head slightly. "His personal effects held nothing of interest." It might as well have been an admission that there may have been the slight chance that my father had been innocent. "Make no mistake, no one else had access to that money." Any other time in my life I would have jumped at the chance to argue my case, or more specifically my father's. But something told me to stay quiet…something that felt a lot like trust.

"In that case, Miss Sava would love to have her father's personal things back…sentimental value and all?"

A beat later Mr. Imami replied with a slow nod. Sebastian had not only negotiated my freedom at great cost to himself, but he had also restored to me what remained of my father. And for the first time in my life, I contemplated the possibility that I may have been the luckiest girl in the world.

✳✳✳

It was midnight when I padded barefoot into the library. The distinct cuckoo of the elaborately carved Black Forest hunting wall clock marked the time. The box full of my father's belongings remained where I'd left it on the eighteenth-century table in the middle of the room. I walked up to it with more caution than necessary, as if it were radioactive. You could definitely make an argument that it was bad for my health. It had been silently torturing me from afar for two days now, denying me even a small measure of peaceful rest. Picking the box up, I sat cross-legged in front of the fireplace that was now cold and dark. Recalling what had happened hours ago put a smile on my face.

He'd found me in the library, searching for a book to read. The lines on his face put there by the burden he carried alone told me it had been another rough day at the office. Later, he would explain that the Dow had lost over seven hundred points, the consequence of which would be felt around the globe—including at Horn & Cie.

Such a remarkable man. Thousands of people depended on him to steer the ship correctly, to make the right decisions often under pressure, and against questionable odds—their livelihoods depended on it. He made carrying all that responsibility look effortless and never asked for anything in return.

As the conversation faded into silence, words became redundant. The longing and hunger in his gaze conveyed all that needed to be said. There was a brief moment of pause, an understanding passing between us, and then we both flew into action. Within seconds, we were both naked. More than one button on his shirt went skipping across the stone floor. My underwear suffered a more brutal and definitive demise. He had me bent forward, over the rolled armrest of the chesterfield sofa before I realized what he had in mind…or more specifically, how he needed it. With my head resting on the cushion, he took me gently, slowly—too gently. I slammed back into his groin, urging him on until the loud slapping sound drowned out my moans and cries.

I closed the door on that line of thought and focused on the box before me. Pandora's box—because I had no idea what I would find inside and what the repercussions would be.

Steeling myself for the worst I took the top off and began meticulously retrieving every item inside, placing each one side by side on the antique Persian rug.

Four flash drives.

Bank statements.

A diary.

His battered, dog-eared personal copy of *Plato's Republic* that he was never without.

A picture of the two of us that had been taken at my engagement dinner.

And lastly, a picture of my mother...she didn't look a day older than nineteen.

I couldn't stop the tears from falling any more than I could stop the earth from spinning. I missed him desperately. Although I couldn't deny that there was still a shade of resentment coloring my memories of him. That last conversation we had played over and over in my mind, even after all these years...

I had picked up the morning paper that day on the way to class, read the headline, and almost cast up my crumpets onto the sidewalk. A picture of my father stared back at me from the front page. The long and the short of it was that he was being indicted for embezzlement. The theft of three million U.S. dollars didn't go undetected in a country that only has a total GDP of fifteen billion. I willed my legs to run, not just walk me to his office. His longtime secretary, Jerina, saw me rushing down the hall with a bewildered expression. Hers became sympathetic almost immediately. Then, something akin to guilt flashed across her face, though it was gone before I had the chance to take a closer look.

"He went home, Vera. They won't allow him back to get his things until tomorrow, and only accompanied by an officer of the law," she told me in a pained voice. An attractive woman in her late forties, I knew she'd been in love with my father for years, and hoped he could return her affection. It never came to be. Whatever he had with my mother was sadly the beginning and the end for him.

By the time I reached our comfortable but modest apartment, I was sweating bullets. I found him still dressed in his immaculate gray suit, sitting at the kitchen table with his copy of *Plato's Republic* next to his cup of espresso, staring out the window absently.

"Papa?" He didn't turn to look at me. "Is it true?" I asked in Albanian.

"Is what true, *Zogu*?" he replied casually, using an Albanian pet name which means birdie. I swallowed the damning words stuck in my throat. It seemed insane to even voice the question out loud, directed at a man I had always held as the standard-bearer of ethics in the world.

"Did you do what they're accusing you of?"

He turned to look at me then. Brown eyes to brown eyes, unwavering, he said, "No." Something inside of me fell back into place. I knew he would never lie to me. Never. After that, I never once questioned whether he was innocent of the crime he was being accused of.

"Hey."

I turned towards the masculine voice coming from the doorway. He leaned against the frame with his arms crossed in front of him, the sleek lines of his muscles in stark relief, the gray sweatpants he wore hanging low on his slim hips. A sated smile graced his face, his lips swollen and bruised by my hungry kisses. His moods had been so volatile lately it was a relief to see him so relaxed. Amazing what good sex could do to a man's mood. I only hoped it lasted longer than an evening.

"The bed's cold without you." His gaze fell on the lid of the box I was holding. Uncrossing his arms, he walked over and stood next to me. "You're going through your father's stuff?"

he asked, his fingers raking through my short hair.

I didn't think he expected an answer. I think he was just surprised I had finally gathered the courage to do it. My attention back on the contents of the box, I said, "It just doesn't make sense…it has never made sense."

He exhaled deeply and lay down with his legs stretched out, his weight resting on his elbows.

"Can you think of *any* reason why he would do this?"

"Not one. He was never interested in anything remotely pecuniary. His hunger was always for knowledge." One glance at Sebastian's expression told me he wasn't entirely convinced. "You don't believe me? Of course, you don't," I said, bitterness coating my tongue. "The man who owns a bank wouldn't believe that some people aren't motivated by money."

"Pump the brakes, darlin'." He grasped my chin and tilted it so we were eye to eye. "At least let me explain before you go judging my thoughts."

"Then it's me you don't believe—don't trust?"

"That's not it either," he corrected, shaking his head. "Did you ever wonder how he could afford a nanny and a private tutor imported from England?"

The question rolled around my stomach like a lead marble, a question that had been slowly poisoning me for the past six years—and the only reason for me to ever doubt my father's innocence.

"We lived a very modest lifestyle. No vacations, one small car. The apartment was a small two-bedroom."

"That's a bit convenient, don't you think? You're a smart woman, Vera, do the math."

His words were arrows that hit the proverbial bull's eye perfectly. The old wound gaped open. As the pain seared through me, I closed my eyes. Until I felt the warmth of his hands wrap around my face, felt the soft brush of his lips on my own. "He loved you. He wanted what was best for you." His voice trailed off. I wiped at the tears threatening to slide down my cheeks.

"What's best for me?" I scoffed, disgust following on its heels. "I could've done without the high-priced education, believe me."

"I always have," he murmured. The sympathy on his face transformed to determination. "I want to show you something." Taking my hand, he pulled us both up off the floor.

"Not tonight, Sebastian," I pleaded, shaking my head. "I've had enough for tonight."

"It won't take long."

He dragged me out of the library and down the hall to a part of the estate I seldom visited. Most of the rooms in that wing were locked up, the furniture covered and the drapes drawn shut. He walked up to a panel of double doors that were beautifully decorated with etched glass. Pushing the doors open, he turned on the lights that revealed the beauty within. Mesmerized, I didn't know where to look first.

The ceiling was entirely covered in etched glass tiles. A gorgeous alfresco graced the walls, and an Olympic-sized pool decorated with Italian hand-painted tiles stretched from wall to wall.

"Wow," was all I could say as I took everything in. Sebastian walked over to a wrought iron lounge chair and sat down. "Why do you have this room closed up? Why is the pool drained?" I asked offhandedly.

Sighing, he raked his fingers through his hair in a gesture I knew meant he was about to discuss a topic he didn't want to. I walked over to him and smoothed his hair back into place while his eyes fluttered shut.

"What is it, lover?"

Clasping my wrists, he brought my hands down and held

them between us. "Remember when I told you that after my parents divorced I spent the summers here with my father?"

"Yes," I replied in a hesitant voice.

"My father and I had nothing in common. Even when he wasn't working, which wasn't often, I barely saw him. Obviously, there were no kids for me to play with so most games were out of the question. That's why I started swimming. Out of boredom, at first. But then I got hooked. On the silence, on the single-mindedness of it. Swimming focused my thoughts...kept the loneliness away."

The last words were barely a whisper. And yet they were spoken loud enough to crack my heart open and leave it bleeding. I bent down to kiss him, but he placed his fingers over my mouth and stopped me.

"I have to get this out," he said, his eyes holding mine. With a nod, I let him continue. "One day my father happened to be walking by and saw me. By then I had been training for months. I was already pretty good—for an eleven-year-old," he clarified, adding a quick grin.

"He never said anything. He just started showing up every day at the same time to watch me. I was so excited. My father had never shown any interest in me whatsoever—other than to make sure I was breathing." Wincing, I laced my fingers through his and squeezed.

"Then he started showing up with a stopwatch, timing me. Everything changed after that. At dinnertime, we talked. We started discussing different training methods, what strokes I needed to work on. He bought me videos of past Olympic meets. It was like we were finally speaking the same language."

"What happened?" I asked, my voice strained from a growing sense of dread. It was like watching a horror movie. I could see where this was leading, and yet I still couldn't stop my stomach from clenching painfully.

"I started winning. I would've killed myself to please him...I almost did," he continued, his gaze falling to our joined hands. "After training with him that summer, I went back to Texas obsessed with being the best. By spring of the following year, I was ranked second in the U.S. for my age group. That summer I flew back and forth for my swim meets, but I couldn't break through to number one. The title was held by a kid from California twice my height."

I held his gaze, willing him to continue. He sucked in a deep breath and exhaled.

"We met for our usual training session. I hadn't slept well the night before. At dinner we'd discussed the last meet, and he didn't say much. He was still pissed about a meet that I'd lost badly. I was tired—I'd been training too hard. During sprints, I kept hearing him shouting, pushing me. So I kept going, way past my lactate threshold...and then I blacked out.

"The next thing I remember was coughing up a shit load of water and my father standing over me, screaming something in German. His face was red and the vein between his eyebrows ready to explode...

"He left for London that day. Marianne said it had to do with work, but I didn't believe that for a minute. I found the doors to this room locked. Bentifourt told me my father had the pool drained, that I was never to set foot inside again."

I hadn't realized that my hands had moved to cover my mouth until he peeled them away and held them.

"We never talked about swimming again. Not when I set a world record in my age group at sixteen, not when I won national championships..." His voice lost volume while his eyes remained on me.

What could I possibly say? Any words would have either been an insult to his feelings, or an outright lie. So I crawled onto his lap and wrapped my arms around his neck, holding him tightly as I stroked the back of his head, comforting him the only way I knew how.

"This is going to sound terrible…however, I'm glad he didn't take an interest in you," I whispered in his ear. "I'm afraid of what he may have molded you into if he had. And in case you don't already know, I happen to think you're perfect."

The last word was smothered by a passionate kiss. The intensity of his feelings was on the lips that met mine, on the fingertips cupping my face. He pulled back far enough that we were nose to nose.

"Whatever your father did," he said, shaking his head, "he did for your benefit, not for his own. You were everything to him. Give him a little credit for that."

In his eyes was a bottomless supply of love staring back at me, offering me comfort and understanding when he'd had so little of it in his own life. Tears of gratitude spilled down my face, tears I made no attempt to hide. And none were for my father.

Chapter Twelve

THE NEXT MORNING I WOKE up abruptly, just as the turn of the earth ushered in a new day. A persistent nagging at the back of my mind made it impossible to sleep. Next to me Sebastian didn't stir. He was on his stomach, a muscular arm stretched out, his long fingers gripping my thigh possessively. Slowly, I pulled away and crept out of bed.

In the box of my father's things I searched for the flash drive I had seen the night before. Cross-legged on the chaise lounge, I opened my MacBook and inserted it. At least a hundred folders popped up. A shock of awareness hit my stomach, butterflies taking flight. There was no doubt in my mind this was a good omen. One by one I opened each of them and began reading.

"What are you doing?"

Glancing sideways, I found him leaning on an elbow, his hair disheveled, a sleepy grin on his face. He looked so happy and relaxed I wanted the moment to last forever. My excitement, however, had other plans; it could only be contained for so long.

"You're not going to believe this," I said, jumping off the chair and into bed. I tilted the screen in his direction.

"Manuscripts. At least thirty of them. It's fiction. Pulpy thrillers...mystery and suspense. And they're pretty good," I said, finishing with a giggle. "My father's name was Tyrone. See," I said pointing. "This must be his pen name." *S. Tyrone* was neatly typed on the cover page.

Sebastian scanned the documents, the remnants of sleep wiped away by curiosity. "The publishing house is in Vienna. I'll contact them today," he said as he read. This new development made joy explode in my heart. Somehow I knew that we were onto something. "Did you know anything about this? These are old. Some of these date back over twenty years." He waited expectantly for my answer, his gaze laser sharp.

"Nothing. I knew nothing about this. He never mentioned it once."

"Then he had a tendency to be secretive," he said softly.

With that, the fragile thread of hope I was spinning snapped instantly. My eyes returned to the documents on the screen. "I guess you're right," I agreed dejectedly. "I need to know, Sebastian. Either way, guilty or innocent, I need to know. Or it will haunt me forever." I looked up into his sympathetic eyes—he, better than anyone, knew what it felt like to be denied closure.

"We'll get to the bottom of it. We'll find out, either way," he replied. And in that moment, hearing him use the pronoun *we* when in truth I couldn't do a single thing to help, my love for him expanded until I could no longer see the boundaries of it.

✳✳✳

For two days Sebastian's executive assistants tried to get in touch with the publishing company. No such luck. The paper trail led back to the owner, one Michael Kreitz, last known address, the outskirts of Vienna. Against Ben's and Gideon's fervent objections, we headed to Vienna in Sebastian's private jet with an entire squadron of security in tow, a Bombardier Global he purchased because of the lowest emissions of its kind. I did my best not to roll my eyes when he proudly rattled off the specs of his toy.

It was my first time on a plane, let alone a private jet, couple it with the fact that I was still acclimating to no longer being a fugitive from the law and to call me anxious would be putting it mildly.

"You're going to punch a hole through the floor of the cabin if you keep that up."

That was my lover's voice, the one seated next to me—I think. I barely heard it through the rush of blood in my ears and the pounding of my heart. Of their own accord my toes kept pressing down like they were pushing on the brake pedal of a car.

My gaze slid sideways where I found him focused on the screen of his cell phone, studiously avoiding my glare. His lips pulled between his teeth in a pathetic attempt not to laugh. "I'd offer you my hand, sweet love, but I already have a fucked-up knee—can't afford to lose a hand, too." When I socked him on the shoulder, he grabbed by fist and kissed the knuckles. Bending closer, he murmured, "I know what'll relax you," his rasp, extra-raspy. Then he took said fist and rubbed it up and down the button fly of his well-worn jeans—where he was already hard.

"That can't be normal. You need to see a doctor about that," I said, amusement replacing high anxiety for the moment.

"I am seeing a doctor. She's doing wonders for it," the beast answered in a filthy tone. His wiggling eyebrows persisted until I could no longer contain the laughter.

"I'm too anxious to read—or nap for that matter," I admitted, fingers tapping on the armrests.

My person was raked head to toe with a sulky look. "Ever hear of the mile high club?"

"Is that an American thing? I don't know how to ski. Besides, what does that have to do with how restless I am right now?"

His brow wrinkled. "Skiing…what?" His voice drifted into nothing. Then too slow blinks and an explosion of laughter filled the cabin. Someone to the left of me cleared their throat and my head swung in that direction. Six large men, including Gideon, stared back at me. Suspicion crept in that this had nothing to do with skiing. I turned beet red. Funny thing though, I didn't get anxious again until we landed. And on the flight back, I got a very good demonstration of what that club was about.

***

If Geneva is a grande dame, then Vienna is a sophisticated maiden. Against Gideon's wishes I opened the tinted window of the car and hung out of it panting like a dog in sheer awe of the architecture. The Schönbrunn Palace made me sigh, the Vienna State Opera made me *oooh* and *aaah*. After which, Sebastian pulled me by the waist onto his lap and kissed me until I was saying those things to him.

The last known address of the publishing house was a modest building in a residential neighborhood. Kreitz Publishing was still penciled into the directory next to the call button. We were the beneficiaries of more than one suspicious glare by the locals. I'm certain it wasn't every day that two carloads of armed men stood on the sidewalk loitering in that neighborhood. We were about to give up when a thin, middle-aged man clutching a small terrier under his arm walked out of the secured doorway.

"Excuse me, are the offices of Kreitz Publishing still on the top floor?" Sebastian asked him in English.

"Publisher has been closed for years," replied the man with a thick German accent. The dejected look on all our faces must've prompted him to continue. "Michael moved to the third floor."

Sebastian's gaze sharpened. "Michael Kreitz?"

The brown and white terrier whined and yelped. "Yes, now if you'll excuse me, Schatzie needs to do her business." As the man stepped out of the way, Gideon moved swiftly, smoothly catching it in time before it closed. Single file, the three of us made our way to the third floor.

"*Ich komme!*" the man on the other side of the steel door shouted after Gideon rang the doorbell at least a dozen times. The door cracked open, security latch still in place, to reveal an elderly man with thin white hair which had been swept from one side of his head to the other. He wore round eyeglasses on his pointy nose. If I actually believed in animal spirits this man's would definitely have been a mole.

"Michael Kreitz?" Gideon inquired.

The mole's suspicious eyes darted back and forth over the three of us. I gave him my biggest, warmest smile to offset the expressions of the two harbingers of doom standing next to me.

"Who are you?" Mr. Kreitz asked in English.

"I'm Sebastian Horn, of Horn Investment Bank." The arched eyebrow I gave him put a smile on his face. "And this is my wife, Vera Sava." At the mention of *that* word my whole body turned to stone. Sebastian slapped an arm around me and pulled me tightly against him. Mr. Kreitz's already small, blue eyes narrowed.

"Sava?"

Everything inside of me lit up at the sound of curiosity in his voice. "Yes, Sava," I repeated with barely contained enthusiasm. "I think you knew my father, Tyrone Sava?"

A slow smile grew on Mr. Kreitz's face, brightening his features. "How is Tyrone?"

My face fell. "May we come in?"

The security latch came off immediately and the door opened. "Please, please," he said, ushering us into the small apartment.

Twenty minutes later we were seated in a room that could have served as the setting for a turn of the century movie about a destitute nobleman. All the walls were covered with walnut bookshelves filled with old leather-bound books. The fine velvet which covered the wing-back chairs was threadbare. Dust covered every square inch of the place.

"He killed himself?" Mr. Kreitz repeated absently.

"I'm afraid so." When I nervously began picking on a hangnail, Sebastian gently took my hand in his. Warm and steady, the comfort he offered spread all the way to my bones.

"Mr. Kreitz, I need to know about the manuscripts I found in my father's personal items…you published them?"

His eyebrows rose comically high. "Published them? He was my best-selling author for close to a decade."

The news made me breathless, joy and excitement exploding in my chest. And then…my joy lost its shine. A thousand mixed emotions began to surface. Anger, suspicion, disappointment…anger. The look on my face must have said it all because his brow furrowed. "You didn't know?"

Automatically my eyes darted to Sebastian who was tightlipped and watching me closely. "No, he never said anything about it."

Mr. Kreitz frowned. "Quite odd."

"Yes. Quite. And I have no idea why he would keep it from me," I reluctantly admitted, my frustration palpable.

My eyes narrowed at the sunshine pouring in, highlighting the dust moats dancing in the air. As a child I was convinced it was invisible confetti that would only come out to play with the sun. Childish fantasy. Much like what I believed about my father. His expression fathomless, Mr. Kreitz's attention followed the shaft of sunlight out the window.

"Your father was a proud man…and a reluctant author. In ten years he came to see me once. To look me in the eye before he signed his first contract." That seemed about right. My father believed you could tell everything about a man by looking him in the eye. He also said you could tell everything about a woman by looking into her heart. My thoughts drifted to the handsome man sitting next to me. I wondered what he thought of my heart—what he saw when he looked in it—because he was the only person I had ever revealed it to.

"He never did a single personal appearance, or book signing. I fought him tooth and nail, but he made me put it in the contract," he said wistfully, a smile on his face as if he were reliving the argument and enjoying it. "It amazed and embarrassed him that readers wanted to meet him." Mr. Kreitz broke off his reverie and looked me squarely in the eyes. "I think he was embarrassed of this work—too low brow for an esteemed professor. Pity, really, he was gifted. And then, he suddenly stopped."

That got everyone's attention.

"Exactly when did he stop?" Sebastian cut in.

His gaze unfocused, Mr. Kreitz pushed his glasses up the bridge of his nose and said, "In 2001...no, 2000. Yes, that's it, 2000." Sebastian's pointed gaze turned to meet mine. Words redundant. By now we had a language all our own; I knew what he was asking.

"Mr. Whitehurst returned to England that year. I enrolled in university."

"Mr. Kreitz," Sebastian started gingerly. "Ballpark...I mean, approximately. What were the royalties for Dr. Sava's books?"

"Let's see...I published approximately three books a year for him over a ten-year period...translated into five languages...international sales..." he kept murmuring to himself. Then he met the anticipation on Sebastian's face. "Approximately?"

"Yes, approximately," Sebastian repeated with a slow smile.

"A little under two million U.S. dollars." His small, blue eyes darted between Sebastian and me. I'd never seen Sebastian speechless. Never. Mr. Kreitz had accomplished the impossible.

***

On the plane ride back home I was a live wire, infused with the energy of a champion. I felt vindicated, burning with the desire to scream from a mountaintop, dance on the ashes of my father's accusers. My father had earned the money to pay for my education with what he believed to be a stain on his reputation.

Sebastian was still speechless. At some point he got tired of watching me tap dance in my seat, pulled me onto his lap, and made love to my mouth—effectively shutting me up. When he got tired of that, he gave me a tour of the beautifully appointed bedroom in the back of the plane, where I effectively shut him up.

The mile-high *high* didn't last though. As soon as we landed, my mood plummeted to basement level when we found Agents Vasquez and Lewis waiting for us on the tarmac. And they weren't alone. Looking like the grim reaper's hotter, younger brother, Ben stood next to them dressed head to toe in black, legs locked and arms crossed over a bulging chest.

The troubled look that appeared on Sebastian's face as soon as he spotted them told me everything I needed to know.

"What now?" he drawled.

Ben's cheek twitched. I'd never seen him look concerned before. He was always in neutral, irreverent in the face of danger. No doubt part of his training. "We got intel out of the driver."

Sebastian's focused gaze moved to Agent Vasquez. Thumbs hooked into her belt, hers met Sebastian's with just as much intensity. "Right before they picked him up he got the green light to take you out—no more warning shots. They're coming after you."

Only hours ago I was soaring with joy. Now I was descending quickly into despair, my fear for him immeasurable. I tried the best I could to put a brave face on, but it was hopeless. Fingers laced, I squeezed his hand, sandwiching it between both of mine.

"We need to get you out of town," Ben stated, because it was too late for suggestions. His pale, frosty gaze narrowed in deep thought. "Somewhere isolated, someplace you don't have habits—somewhere easy to see them coming."

Sebastian and Ben exchanged knowing glances.

"A boat," Sebastian stated. Ben agreed with a simple nod.

Chapter Thirteen

THE NEXT DAY WE LEFT for the French Riviera in a helicopter piloted by Ben. Not even Sebastian's filthy jokes could dissuade me from feeling anxious. I spent the entire flight with my heart in my throat and my short nails digging into his skin, which I only noticed when we landed. As soon as I spotted the red, crescent-shaped marks, I frowned and kissed his arm. Sweet man. He hadn't said a word about it.

By the time we landed, I was ready to fall to my knees and kiss the solid ground beneath me. There was no time, however. We were immediately escorted to a car and driven at warp speed into Cap Ferrat by Ben. Standing on a concrete pier that stretched for miles, my eyes climbed higher and higher until I was gazing up at a ship.

"We're going on a cruise?" I asked, in a delighted voice, my naïveté on full display. Sebastian's brow wrinkled. Then it dawned on him. His chest rattled with the deep sound of laughter that exploded out of his mouth. "No, babe. This is our boat."

"Just for us?" This couldn't be right. It was a cruise ship. I wrinkled my nose, the heat of the sun turning it fifty shades of red. I lowered my sunglasses to get a better look at it.

"Hmm."

"But…have you invited more people?" I looked around for a moment. My gaze returned to the "cruise ship."

"No—unless you mean those guys," he said, smiling, a mix

of love and amusement flashing in his whiskey colored eyes. I glanced around him and watched twenty armed men loading weapons onto our boat. No, we were definitely not taking a cruise.

***

Some people believe that with time you can become accustomed to just about anything. Time had done nothing to make me at all comfortable with this level of opulence. If anything, every day brought more evidence that I was a figurative and literal foreigner in a foreign land, an imposter. *Alice* wasn't meant to live in *Wonderland* after all. At some point she had to return to reality…didn't she?

On our way to Sardinia, we stopped in Corsica, dropping anchor just outside the Bay of Calvi. We were not alone in this; a number of megayachts were parked outside the bay because they were so large they would've run aground.

The vista was a feast for the senses. The red and gold craggy Corsican landscape jutted out and embraced the bay, the crystalline water a patchwork of blues and greens resembling spilled jewels glistening in the sunlight.

I whiled away the morning on the deck of the yacht, seeking refuge from the blistering sun under the shade of the enormous canopy of a lounge chair. The *sirocco* kicked up, a blast of dry, hot air carrying with it the sweet scent of North Africa. For the first time since we'd left Geneva, I let myself relax, closed my eyes and surrendered to the serenade of the wind.

The Mediterranean sun was not a friend to my pale skin, which hadn't seen a bathing suit in more than a decade. As I finished slathering every square inch of my body with zinc sunscreen, Sebastian emerged from below deck with his red swim trunks hanging dangerously low on his hips. He stretched his arms overhead and bent his head left and right, the motion causing his trunks to drop low enough that I could see…well, you get the picture.

"See anything you like?" he drawled, wiggling his eyebrows. His sense of humor was returning in small increments, more and more of it the farther we traveled from Geneva. That alone made the trip worthwhile.

I see the bite marks I left on your hipbone, I thought, though I kept that to myself. "Yes—and so will the captain and the crew if you don't pull up your trunks."

The remark only earned me another mischievous smirk. He was about to dive in when I said, "Let me put some sunscreen on you." Beneath the constellation of freckles that had sprouted up on his shoulders practically overnight, the skin was turning a little pink. When I held up a bottle of waterproof fifty, he wrinkled his nose at it, and shook his head.

"I'm not a delicate china doll like you," he replied in a low, sexy voice and dropped a quick kiss on my pursed lips.

Delicate…hmmm. I dug a finger right into the newly pink skin at the top of his shoulder blade and he winced, shying away from the pressure.

"Right, my pretty pink rose. Guess who's going to be looking for the bottle of aloe tonight." I finally got some on him, even though I had to suffer through more complaints and assurances of his manliness.

Already having given up all pretense of reading a novel, I slipped on the Victoria Beckham sunglasses which Sebastian had purchased on the sly—the sunglasses which I had refused to let him buy after almost swallowing my tongue when I saw the price—and watched him do laps up and down the length of the boat.

I couldn't take my eyes off of him. My very own merman. His skin gilded, sunlight glistening off the curved planes of his slick muscles, the graceful motion of his arms as they arced and sliced through ultramarine waves. I used to roll my eyes at the silly romantic novels the other girls at school would read. Now I was writing odes in my mind to the man's gluteus. Oh how low the mighty had fallen.

"Come in," he yelled, motioning with his arm.

"I like the view from here." The merman's smile was wide and bright, lighting up his whole face.

In the distance three tenders approached at a high rate of speed. The seemingly invisible armed guards aboard our yacht manifested out of nowhere. Their automatic weapons pointed at the intruder, it was an ugly reminder that although the scenery had changed, the danger had not lessened. Sebastian stopped swimming and bobbed up and down in the water, watching with narrowed eyes. When a smile broke across his face, I knew there was no threat.

"Hani, what's up, man?" Sebastian called out, amusement and surprise in his voice. After which, he lifted himself into the tender and a lot of hugging and back slapping began. The tender pulled along the side of our boat and Sebastian and the man he called Hani, along with his team of heavily armed guards, boarded the yacht.

Hani was average height and slim. He wore a short, neat beard and a smile that I got the impression was perpetual. He also had the most striking, rather unforgettably large, aquamarine colored eyes.

Over an assortment of grilled fish, from fresh *branzino,* a wild caught Mediterranean sea bass, to *langoustines,* the two men spent the entire lunch reminiscing. I soaked up every word. This was a glimpse into the life of the man I loved that I was too much of a coward to ask about. Because if I could pretend he didn't have a past, then I didn't have to face mine.

"Praise to Allah, he saw me go under the water." Hani had explained that he and Sebastian had met when they both attended Stanford. Pouring himself another glass of

Pellegrino, he continued, addressing me directly, "It was stupid of me. Maverick's is one of the most dangerous places in the world to surf. I'm one lucky bastard that a world-class swimmer was there that day to pull me out and drag me to safety."

I glanced at Sebastian and found a soft smile on his face as he watched his friend tell the story. *Boy Scout*, I thought—the nickname given to him as a child. As much as he hated it, it fit.

His expression suddenly sober, Sebastian said, "I have a favor to ask."

"Anything," replied his friend.

"I need you to find out as much as you can about a charity called The Crescent Foundation, they work with other agencies to assist displaced Muslims." Hani looked at the name of the organization on the screen of Sebastian's cell phone.

"Is this personal?"

"A good friend is involved and I want to make sure there's nothing shady going on."

Sebastian had tossed and turned all night long, restless, sleeping in short intervals until dawn filtered into the porthole. After that, he stopped pretending and went for a swim. I knew it had to do with Charles and the case, though I didn't pry. When he was ready, I hoped he would explain what was going on in his head.

"I'm happy to help," Hani said, nodding briefly. "Come tonight. I'm having a small get-together on my boat." Turning, he pointed to a megayacht that could have swallowed up the one-hundred-foot one that Sebastian had chartered. "I'll have the information for you." And with that, he placed a brief kiss on my knuckles, slapped Sebastian on the back, and boarded his tender.

"See you around eleven," he shouted over the loud roar of the engine. His high-powered tender kicked up a froth of white. Waving, he sped away, his security team following closely behind.

Chapter Fourteen

A SMALL GET-TOGETHER...*RIGHT*. The party was well underway when we arrived around eleven. Nearly three hundred people crowded the open decks. Music courtesy of a celebrity DJ pumped obnoxiously loud. I'm not ashamed to say I was completely star struck. Models and actresses rubbed elbows with Arabian princes and world-class soccer players, a Pulitzer prize-winning writer talked animatedly with a Russian oligarch. Everywhere I looked there was a face I recognized from television or magazines.

Totally unfazed, Sebastian took in the scene. He looked rather bored actually. But instinct told me it went deeper than that, that the boredom was hiding a darker sentiment.

"Stay here, I need to hit the bathroom," he instructed. I nodded, though a little uneasy about being left alone. "I'll be right back," he said and pressed a quick kiss on my lips when he noticed the dubious look on my face.

I walked around aimlessly, overwhelmed by the music, the din of women laughing and squealing, the cacophony of conversation. Pushing past scantily clad bodies, I cut through the drift of expensive perfume hanging in the air, and found a small corner at the back of the boat to hide, to get away from the critical stares of these people I had absolutely nothing in common with. It dawned upon me then, why Sebastian shied away from this, why he was so closed off and guarded—what growing up in an environment such as this could do to a person who was sensitive and thoughtful. Skin to sweaty skin, pressed between all those beautiful bodies, I had never felt so alone, so lost...forever a stranger in a strange land.

Eventually I got tired of waiting. After what felt like an eternity, I went in search of him. As I walked through one of the cabins, I heard his distinct voice drawling, "Someone's waiting for me. What do you want, Delphine?" The impatience in his voice was pronounced.

"You won't return any of my phone calls. I just want to know how you are. I'm worried about you," I woman replied, her accent American.

"No need to worry about me. I'm good—great actually."

"Well, I'm glad to hear that...you look good."

There was a heavy pause, and then he said, "I'm getting married."

I reached out to hold onto the wall, my muscles shaking, my knees giving out, too many thoughts and feelings hitting me at once.

"What?" she exclaimed. "Is this your idea of a fucking joke?" Her tone instantly sounded alarm bells. Clearly Delphine was not happy about the news, regardless of whether it was true or false. "Boy, you moved on fast. Did she mean anything to you? Did you ever really love her?"

"How dare you ask me that," he growled in a low voice.

Reacting without thought, I plastered a smile on my face and stepped into the room. "There you are."

He wrapped his arm around my waist and crushed me to his side. I had to loosen his grip just to be able to breathe. She was beautiful, there was no debating that, tall and reed thin, long, black hair cascading down her suntanned back. Impulsively, I reached up and ran a hand through my short hair. Her intense, dark eyes traveled from my Blahnik high-heeled sandals, to my Tom Ford dress in a thorough inspection. Something about her looked familiar. As a matter of fact the shape of her features reminded me a lot of…

"Vera, this is Delphine—India's sister. Delphine, this is my fiancée."

My stomach sank and goose bumps swept over me from head to toe. "It's a pleasure to meet you," I said, stretching a hand out.

Her eyes shot straight to my bare ring finger. Then she took my hand in a weak grasp, and shook it briefly.

"Congratulations," she said in a flat, dry tone. It was pretty clear she didn't believe congratulations were in order. Immediately, her eyes, filled with resentment, returned to Sebastian. "It's good to see you." The longing in her voice fanned the flames of my possessiveness.

"Darling, we should go find Hani," I said, laying it on thick and knowing it really was beneath me. Sebastian laced his fingers through mine. "Be well, Delphine," he said and dragged me out of the cabin. The weight of Delphine's stare caused me to glance over my shoulder. She stood perfectly still, her eyes glued to his back. Something about it made me crowd closer to him.

On deck, he parted the wall of bodies with ease, pulling me along. "Let's get the fuck out of here," he said.

Just then, Hani's voice rose above the noise. "Sebastian!" We both looked up and Hani waved, motioning for us to join him on the top floor of the yacht.

We climbed the steps to the third deck. Meanwhile, Sebastian's jaw held a tightness I recognized as discomfort. It worried me that he was pushing himself too hard. Hani waved us over to the table. Seated next to him were three, young women, by the look of them, models. Snapping his fingers, he said something in a low voice and, without a word, the girls stood and left the table. Hani picked up the bottle of Crystal.

"Champagne?"

"Not for us," Sebastian answered without a glance my way. The fact that he hadn't bothered to ask me rankled but I pretended otherwise. The tension surrounding him was palpable, his encounter with Delphine still looming over him like a black cloud. I made a mental note to ask him about it later. Hani shrugged and placed the bottle down.

"Did you find anything out?"

"Yes," Hani answered, his face a mix of interest and concern.

"I owe you, man."

"Yes, you do. It wasn't easy...the charity organization is based in Beirut." Hani's dark eyes looked troubled. "On the surface, everything looks tidy."

"Shit." Sebastian tilted his chin up, his gaze taking in the night sky. Overhead, countless stars twinkled while turmoil churned down below. "And?"

I didn't miss the way Hani scanned the surrounding area left and right before speaking. In a low voice, he replied, "And the doctor that runs it has ties to Hezbollah. Distant ties, but ties nonetheless—at one point he was the personal physician for a top-ranking Hezbollah leader."

His eyes slamming shut, Sebastian mumbled a low, savage curse.

"Could be nothing," Hani offered. Sebastian's piercing gaze slid back to his friend. Sighing deeply, he said, "Highly unlikely. But I sure as fuck hope you're right."

✳✳✳

Lost in his dark thoughts, Sebastian didn't utter a single word on the trip back to our boat. Once we were back on board though, he wasted no time. Taking my hand, he led me below deck and straight to the bedroom

As always, he stripped me slowly, with infinite care, as if he were unwrapping a priceless artifact. Except this time it made my blood boil. The more clothes he carefully peeled off of me, the angrier I became. His mind felt a million miles away. Even his touch felt plastic, bloodless and foreign. I began tugging roughly on his linen shirt. When a few buttons flew off, he scowled at me and placed his hand over mine.

"What?" My voice was intentionally sharp.

"Easy," he warned.

I scoffed, and the v between his brows deepened. Undeterred, he continued his careful divesting of clothes until we were both naked and lying on the bed. The moonlight streaming in through the porthole made the room look dreamy and incandescent while my mood was quickly sinking to black.

The petal-soft kisses started at my ankles, traveled over the soft landscape of my inner thighs, over my hipbone and belly. I had never once shied away from his touch. This time, however, everything felt off. By the time he reached my collarbone, he could sense I wasn't aroused; we had always been acutely aware of each other's needs and this moment was no different. His fingers languidly stroked between my thighs. The dryness was unmistakable. His eyes flickered to mine and lingered on the tightness of my pursed lips. "What is it?"

It took me a moment to screw up the courage. Looking him dead in the eyes, I said, "I want you to fuck me—hard."

I could count on one hand the times in my life I'd used that word. My heart sped up, drumming inside my chest like it wanted to be free of my rib cage. His eyes narrowed as he examined the degree of my intent.

"No."

As simple as that, he had shut me down. Then he leaned in for a gentle kiss. Anger exploded within me. I pushed him off and slapped him across the face hard enough that the sound echoed in the room.

To call his expression startled wouldn't even begin to do it justice. Blood surged up his neck and over his face, the throbbing vein at his temple looked like it would burst any moment, his jaw so tight it could've pulverized his molars.

"What the fuck!" he shouted.

I struck him in the chest, and his eyes narrowed. When I tried that again, he caught my arms and pinned them over my head to the bed. With feline stealth he pounced, his powerful body straddling mine, raised over me. I glanced down and found him startlingly erect. He was so hard it was almost touched his stomach. When my gaze lifted to his, there was a lewd smile on my face. Complete consternation overtook his expression.

"What the hell is wrong with you?"

"I'm sick and tired of you treating me like I'm something breakable! I can't stand it another second!"

His grip on my wrists tightened as I fought him—tight enough for it to be painful. "Stop fighting me. I don't want to hurt you," he growled.

"You can't hurt me, you dolt!" Apparently I was making up for lost time because I didn't fight the impulse to call him every name in the book. "How many bloody times do I have to tell you that!"

His eyes became two golden slits. His expression darkened to the point that it made me pause. Once unleashed, the fury took over. He looked like that full-sized tiger I hadn't seen in a long time.

"You know what—sometimes I *do* want to hurt you." Raspy and low, his voice was positively primitive. "I want to dig inside of you, and tear you up just for existing—for making me love you!" Crouched low, his hips were pinned to mine. His erection pressed uncomfortably into my abdomen. "I want to get into your molecules and become part of your DNA. I want to be as vital to you as you are to me." Burning through my veins, a flush of intense heat traveled to the crease between my thighs. "You're pissed because I treat you like you're precious? You ARE precious to me! Fuck! As precious as my own heart—it's self-fucking-preservation!!" he shouted, inches from my face.

I broke one wrist free of his hold, and snatched his hair in a punishing grip. My lips crashed into his. He gave back in equal measure. We devoured each other. Squeezing, stroking, pushing and pulling. I squirmed until he was perfectly positioned over the apex at my thighs, and rubbed against him. Neither one of us held back. The friction turned into sparks of pleasure. I erupted instantly, screaming out his name.

His breathing was beyond harsh, the tendrils of his control visibly snapping. On a heavy exhale, he shifted and with a powerful thrust, buried himself to the hilt. The hard impact of our hipbones made me sigh in relief.

We weren't gentle or considerate. Our bodies slammed into each other without thought to pleasure or pain, without any sense of vanity. It was sweaty and coarse and starkly beautiful.

In the heat of the moment my short nails left a scarlet trail on his lower back and buttocks. Whispering words of encouragement in his ear, I urged him on until he turned wild, shoving me over the edge of a second orgasm forcefully. I came so hard spots floated in my eyes. And as I fell back to earth, a river of tears ran down the sides of my eyes and soaked the pillow, an overwhelming sense of relief unlocking the surfeit of emotion that had been trapped behind that steel door.

A moment later he reared up and found his own release. His face crumpled while his eyes remained open, staring into mine as he emptied himself inside of me…emptying the hurt I had inflicted, the distrust, the fear.

The look on his face eased all my concerns. The full weight

of him collapsed on top of me. I wrapped my legs and arms around him and held him close, soaking in the sensation as if it was the first time. After weeks of dancing carefully around each other, something fell back into place. We were us again. We had somehow found our way back to each other—no piece left behind.

"You are," I whispered in his ear, my voice cracking. "Now and forever."

"What?" he murmured in a vulnerable, almost inaudible voice. The vibration on the delicate skin of my throat made me shiver and tighten my hold on him.

"Vital to me."

Chapter Fifteen

THE ROAD WAS RIDICULOUSLY NARROW and treacherous, one lane in each direction. Hugging the mountainside, it snaked up higher and higher with no end in sight. I tried to keep my focus straight ahead, and not on the passenger side window that overlooked the steeply plummeting cliff. Every so often, I checked the rearview mirror to see how the large SUV with the security team was faring. They hadn't driven over the side yet so that was good.

"Are you going to white knuckle it all the way to the top?" The amusement in Sebastian's voice got my attention.

"This better be worth whatever it is you have planned."

"I think so," he crooned. With his eyes concealed by silver Oliver People aviator glasses and thankfully fixed on the task at hand, I couldn't get a better read on him. The small curve of his lips remained though. He seemed happy. That's all that really mattered to me.

We made love several more times the night prior. Never as fiercely, or with the same savagery of the first time, however, it still felt like he had broken loose of whatever it was that was holding him back. He was present in every kiss, every touch.

Needless to say, I woke up battered and bruised. When he saw me crawling to the bathroom hunched over, he raised an eyebrow. "I know I asked for it," I grumbled with a smile on my face. I turned on the shower as hot as possible, and let it pummel my muscles for ten minutes until he joined me and soothed all the aches away. Afterwards, we took the tender into Porto Cervo, the main port of northern Sardinia. And when I say port, I mean only megayachts allowed. Originally developed by the Aga Khan, it's now legendary as the playground of kings.

The top of the mountain was a flat, cleared parcel of land, deserted except for a small white church no larger than a cottage. My senses feasted on the breathtaking view. There was so much to take in my eyes didn't know where to land first. The bleached stucco highlighted the exquisite glass windows stained in primary colors. Overlooking the Mediterranean, it sat precariously at the edge of the cliff, lording over everything below.

I stepped out of the car and walked over to it. I wondered if they still held services at the church, or whether it was a historical landmark. A tug on the handle revealed that the doors were locked. In a daze I walked around the side of the small building until I reached the edge of the cliff, standing as close to it as I could without getting vertigo. The strong Sardinian wind blew under my white, cotton sundress, ballooning it up, and whipped my short hair around. Now a razor sharp, chin-length bob since Sebastian insisted on a hairdresser coming aboard before we sailed from Cap Ferrat.

"Was it worth it?" Sebastian's raspy voice called out from behind me.

Glancing over my shoulder, I found him a few paces away, leaning on his cane—something I had insisted on, argued about. I was glad I had; the virgin, rocky terrain was a serious hazard to his knee. One hand was casually stuffed in his beige, linen pants while a slightly mischievous smile graced his face. The breeze blew his long hair in every direction until he tucked it behind his ear.

"Every tired step, every lonely, sleepless night, every day I went without food—you are worth every minute of it."

The amusement dropped off his face, his expression solemn all of a sudden. I knew what that meant. I knew he wanted to wipe away every bad thing that had ever happened to me, but I didn't. In hindsight, I could admit that it made this moment all the sweeter.

His soft eyes caressed mine. "That's not what I—"

"I know what you meant," interrupting, I clarified. My eyes returned to the horizon. At this height, I could see the curvature of the earth, the sea a convex mirror reflecting dapples of sunlight that looked like the scales of a fish. Everything seemed calm, peaceful from this vantage point.

He came up behind me and wrapped his arms around my waist, pulling me back into the safe harbor of his body. The cane fell away with a thump. He placed a string of kisses on the side of my neck before his chin came to rest on my shoulder.

I don't know how long we stood together like that. Apart from the world. In a bubble where only the two of us existed. Away from responsibilities and expectations. Away from all the reasons that two people from completely different worlds could never make it as a couple in this one. I could've stayed like that forever.

"Run away with me," I murmured.

I felt his smile on the sensitive skin of my neck. "Where would we go?"

"We could live on that tiny island over there," I said, pointing to a rocky outcropping just off shore. "You could fish, and I'll make a fire and cook it."

"You know how to make fire?"

A beat later, I answered in a sullen voice, "No."

"What about water?" he said chuckling. The small island had no trees, which meant no leaves, ergo nothing to collect rainwater.

"Crap," I grumbled, defeated by his brilliant logic. "We're

going to have to swim back to civilization. And since I'm not a very good swimmer, you'll have to tow me in."

He turned me to face him. His eyes traveled from my eyes to my mouth, studying me with an intensity and seriousness that said it was important he remember this moment…that it might be the last time. The amusement dropped right off my face, a twinge of panic parking itself in my gut. When I reached up to cup his face, his eyes fluttered shut, as if he was summoning courage for what was to come next.

"What's wrong?" I said, the worry making me speak more harshly than I intended.

"I love you, Vera." I rushed to return the sentiment, but he stopped me with a sweet, closed mouth kiss, whatever I was about to say banished by the touch of his lips. Pulling away far enough to peer into my eyes again, he said in a gravelly, anxious murmur, "I can't get down on bended knee, but I am throwin' myself at your feet. Will you do me the honor of being my wife?"

My eyes instantly began to water, tears sliding down my face unimpeded. So much for not being a crier. Then again, everything I knew to be true had been turned upside down the day I'd met this man, this incredibly wonderful man. There were a million reasons it was a bad idea for him to bind himself legally to me. However, there was one that trumped all the rest. Was it enough to sustain a lifetime together? The cynic in me scoffed at the notion. And yet the disappointed romantic in me was reminded that I had left disappointment by the wayside the minute he walked into my life.

I linked my hands behind his neck, love and hope undoubtedly living openly in my eyes, and jumped into the unknown. "I would be honored to be your wife."

I knew the moment my words hit their mark and sunk in, when he allowed himself to believe them. His face split in a blinding white grin that he only brought out on very special occasions. I would've done anything for one of those smiles.

He crushed me to his chest and dropped kisses on my mouth, my temple, my nose in a frenzy of unbridled joy. Lost in the moment, I giggled like a teenager, the sound fading as a strong gust of wind carried it away.

A wild glint sparked in his whiskey colored eyes. "When do you want to get married? Tomorrow?"

"What?" I shouted, shocked back to reality.

"We can fly to Venice and do it there," he added quickly, his expression eager. It was then that I realized he was serious. Questions were thrown at me in such rapid-fire succession that I only caught every other word.

Church?

Fly everybody in?

Just us?

"Sebastian," I said, interrupting.

Not registering my prompt, he continued full steam ahead. "The jet is waiting for us at the airport. We could do it today if you want?"

"What?!" I kept repeating like an idiot. He did that to me often.

"Shit, I almost forgot," he said, digging into his pants pocket.

I could no longer blink, my eyebrows as high as my hairline. A deep, blue egg sat in the middle of his wide palm. A shade between cornflower and electric blue, the stone glowed, pulsed with life as if lit from within.

"It's a Kashmir sapphire, rare, one of the first mined by R.V. Gaines in the 1940s."

I barely heard him I was so mesmerized by it. Cautiously, I picked up the ring. The stone was set in a very delicate platinum and diamond band that only complimented the audacity of the gem. Turning it left and right, I watched it catch the light and reflect it back like velvet nap.

"It's said that sapphires are a guide for travelers and seekers." His eyes were downcast, his brow furrowing thoughtfully. He slipped the ring on my fourth finger. It fit perfectly. I wasn't surprised he knew my size, Sebastian had always expended more energy on me than I was comfortable with. I held my hand up. The oval stone almost covered the entire length of skin between my knuckle and the base of my finger.

"I saw it and thought of you...my traveler." He raked my hair back and held my face tenderly. "Unpack your bags and stay a while," he whispered, his lips hovering over mine. "Stay with me."

I'm the one that hurried to close the distance between us, kissing him with everything I had. Not for the ring, although it was beautiful, or the magnificent location, very romantic. But because of who he was—my lover, my friend, my conscience, my heart—so bravely baring his soul. My world began and ended with him.

To this day, I know less about the magic that causes two people to fall in love than I do about quantum physics. Such mysterious alchemy. But what I knew to be true from that moment on was absolute. Regardless of time and distance, we would always find a way back to each other.

✳✳✳

The next day I was on the deck of the boat, reading while Sebastian was busy videoconferencing the office, when one of the security guards hired by Ben handed me a heavy, manila envelope.

"Mr. Horn is below deck," I informed him. He shook his head, and said the envelope had been expressed from Geneva for me. My stomach churned nervously as I opened it and gingerly removed the stack of official looking papers. A typed letter from Mr. David Bernard, Esq. was clipped to the front.

Dear Vera,

Hope this letter finds you well. Let me begin by offering my congratulations on your engagement. With a conflicted heart, I write this letter in an appeal for your help. Please don't take this as a slight on your intentions regarding Sebastian, however, for the sake of the bank and the integrity of Sebastian's position, it would be best if you would sign the papers I have enclosed. I'll spare you the legalese. It's a binding contract stating that, in the event of a divorce, you have no claim on the bank. In the event of his death, you will receive a small portion of his inheritance, the rest will go to The Horn Foundation.

Without it, I'm afraid it will seriously complicate bank business and compromise Sebastian's standing with the clients. You should know that I have discussed this with Sebastian and have met with complete and utter resistance. I hope you prove more reasonable.
Best Regards,
David Bernard, Esq.

Without hesitation, I slid the pen from the envelope and signed all ten locations on the contract where the highlighted arrow pointed. Placing the papers back in, I handed it to the security guard and told him to send them back to Geneva for overnight delivery.

I hated keeping it from Sebastian. However, I knew that sharing the information would open an argument of epic proportions and my force of will was nothing compared to his. He was in a completely different weight class than me…I didn't stand a chance.

Strangely, as I signed my name on the dotted line, a yoke I was unaware of carrying around magically lifted. All the reasons I debated with myself regarding the possible cost to Sebastian's reputation by becoming his wife seemed to dissolve under the power of the pen. Without any claim to his fortune, we would be back on even ground. At least, we would in my eyes.

***

"Wake up," whispered a sexy, gravelly voice. Drifting on a sea of tranquility, a merman appeared in my dreams. His eyes supplicating, his voice calling me home. "Wake up, wake up."

There was mischief in that voice. I reached out to stroke his face but he caught my wrist and playfully bit my thumb. Then he wrapped his full lips around it and sucked. My body was suddenly burning. The sea of tranquility transformed into a wildfire of lust.

My hands stroked across his smooth, muscular chest and traveled down to his full-blown erection. Steel wrapped in velvet. It pressed against my hip begging for my attention. My hips, as if summoned by their master, turned to press into the merman's impossibly hard sex. Pushing and pulsing, gentle pleasure coiled into something much more potent.

"Wake up, sleeping beauty. I want to show you something and if we start that, we'll miss it."

This merman was very bossy. My eyes blinked open to find Sebastian's face hanging over me.

Wearing a crooked smile, and wicked intentions, he said, "Can you let go of my dick, babe?"

Barely conscious, I looked down and saw my hand fisted securely around him. Poor man. I peeled one finger off at a time. "Jesus, did I almost rape you in my sleep?" I croaked, my eyes falling shut again.

"Trust me, I was willing."

He grabbed both my wrists and pulled me out of bed. "Noooo," I whined.

"Yes," he replied chuckling.

Another fifteen minutes of cajoling and he had me semi-dressed and walking up four flights of stairs to the top level of the boat. As soon as I reached the last step, I got it. I knew what he wanted me to see…and it was worth it.

The image my eyes beheld was so awe inspiring, so absurdly romantic, that it brought a tear to the eye of a cynic like me. Without any pollution, electric or otherwise, nor clouds to speak of, the full moon was so large and perfect hanging low in the night sky that it looked Photoshopped. And on the opposite side, an infinite amount of stars sparkled down on us.

Lacing his fingers through mine, he led me to a lounge chair that fit us both comfortably. We lay down, him on his back, me wrapped around him, my leg pressing against his sex which was growing hard again. He tucked one hand under his head, and all the muscles of his arm and chest popped up. I'd never seen a more innately sexy man. No artifice whatsoever.

A falling star streaked across the night sky. Staring in wonder at the show Mother Nature was putting on just for the two of us, I murmured, "Am I still dreaming?"

He looked down at me. In his eyes there was more love gleaming brightly back at me than there were stars above. "If you are, don't wake up. I want to stay a little longer."

Chapter Sixteen

THE NEXT DAY WE DISEMBARKED in Sardinia. Sebastian's private jet was waiting for us at the airport of Olbia, where private jets came and went as regularly as taxicabs. Two hours later we landed in Venice and checked into the Gritti Palace hotel where Sebastian had reserved an entire floor of suites. A week after landing in Venice, we were married on a humid Sunday in the middle of September. My head was spinning at how quickly and efficiently Sebastian arranged everything. All I did was stand back and let the inexorable force of my beloved control freak take me wherever he wanted to go.

Hanging out of the open window, I watched the *vaporretto*, the water taxi, steam by on the Grand Canal and took in the incomparable view, almost surreal in its beguiling beauty. My spirits soared so high I could have flown out the window. A cacophony of different languages, from German to Japanese, drifted up from the narrow sidewalks down below. I smiled and waved at a Japanese tourist who lifted his camera to take a picture of the grand historic building.

"It's just a wedding, my love. Does it really matter where we do it?" When my question was met by silence, I glanced over my shoulder.

Since Sebastian was raised Baptist and stopped practicing ages ago, Roman Catholic law wouldn't allow us to be married in a church. Not unless we wanted to post banns and wait a month. It didn't stop him from trying though. The word *no* was a difficult concept for him to grasp.

Seated at the breakfast table bare chested with his pajama bottoms hanging on his hips in sheer desperation, he looked sexier than anyone had a right to. No shame whatsoever—I loved that about him. His heavy-lidded eyes met mine over the rim of his coffee cup. My attempt to reason with him was answered with a frown and an emphatic, "Yes."

Placing the cup down, he licked his lips and stalked over to me. A big cat hunting prey. He blanketed my body from head to toe, caging me with his arms and thighs. A low groan rumbled in his chest as he pushed the erection tenting his pajama bottoms against my rear end. He crammed himself snuggly between my cheeks and heat radiated to every point in my body. A slow burn that made me soft and compliant. His hips rocked slowly. His warm palm cupped my breast. He knew my weaknesses, knew how to turn them into his strengths, how to mold them into desire.

My eyelids grew heavy, my eyes lost focus. But I caught it nonetheless—the shadow of a woman in the building across the canal. Partially hidden behind a heavy silk curtain, she was watching us. My eyes tangled with her tip-tilted dark ones. She was older, maybe sixties, and by the easy grace in her posture and the way she held her cigarette between her long fingers, sophisticated. A dark flush of embarrassment crept up my neck, and yet, I possessed neither the will, nor the want to stop him.

He bit and kissed a path down the curve of my neck. An act of possession, of ownership. It sapped all the strength from my legs. Pressing his groin harder into my rear end, he trapped me against the wall below the window frame. His hand covered mine on the sill, his tan fingers resting between my paler ones.

A sudden realization crashed down on me. Everything that came before him, everything that I thought I was, had been a sham—the imitation. This is who I really was, my natural state. With him I felt alive for the first time in my life.

His other hand found the crease between my thighs and petted me over my nightgown. With no means of escape, I was tortured ruthlessly. "Now what were you saying?" he crooned while his other hand slipped beneath the gown and brushed my nipple.

"I...I don't think you should take it personally that the Pope wouldn't speak to you," I said, my voice cracking and breaking as I jumped between laughter and lust. Biting my lower lip, I managed to squeeze out, "I think he has more important matters to attend."

"I'm 'bout to atten' you in a minute, darlin'." His accent, thick and rich, ratcheted up the heat between us times ten; the shameless seducer knew what that accent did to me.

He gathered the hem of my gown and lifted it to my waist, pushed his bottoms down in one efficient motion. Kicking my legs apart, he spread me open with his fingers, his palm petting the place I was dying for him to touch.

My world turned into pure sensation. The velvety heat of his sex pressed between my cheeks. The crisp feel of the hair between his legs. The unyielding muscles of his abdomen pressed into my lower back. Pleasure tugged and tugged at me.

On pure instinct my hips rolled, my back arched, seeking him, wanting...needing. So much need. Thrusting powerfully, he buried himself inside of me to the root. My scream of approval reverberated off the ancient hand-painted walls of the hotel.

Deep and slow, he pumped into me. So deep I couldn't tell where he ended and I began. My eyes cracked open to discover the woman across the canal was still watching us. Shame blazed a fire across my cheekbones, but there was nothing to be done for it. I was lost to everything other than him, his body, the scent of sex that drifted languidly around us, the deep, raspy voice that murmured deliciously filthy things in my ear.

For reasons I couldn't even begin to understand this man ignited something in me that I never knew existed. In his arms I wasn't proper, or quiet, or measured, or apprehensive. I was a wanton thrill-seeker, a risk-taker. I was adventurous and carefree. And more in love than I ever thought possible.

"This is everything," I heard him murmur right before he had me screaming my release from the rooftops, his following in its wake.

Hours later, after we showered and attempted to put clothes on, I was watching him button his shirt, watching him conceal muscles honed by years of intense swimming, when I asked, "Why is this so important to you?" The question was meant to be lighthearted, casual. His large eyes, filled with profound emotion, left me to focus on the buttons he was fiddling with.

"I'm marrying the woman I love," he replied in a voice serious and true. "I don't intend to do this ever again. I want everything to be perfect."

That sobered me instantly. The naked sentiment hit me in the chest, my throat closing up at his sincerity, his courage, his ability to wear his feelings for me on his sleeve. Something I still had a very hard time doing.

***

In a shocking turn of events, the Roman Catholic Church did *not* bend to his will like the rest of us. He huffed and puffed all week at not getting his way, while I did my best not to laugh and crow *I told you so*. I was marrying a hopeless romantic after all—I had to remind myself to handle his feelings with care.

Mrs. Arnaud, Mr. Bentifourt, and Charlotte flew in on the

private jet three days before the wedding. Ben took a separate flight for reasons no one had a bloody clue about. Held in a historic villa overlooking the canals, the intimate civil ceremony was officiated by the Mayor of Venice.

I grabbed a hand towel and wiped my damp palms on it.

"Nervous?" Marianne asked while she buttoned the thousands of tiny, fabric covered buttons that trailed from the top on my spine to the hem of my train. My eyes met hers in the etched Venetian full-length mirror we stood before.

"We come from such different worlds…can this last a lifetime?"

In the subsequent heavy pause, her vibrant eyes skipped from me, to the buttons of my dress. "You are looking at it from the wrong angle."

"Meaning?"

"In which ways are you alike?"

The proverbial bull's eye. I was so wrapped up in listing all the ways we were different that I ignored the way in which we were alike. The most important way, the most fundamental way.

"Our souls…our souls are alike." She smiled back knowingly. Tears pooled in the corners of my eyes. "I love you, Marianne."

"I love you too, *chérie*."

The room, already breathtakingly appointed with authentic antiques, was decorated sparingly with large vases of white lilies. I stepped into the room wearing an ivory, Chantilly lace gown by Valentino that had been hand delivered from Rome. God only knows what he did to swing that because it fit me perfectly.

Charlotte served as my maid of honor and my personal attendant—I couldn't move an inch without her fussing with the train of my dress. She wore a grin as bright as the sun, and a lavender Chloe dress I had no idea where she'd gotten until I heard her thank Sebastian. Ben served as best man, looking uncharacteristically surly throughout the entire ceremony—though that did nothing to diminish how handsome he was in his tailored blue suit—handmade no doubt, no way was he getting that body into anything off the rack.

Mr. Bentifourt walked me down the aisle wearing an appropriately solemn expression for the occasion. As he handed me over to Sebastian, he patted my hand and gave me a warm smile that lit up his whole face.

And Sebastian…well, I'm not embarrassed to say he looked like he'd stepped out of my dreams, dreams that in no way could I ever have anticipated manifesting into reality.

In front of the arched windows, towering over everyone, he stood completely still, his posture relaxed, wearing a handmade blue suit that hugged his impressive frame perfectly, and an ivory silk tie.

He looked like a gilded mythical god, his hair shot through with streaks of pale blond from hours spent in the Mediterranean sun, his skin the color of raw sugar making his eyes glow a deep, reddish gold. I watched a million different emotions, large and small, rise to the surface and recede. But the smile in his eyes…that smile always remained.

Sebastian lifted my veil, then took my hands in his. His palms were damp, otherwise I would've never known he was nervous. Sweet man. I squeezed and he squeezed back. As the mayor murmured the words that would bind us together, a peace unlike anything I'd ever experienced before descended upon the room, permeating every corner. Within me something transcendent of shape or definition aligned and clicked into place. In the eyes of the man standing before me, I saw my joy, my future, all my hopes and dreams living there.

I recited my vows without reserve. No matter all the obstacles I may have contemplated until that very moment, as I stood before him, basking in the love that emanated from every fiber of his being, I knew what I was doing was right. Because in the end, this thing between us proved stronger than both our wills combined. Because there was no question that all roads would forever be leading me back to him.

***

"One more," I said squirming, an apologetic look on my face. Sebastian gave me his best "I'm trying to be patient" look but he wasn't fooling anyone. "Can I please see the one with the double strands of turquoise?" I asked the street vendor in Italian. He reminded me of an Impressionist painting I'd once seen in a schoolbook. Playing off the bright orange kaftan he wore, his black skin looked nearly blue. Although he nodded patiently, a sweet smile on his face, I suspected he was just about as annoyed with my inability to make a choice as Sebastian was.

"We can get a real one at the jewelry shop on St. Mark's Square."

"This is real," I said, holding up the turquoise bracelet for his inspection.

He frowned. "I meant precious." Turning to the street vendor, he said, "How many euros?"

"Fifteen," the vendor replied in English, his accent thick.

"We need to get going. We're too exposed here," Gideon stated. The naked concern in his voice pecked at me. Gideon was perpetually Mr. Cool and Collected. If he was alarmed, there must've been good reason.

My attention broke away from the table of colorful bracelets and moved over my shoulder, where I watched Gideon furtively scan the narrow, cobblestone street flanked by ancient buildings. The look on his face made me uneasy. Sebastian handed the street vendor a twenty-euro bill and told him to keep the change, his face now tight with a heightened sense of awareness.

"Let's go," he ordered. Clasping my wrist, he pulled me along.

All heavily armed, Gideon and two of his men, who had been with us since we sailed from the French Riviera, created a boundary between us and the flow of tourists that moved up and down the narrow street. In a well-orchestrated effort, we walked methodically, on a mission to reach the safety of our hotel.

The din of the crowd was making everyone jumpy. Someone shouted. My head swiveled in the general direction, and yet we didn't even pause to see what the commotion was about. A car horn blared a street over. I jerked in surprise, and still we kept marching at a brisk pace.

Watching Sebastian eating up ground, you would never have known that his knee was injured, or how hard he worked to make it look like he wasn't. I worried about how much pain he would be in later. When I squeezed the hand I gripped tightly, he squeezed back.

A revving of a motorcycle engine could be heard in the distance, the sound growing louder by the second. We'd just reached the intersection, ready to turn the corner, when people began to scatter. A second later, mass confusion took over.

At the top of the street, a motorcycle was quickly approaching, flying down at a high rate of speed. Like bowling pins, bodies dove out of the way. It was too late to run. Too late to retreat. We were boxed in by the ancient buildings closely packed together. The security team instinctively got into position.

And then it seemed to happen simultaneously all at once, and also in slow motion, as if I were floating above the scene watching from a third person perspective. But I wasn't...I was right in the thick of it.

A black Ducati screamed towards us, the rider's identity

obscured by a helmet with a black visor. Sebastian's grip on my hand became painful. He jerked and pushed me into a store, turning so his back was to the street. He was shielding me while exposing himself. I didn't scream. I didn't have time to.

Pop pop pop. It sounded innocuous, like balloons popping. Or fireworks on Bastille Day. Not the sound of death. Not the sound of vengeance. Next came the sound of glass shattering. It was loud. Female screams right on the heels of it. The air was crushed from my lungs as Sebastian fell on top of me. I gasped and grappled for breath, but two hundred and twenty pounds of bone and muscle made it impossible. I didn't have the strength to push him off, nor the air to speak. He didn't make a sound and he didn't move. Up until then, I was operating on adrenaline, numb from it. Now, for the first time that afternoon, I knew true fear.

"Fuck."

His voice was music to my ears. That word was suddenly the best ever to be invented in the English language. When he managed to push himself up on his elbows, I took a long, deep breath that hurt my lungs. A violent coughing fit ensued.

"You okay?" he asked. A nod was the best I could do. I grabbed his face and inspected him closely. Even with broken glass all over his hair and shirt, he seemed uninjured.

Gideon stormed into the store. "Everybody okay?"

We both nodded. Once Sebastian was standing, they hoisted me up. Sebastian immediately went to work brushing the broken glass from the store window off my yellow sundress.

"Did you get him?"

Police sirens approached. All heads swiveled in that direction.

"Too many people in the line of fire."

"Damn it."

"Venice is no longer safe," Gideon deadpanned. He wiped his sweaty brow with the sleeve of his linen shirt. At the sight of my scraped and bloodied hands and knees, his eyes grew soft and concerned.

"Time to go home." Sebastian's countenance and tone could've frozen hell. The honeymoon was officially over.

Chapter Seventeen

I COULD NOT HAVE DREAMED of a worse way to end what should have been the best few weeks of my life. Anxiety, escalating to monumental proportions, had me living on the edge of a razor blade. Every night since the attack in Venice, I had woken up in a pool of sweat. And every time Sebastian asked what the nightmare was about, I dissembled. I couldn't very well explain that I found new and more grisly ways for him to die in my arms each night.

Upon our return, we holed up on the estate. Interpol and the FBI were contacted as soon as the attempt on Sebastian's life took place. The day we arrived, Agents Vasquez and Lewis were there to meet us for a debriefing. Mr. Bernard was at the bar, pouring himself a drink, when we entered the living room.

"They're getting desperate. They know that any day now the so-called audit for tax evasion will start," said Agent Lewis. She pushed off the doorframe she was leaning on and joined the rest of us that were seated.

Across from us on the couch, Agent Vasquez bent forward and placed her elbows on her knees. Clasping her hands into a single fist, she asked, "Who's next in line to be CEO in the event of your death?"

"David has specific instructions. If I don't have an heir, the bank would go directly into escrow to be prepared for sale. In the meantime there would be an interim board elected. With

Charles being the largest account holder, he would automatically qualify to be a member. Day to day operations would be handled by Shay Savitch, my executive vice president."

"What about a wife? Any provisions for a wife?" Lewis inquired casually.

"I don't have a prenup. Now that I'm married, my wife inherits everything."

My gaze cautiously met David's, whose dark blue eyes stared back at me in collusion over the rim of the cut crystal glass he sipped.

"So we can assume your wife's a target as well now," Vasquez added.

Sebastian's burdened eyes flitted to mine. He squeezed my hand and replied, "Unfortunately, yes."

Vasquez and Lewis exchanged an understanding. "It's time to move on Mr. Redman. Tomorrow. At the office. Mrs. Horn, it's best you be there too. Venice indicates there may be a leak at Interpol—you could be in danger."

Mrs. Horn…the first time anyone had ever used my married name.

"She'll be there," Sebastian assured them.

"We'll be in touch with the details."

I turned to study Sebastian's reaction and found none. His complete attention remained on the two agents seated before us. Composure was written all over the perfect angles of his face, his expression as placid as a frozen lake. *He knew.* The knowledge came to me suddenly. He'd known all along that Marcus was involved.

"Why?" My voice sounded disembodied, untethered from me.

Agent Vasquez's eyebrows rose up her forehead. "In the four years Mr. Redman placed the trades for Mr. Hightower's account he earned a cool fifty million."

"But he was already wealthy. Why would he do this?" I asked, my tone incredulous.

"Because of me," Sebastian answered. "He was sticking it to me." His voice may have been present, but his mind was far away. "He's trying to take me down."

***

By late morning, with Justin driving and Bear riding in the front seat, we were pulling in front of the turn-of-the-century marble building, everyone ready to play their part. Both national and international agencies had their people in place. Security at the bank being some of the most sophisticated in the world, Bear and Justin remained in the lobby while I took the elevator up to the top floor.

I should've been paying more attention to my surroundings...I should have. But I wasn't. I was glancing down at my phone to read a text Sebastian had sent me, a text that told me to remain in the lobby until Gideon came to fetch me.

I only glanced up when I heard someone step in right behind me. Marcus stared back at me with poorly feigned innocence in his opaque, brown eyes. That ultra neat, boyish exterior didn't fool me. For a moment his expression was one of surprise, but it quickly settled into something darker. Something malicious. Something that made all the hair on the back of my neck stand at attention.

"Well, if it isn't the little illegal immigrant shacking up with my dear brother."

My posture altered. It snapped ramrod straight. "Stepbrother. You don't share blood, thank God." I don't know where I found the courage to say that.

His mouth hooked up on once side in the most smarmy, smug smile I'd ever had the displeasure of witnessing. "I'd really like to know what it is about you that has him so twisted in the head. Is your snatch made of gold?"

I was starting to sweat. Two minutes of courage was all I had in me, and the elevator ride suddenly felt endless. My gaze darted to the numbers illuminated at the top of the car. Moving swiftly out of his relaxed pose, he stood in front of the panel and hit the stop button.

"What the hell!"

I was too scared to reach around him, to touch him in any way. I knew from past experience with him that he wouldn't think twice about manhandling me. Just how far he would go, I had no idea.

"Do you know that your boyfriend—pardon, your husband—likes to fuck my wife?" Examining me closely he added, "You know. Then you also know that he likes to choke her while he's doing it, likes to watch her fight for air while he comes inside of her." He knew exactly where to hit me, where my Achilles heel was, and he went at it without mercy. The anxiety and discomfort was all over me, impossible to hide as I desperately tried to fend off his psychological assault. "Sometimes he likes to tie her up—"

"Let me out, you son of a bitch."

"Sometimes he likes to fuck her in the ass."

"Let me the hell out of here, or I'll scream!" I started pounding on the metal door.

"Do you know how I know that? He leaves bruises, his handprints all over her for me to find."

"Help! We're stuck!" I screamed at the top of my lungs, and banged and banged and banged with flat palms on the brass doors.

Undeterred, Marcus carried on in an unhurried pace, as if he were reciting a poem, something pleasant. He certainly looked like he was enjoying himself. "But he doesn't anymore because he's too busy fucking you. Which leads me to believe that you must be the lay of the century. And maybe, just maybe, if I fuck you, that magical cunt of yours can help me forget about my wife—just like Sebastian has." By now I was going crazy on the door, my hands red and swollen from the effort, my voice hoarse from screaming.

All of a sudden, the double doors opened on the top floor, and a room full of men in expensive suits stared back at me with matching neutral expressions. The one expression that wasn't neutral was Sebastian's. He took me in from head to foot slowly and thoroughly.

I could almost imagine the picture I painted: red faced, sweaty, breathing heavily. When his fiery gaze darted to Marcus, there was no doubt what was coming next. In a couple of long-legged strides, Sebastian was on him in seconds, Gideon thankfully there just as quickly. Both men, swinging wildly, landed punch after punch until some of the other employees joined in to separate the two.

Agent Vasquez, standing next to the Interpol agents, stepped forward. "Wanted to do this a little more discretely," she said, an annoyed look on her face. "Marcus Nathaniel Redman, you are under arrest for money laundering, financing of terrorism, intent to harbor assets for terrorist organizations..."

The list was so long I stopped listening after a while.

As soon as the Interpol agents had Marcus in handcuffs Sebastian ordered, "Get him out of here." His gaze, still burning with anger and vengeance, focused in on me. "In my office." As soon as we stepped inside he turned and barked, "What did he do to you?"

"Nothing. He didn't touch me."

"Bullshit." He took a handkerchief out of the interior pocket of his jacket and I grabbed it from him. I stroked his face and pressed it under his nose absorbing the dripping blood.

"I swear he didn't. It was all talk. He was just taunting

me."

Suddenly uneasy, he said, "What did he say?" His eyes unblinking.

"Nothing I ever want to hear again, let alone repeat."

"Vera," he pleaded.

"No, Sebastian. I'm not discussing it."

I told myself it didn't matter. I told myself it had all happened before me. But when my head hit the pillow that night, I stayed awake 'til dawn with those ugly images running through my head.

Chapter Eighteen

THE ROAD TO MONTREUX WAS breathtaking in its bucolic majesty. Steep, emerald green mountains jutted up arrogantly, penetrating the cerulean blue sky with impunity. Their permanence inspired awe, their stark beauty admiration.

My gaze moved from the open sunroof of the Bentley, to the man in the driver's seat. Sharp angles, stark beauty, fierce and arrogant. I smiled at the similarities. Lost in contemplation, he was quiet for most of the hour-and-a-half drive. I could feel the tension pulling him apart. We had no idea what awaited us at Charles'.

After Marcus was arrested, Interpol and the Feds moved quickly on The Crescent Foundation, freezing assets and arresting one Dr. Farshid, the head of the charity. Marcus gave them all up, no coercion necessary. Two days later we were on the road to Montreaux.

"You love him," I claimed the obvious.

"Charles? He was like a father to me." Then, shaking his head, he clarified, "He was more than that—he was a friend when I had nobody."

My chest caved in on itself, an enormous weight squatting on it. It wasn't the first time he'd mentioned how alone, or how lonely his childhood had been.

"Ben?"

"We couldn't speak much when he was training. Then the war."

"And your father?"

His eyes slid to mine. He scoffed. "If it hadn't been for Charles, we would never have reconciled. He's the only one that ever got through to him."

"As hard as I try, I can't understand your father. Loyal to his friend, and yet, neglectful of his only son? It's just bizarre."

"Preaching to the choir. I've been trying to figure it out for thirty-five years, and I still don't have a clue."

"Are you going to be okay?" No explanations were necessary. He knew what I was implying. There was so much at stake. We both had harbored hope that Charles was somehow innocent of everything other than poor judgment, but after Marcus' arrest that chance had withered away.

"I have to be—don't I?" he said in a resigned voice, his disappointment palpable. The one person that had ever been there for him, and he would soon lose him as well.

Impulsively, I sifted my fingers through his hair and his expression softened. Sighing deeply, he trapped my hand and brought it to his soft lips. One, two, three kisses on my knuckles. His touch reverent. He was always reaching for me, always so affectionate. Baring my open wrist, he brushed his lips on my pulse, making me shiver while certain other parts of me grew hot and bothered.

"Pull over."

His face snapped in my direction. In the mirror of his sunglasses, I saw my reflection. Cheeks flushed. Spark of lust in my eyes. There was no doubt where my thoughts were headed. His brow wrinkled and pulled together in question. Sliding his sunglasses off, his eyes where two, mischievous crescents trying to assess the situation.

"Pull over now," I repeated more forcefully, pointing to a deserted clearing off the road where he could park the car. I almost laughed when he did as he was told. He parked the Bentley under the shade of a tall conifer.

"Vera…" he drawled, his husky voice filled with wonder and poorly hidden excitement, my name a supplication on his lips. How could one word imply so much?

Before the engine was off, I had my greedy hands on his belt buckle, undoing it and yanking the tiresome thing from his waist. He chuckled as I quickly ripped open his pants. His eyes bright, scintillating with anticipation, complemented the smile kicking up the side of his sensual mouth.

"What's gotten into you?"

"You," I replied, a fierce need to please him, to make him feel loved seizing the reins of my self-control, overriding the sense of propriety that I still held onto. I wanted to do things with him, and to him that, in my wildest dreams, I would've never entertained with anyone else. But most of all, I wanted him to never feel alone again.

My eyes held his as I fisted him tightly and lowered my head. I watched amusement turn into lust, turn into pleasure.

"You've gotten into me," I murmured, licking the broad head of his shaft, slick with the evidence of his excitement. Salty like the Mediterranean. Like tears. I traced the slit with the tip of my tongue and heard a strangled moan surge out of him. His hands gripped the steering wheel hard enough to bend steel, his fingers flexing repeatedly. I took him down my throat, and watched his head fall back on the headrest, his eyes drunkenly fluttered shut. I cupped and stroked and squeezed his sac, heavy and velvety and warm in my hand.

"Fuuuck me," he mumbled, the words barely comprehensible.

I intend to, I thought. And went about doing just that.

***

We followed an endless gravel driveway that led to a late eighteenth century manor abutting Lake Geneva. The car hadn't even come to a full stop and three very large and very intimidating men were already on the front steps. As soon as we parked, they began opening car doors, the trunk, unloading our bags. The bulge in their closely tailored black suits was easy enough to spot from a mile away. I glanced at Sebastian and caught the cautious look in his eyes, the heightened sense of awareness reinforcing his posture.

"My dear boy!" The jovial greeting caused both our heads to turn in the direction of the open doorway. Charles stood with his arms stretched out, looking like a character in *The Great Gatsby*. His white linen suit was without a wrinkle, the grin he wore infectious. Sebastian smiled back tenderly. Some of the concern that only moments ago was stamped on his features faded. "Come in, come in. Lunch will be ready in ten."

Charles walked back into the house with us trailing close behind. Catching Sebastian's attention, I mouthed *"dear boy"* and raised an eyebrow indicating my delight at this. He shrugged, and the side of his mouth hooked up.

"I was expecting you half an hour ago." Charles threw the remark over his shoulder.

"Yeah, we...uh—took in the scenery," Sebastian answered.

Charles glanced directly at me and said, "And how was it?"

The second I caught the twinkle in his eyes I turned cherry red. Pursing my lips to stop from laughing, I said, "Majestic."

The interior of the manor looked like a world class museum. Artwork worthy of the Hermitage, spanning from the fourteenth to the twenty-first, covered the aged stucco walls. Furniture that looked too precious to sit on crowded every room. Fabrics in jewel tones, emerald green to royal blue, from the most luxurious mills in northern Italy, covered every chair and sofa. I was afraid to touch anything.

"Your home is amazing," I said as we walked from room to room, looking around with an awed expression I couldn't have concealed even if I wanted to.

"My dear girl, this is just the summer house. My home is in England."

Shocked, my eyes slammed into Sebastian's while a small smile played on his sensual lips.

***

Lunch was served on the veranda. The table was adorned with heirloom quality crystal and silverware complete with food you could only find at a Michelin rated restaurant. Bordering the lake, the patio was trimmed by stone balustrades topped with vases overflowing with shocking pink geraniums and purple petunias.

It was a scene out of a movie and I, the spectator. That's how I felt most of the time anyway. I cupped my fingers over my eyes and looked out at the horizon, the water as smooth as glass, the sun blinding. One of the butlers unspooled the candy-striped awning over the table, shielding us from the steady glare.

"Any news on the foundation?" Charles inquired. The butler brought him a bottle of wine, which Charles inspected before giving him a curt nod. Charles tasted it and gave him the green light to pour.

A strange melancholy washed over me. Here we sat, exchanging pleasantries while overlooking a small slice of heaven, when in just a short period of time everything would change.

I turned to watch my husband. He could never hide anything from me and this moment was no different. Even though he wore a smile, even though his countenance was relaxed, all I saw was sorrow.

"The girls school in Zambia is finally done, thanks in part to George Bush. Bono brought him in and we got the additional funding needed when it ran over budget.

"Bono and Bush. What strange bedfellows," Charles

remarked with a saucy grin.

"Effective ones," Sebastian countered.

"I'm traveling there at the end of October. I'll swing by and take a look."

"Do you go there often?" I asked Charles.

"Not as much as I used to when Hen, Sebastian's father, was around," he responded, his features swamped by an unambiguous longing. "Africa," he continued, looking out over the postcard scenery. "She's a seductive mistress."

"Why is that?" Sebastian's voice held genuine curiosity.

"It's the mystery—she's elusive. Every time I go back, instead of knowing her better, I realize I don't know her at all. I can't ever get enough."

"The only time I ever saw any real emotion on my father's face is when he spoke of her." The look on Sebastian's face spoke of disappointment, of a father that gave so much to others, but never had anything left to spare for his only child.

I watched Charles' expression transform. The silent debate being waged was in his eyes. "Did I ever tell you about the first time your father and I went on safari?" Suddenly interested, Sebastian's gaze returned to Charles. He shook his head. "It was my twenty-seventh birthday," Charles began, his hands curled into fists, his thumbs rubbing nervously. It was clear that some dark sentiments lurked behind this story.

"I had a falling out with my family and was quite down about it so your father surprised me with a trip. By the time we arrived in Botswana, there was a coup in progress—a failed coup, as it turned out." Charles chuckled. "The Swiss consulate put us in touch with a UN aid worker who could get us on a plane back to Joburg. Layla Assefa, an Ethiopian ex-pat raised in Italy—father owned a chain of hotels there. Smart as a whip, beautiful. She was something." Charles' gaze roamed far away, an insightful smile on his mustache covered lips. "I left after a week." His sharp gaze snapped back to

Sebastian, loaded with meaning. "Hen came home four months later—and only because Egon threatened to disown him."

Sebastian's attention was riveted on the story.

"If you think your father was cold, you should've met your grandfather. Egon was furious. Hen wanted to marry her. Can you imagine? They fought viciously. All for naught, she died two weeks later when her plane crashed in the desert...your father was never the same after that." A hushed silence fell over the table. Charles took a long sip of his wine.

Sebastian looked like he'd been punched in the gut, his expression one of total shock. Then it morphed. A carousel of emotions each took a turn manifesting on his face until only one remained. Resentment.

"This was all about a woman?"

Charles' milky, blue eyes met Sebastian's squarely. "A woman he loved with every breath in his body," Charles clarified. Then he looked pointedly at me. "Don't judge him too harshly. There's a lot more of him in you than you'd like to believe."

***

I awoke from a nap and found myself alone in the elegant bedroom. I never napped. However, the champagne that Charles had popped opened at lunch, though delicious, had proven itself as powerful a sedative as a blow to the head.

A pang of unease hit me. There was once a time when self-preservation trumped everything, even love. Until I met him and my best laid plans were blown sky high. With stealth, he'd crept under my skin and seamlessly adhered himself to every vital part of me. It wasn't that he was there which made me nervous—it was the thought of what it would feel like to have him ripped away from me.

Kicking off the blanket, I jumped out of bed in search of the man in question. Out on the balcony, I was assaulted by what can only be described as beauty in its most profound definition. Flowering trees and impeccably manicured gardens bordered the lapis blue lake. Tiny sailboats loitered on the water, the wind turning uncooperative. On the horizon, white-peaked mountains lorded over all of it. Sebastian was nowhere to be found, not even in the garden down below. Thus I threw on my skinny jeans and a white linen shirt, and went in search of my husband.

My husband.

Every time I caught a flash of the platinum band around my finger a silly smile broke out on my face. The engagement ring was tucked away in a safe, back at the estate. I was too scared of losing it to get any enjoyment out of seeing it on my hand.

My search of the first floor proved fruitless. The dock came next. Overhead, a quilted gray blanket had unfurled across the sky, as gloomy and brooding as the tall blond I found standing on the edge of the wooden pier. With his hands stuffed in the back pocket of his jeans and his hair windswept, he looked more like a moody male model than a stuffy banker.

"What are you thinking about?"

Looking over his broad shoulder, the smile he gave me barely reached his eyes. "Come," he said, ignoring my question. His Highness held out his hand. As I placed mine in his, the thin platinum band wrapped around his finger caught my eye, reminding me that I was just as much his, as he was mine. Fingers laced together, he helped me step into a red, lacquered rowboat and followed me in.

We were both quiet while he rowed. I pretended to be engrossed in the scenery when in truth I hid behind the absurdly expensive sunglasses he'd bought me, and surreptitiously thieved glances at him. I wondered if that was weird—to be so enthralled with one's own husband. Did other women feel that way about theirs? Maybe it *was* weird, I decided. But with him in the picture, there wasn't anything on the planet that could've stolen my attention away.

"Do you think Charles was in love with your father?"

Sebastian didn't react at all to my question, which told me it had crossed his mind as well.

"Maybe...but it's just an assumption." Shrugging, he added, "I've never seen him with anyone."

"How lonely that must've been for him. To be constantly near someone he loved who could never return his feelings." Sebastian scoffed, his jaw tight, his mouth set in a grim line. "What?"

"Nothing."

He was pissed. It was definitely something. "Spit it out."

"Do you know how fucking infuriating it is to know that he was so accepting of everyone else?" Head shaking, he muttered something to himself. "I couldn't even sneeze without incurring his wrath!" He raked his fingers through his hair. "*If* he noticed me at all." He'd stopped rowing, the boat drifting aimlessly along the shoreline.

My heart ached for him. After the revelations at lunch, I was getting a pretty clear picture of the father/son dynamics, and it wasn't pretty. Sebastian was fruit of the poisonous tree. The result of a marriage Heinrich didn't want, to a woman he didn't love, because the one he did was stolen from him. And Sebastian was made to pay the price.

The man sitting across from me gazed out at a faraway point, his countenance brooding, his anger doing a poor job of covering up the pain. "Look, your father took his once-in-a-lifetime love, his heartbreak, and turned it into something ugly and cruel."

The magnetism that existed between us, constantly drawing us together, would not quit. As if summoned by some invisible force, I got up and straddled his lap. My legs and arms wrapped around him while he watched me expectantly.

"He took his disappointment out on an innocent child. And what have you done? You've taken all that pain and turned it into something good. You're kind, and loving, and selfless, and generous, and you're—" His eyes were large in his face, drinking in every word. "You're kind of a catch." His lips twitched and twitched, an amused glint appearing in his eyes. "And I thank God every day that I'm the one that caught you."

Turning sulky with lust, his gaze lowered to my lips. "Damn right," he muttered. "What are you gonna do now that you got me?"

"Well," I said, placing a soft kiss on his brow, on his temple, on his nose. "How much time do we have?"

He smacked a kiss on my lips. "The rest of our lives."

"No need to rush, then."

With that, he proceeded to show me just how slow he could go.

✳✳✳

We whiled the rest of the afternoon away in our bedroom. However, we couldn't ignore that the time was fast approaching for Sebastian to confront Charles. I could feel an ominous cloud slowly descend upon him as the minutes passed, marked by the antique cuckoo clock in our room. Sebastian didn't argue when I told him I wanted to sit this one out. This was sure to become a very intimate moment for the two of them, and I didn't need to add more stress to an already unpredictable situation.

He was super quiet as he dressed for dinner in his gray gabardine slacks, and a white cotton shirt. When his fingers tripped over the buttons, I got off the bed, pushed his hands aside, and did it for him. Blowing out a deep breath, he planted his hands on his hips while I worked. "I fucking hate this."

There was nothing I could say or do that would assuage the pain of having to send the person he loved to jail. So I remained quiet and let my nearness speak for me. "Come find me as soon as it's done," I said, punctuating it with a kiss. A quick nod later, he was out the door.

By eleven I was on pins and needles. Impatience got the best of me eventually. I debated for all of a minute whether I should go in search of him. As soon as my feet hit the top of the marble staircase, I heard the unmistakable sound of two people arguing.

"Why?" Sebastian's distraught voice drifted up from the ground floor. "My father trusted you."

"You still don't get it. That shouldn't surprise me. You've always been naïve—straightforward. I blame your mother. It's the American in you."

Taking the stairs by two, I chased after the voices, finally reaching the room they were emanating from. Charles' study.

"Then make me fucking understand, Charles!" Sebastian shouted, his temper spinning out of control.

"Who do you think allowed me to place the trades through the bank?"

Sebastian swore savagely.

"The bank was failing," Charles continued. "It was in dire need of fresh blood to sustain it. A number of the other boutique banks had already been swallowed up by larger conglomerates. Hen was not the charmer you are—that shouldn't be a surprise—and set in his ways. I brought in a couple of sheiks, an Israeli arms dealer. But there was only so much even I could do. He thought they should court *his* favors. Arrogant prick. I loved him dearly, your father, but he was that.

"When the situation finally became dire, I approached him

with a deal I'd been working on. They needed someone to take exploding profits earned from the opium production increase in Afghanistan. You know what happened after the Americans pulled out; the trade increased exponentially and all that cash had to be—"

"Washed," Sebastian finished.

"They came to me, and asked if I could place some trades. Any profits the trade earned I kept, and the losses they paid. In return, I was to send half the amount of the initial investment to a charity."

"They?!"

"I always dealt with a middleman."

The next time Sebastian spoke his voice was so quiet it was barely audible. "They've already killed India…they're trying to kill me."

"I…I had no idea…not until you were shot…you must believe me." Charles' voice was as small as it could possibly be.

"And Vera? They won't be able to identify your remains if anything happens to her."

"I'll make it right…I'll talk to them."

"It's a little late for that." Sebastian's fury was back. The silence emanating from Charles explained everything. "That fucking charity was a front," Sebastian continued. "The money is funneled to Hezbollah. You were directly funding terrorism."

"I didn't know." Charles' voice faded away, until there was nothing left.

"You son of a bitch—you didn't want to know!"

The heavy silence that followed devoured time. I couldn't stand idly by any longer. Pushing the doors of the office open, I stepped inside and scanned the room.

Sebastian stood near the fireplace, his stance defiant, his muscles so rigid he looked as if he was about to shatter.

Charles sat slumped down in a leather wing-back chair behind a stately antique desk. He suddenly seemed his age, defeat written all over his face and his posture. He barely acknowledged me.

Swirling the liquor in the crystal tumbler he held, Charles stared into the glass with a vacant expression and murmured, "What are you going to do?"

Sebastian glanced up from the empty fireplace and stared a hole through the man he loved more than his own father. The man complicit in his attempted murder and the murder of his wife. Hands stuffed in his pockets, he shrugged his wide shoulders and shook his head as he dejectedly answered, "There's nothing I can do. The Department of Justice is in charge of it. This is just a courtesy they allowed me. They have everything they need to tie you to multiple terror organizations…a witness willing to testify."

Charles' eyes snapped up in surprise. "Who?"

"You know who."

"Marcus," Charles volunteered. His eyes falling on the liquor he held. Raising the glass to his lips, he drained it in one gulp.

"You're surprised he would cut a deal?"

"Not surprised—no," Charles said, resigned of the now clear and inevitable outcome. "How much time do I have?"

Sebastian stared at him, pain etched on his perfect features. "None," was his soft reply. Walking over to me, he took me gently by the arm and ushered me towards the door. "They're camped outside. They'll arrest you by morning." Then before we walked out, without turning around he said, "I loved you. I loved you in ways I never loved my father."

Jesus. To be held in contempt by his father for no fault of his own, and betrayed by the man he loved most was a blow I don't think many could recover from.

We made our way up the marble staircase at a glum pace.

Needing to be as close to him as possible, I wrapped myself around his arm and kissed his bicep. "I don't know what to say. Sorry doesn't seem enough." He looked down at me, his eyes soft and loving, accepting anything I was willing to give. He deserved so much more. He deserved the best. He'd received so little support in his life that his standards were sadly low.

A shot rang out as we reached the top of the staircase, sundering the quiet.

Sebastian's eyes were wide and startled. In a frenzy, he turned and hurried back down while I chased after him. Watching him leap down the steps a few at a time, I was certain he'd hurt his injured knee, though he would only feel it later—when the adrenaline wore off. When I finally reached the bottom, five armed men ran past me in the direction of Charles' office. I was the last to arrive.

Charles was slumped over on top of his desk, a pool of blood growing around his head. A handgun lay on the floor close by. Sebastian had his fingers on Charles' pulse. His face was a solid mask, as still as death. Only I knew better. When the pain was most unbearable was when he retreated behind the walls of his fortress. I could almost hear the sound of his heart splintering apart into jagged pieces.

"Call the police," he told to the security guards. They were the last words he spoke willingly for the next two days.

Chapter Nineteen

ONCE WE GOT BACK TO Geneva, our life was summarily highjacked, governed by meetings with the FBI and Interpol. With the case winding down and details to tie up, Sebastian was busy keeping bank business running as smoothly as possible while simultaneously appeasing clients that were wary of all the attention by both the Swiss and American governments.

A melancholy atmosphere hung over everything. We stayed mostly at the apartment. Dealing with the fallout of what Charles and Marcus had done was taking up so much of Sebastian's time that he didn't have any to spare for the trip back and forth to the estate. Which meant that I spent all my days and some of my nights alone, with nothing to do except clean and cook. When Sebastian suggested we get a permanent housekeeper for the apartment I almost murdered him with my eyes. The only bright spot was that I got to see Charlotte more often. Little did I know when we met for lunch that day that would soon change as well.

"So...what will you do now?" Her big brown eyes wide, she stared back expectantly as we made our way to the brasserie on the corner. A crisp breath of wind painted two circles on her dimpled cheeks and blew her curls in every direction. We both shivered as we walked into the headwind.

"Well, I have a month and a half until my interview for the residency position, and that's in no way a sure thing." At the smirk and raised eyebrow she gave me, I added, "Don't look at me like that. I refuse to let him meddle in this. If I get it, it will be on my own merit."

"Boooring. You are so bloody boring."

I chuckled at her usual dramatics. "You'd be surprised," I teased, my eyebrows wiggling.

"You dirty girl. Don't leave out any of the filthy parts." Something close to wistfulness crossed her face. She was definitely hiding something behind the jokes and sarcasm.

"Why aren't you dating? And don't give me that crap about *living on the estate makes it difficult* again."

The amusement dropped off her face all at once. Her steps slowed. "There's a reason I wanted to see you today."

"I don't like the look on your face."

Without preamble, she said, "I'm leaving in a few days."

I stopped walking and turned to face her. "Leaving? Like on vacation?"

She bit her bottom lip, her brow wrinkled. "Not exactly," she replied, her voice dropping in volume.

"Then how exactly?" The churn in my gut told me I wouldn't like the answer.

"For good."

The bottom officially fell out of my stomach. "For good?" I repeated, grief-stricken. "What do you mean for good? And where are you going?"

"Back to England."

"You're being deliberately vague."

Her eyes darted around, searching for cover from my scrutiny. "It's my mum. She's sick."

"And the dog ate your homework? You've never once mentioned your family." Blowing out a deep breath, she continued. "I need to go deal with a problem that I've put off for years. Please don't ask me anymore."

"Why not? Maybe I can help."

The wind kicked up again, her hair streaming across her face. Pushing the curls away, she said, "You can't. Believe me, I wish you could, but you can't." Her expression convinced me that she truly believed it.

"Are you ever coming back?"

"I want to...depends how things go."

"Promise me that you'll call and let me know how you are. I won't rest otherwise. If you make me worry, I'll come looking for you."

The edges of her plump mouth curled up faintly. "Worse than a Sunday school teacher."

"Count on it."

"Okay, I promise."

"Now let's get inside and get drunk—give you a proper send off."

"You get drunk. I'll drown my sorrows in an extra-large crème brulée since I won't be seeing any for a while."

"Deal."

We spent the rest of the lunch laughing, talking about anything and everything other than the secrets I knew she was keeping from me. I just prayed that when the time came, she wouldn't hesitate to call.

***

It was almost midnight when I heard the sound of the alarm beeping. Ten minutes later he walked into our bedroom tugging on his tie. I placed the book I was reading on the bedside table and examined the handsome man standing before me. Hair disheveled like he'd run a worried hand through it, shoulders sagging under the enormous burden he carried, jaw tight and lines of fatigue written across his face.

"Come here," I said. Without a word of objection, he walked over to me. I rose out of bed and made quick work of his clothes, peeling each article away from a body a Greek god would envy. "What's wrong?"

Without mincing words, he came right out with it. "Your father was most likely innocent, and mine was a crook." He chuckled humorlessly.

"Tell me."

The sound of his tired sigh said more than I needed to know. "In ten years they nearly doubled the three hundred million. It's not a huge sum but enough to cover any bad trades they may have made. Enough to keep the balance sheets in the black."

"Not a huge sum?" I mumbled.

"I don't know why I didn't see it immediately," he murmured, his expression forlorn. "My father was a total control freak." He said this as if this should surprise me, as if he was admitting some big family secret. I swallowed the snort desperate to erupt out of me. "He knew every move we made at the bank before I told him."

"Lie down." I knew then how drained he was because he did exactly as he was told. I grabbed the lotion from the drawer in the bedside table and began on his injured knee. "Nobody wants to believe the worst of their parents. Take it from me."

The arm covering his face muffled a primitive growl loud enough to wake the neighbors. "Jesus...that feels almost as good as you riding my cock," he mumbled.

My eyebrows nearly reached my hairline. "Charming. Did you eat?"

"Not hungry," he answered, moaning as my skilled hands worked on his thigh.

"Darling, I know you're tired, but I need to talk about a job that Dr. Rossetti mentioned before we went to Italy."

"Hmm."

"For a physician's assistant at a free clinic."

"Hmm."

"I'm going in tomorrow for the interview."

"'Kay." Ten minutes later, I glanced at his face and found him asleep. His sensual lips softly parted, the lines of worry now smooth. The satisfaction I felt knowing I could do that for him was ridiculous. Enveloped by a new sense of ease, I crawled in beside him, covered us up, and fell soundly asleep. At dawn the feeling vanished when I discovered the bed empty.

***

The clinic was located in a modest neighborhood. I actually checked the address twice before giving it to Bear, who drove me. The building looked freshly painted and the waiting room cheerful. I didn't know what I was expecting, but it wasn't this. Whoever was organizing the fundraising was obviously doing a very good job.

Inside, the sound of patients crowding the waiting room, I'm ashamed to admit, excited me. This was what I was meant to do. With all the drama of the past few months, I'd lost sight of what was really important to me.

At the check-in desk, I stood quietly waiting for the twenty-something receptionist to notice me. With her attention completely fixated on the mess piled on top of her desk, it looked like that would be a while.

"I'm here for the physician's assistant interview."

"Muller, Muller...where the bloody hell is that file," she mumbled to herself while she searched under stacks of paper, an index finger with a broken nail tapping anxiously at her bottom lip. "What are you here for?"

I took her in. The untidy bun, the fraught expression she wore—it was clear she was in way over her head.

"The interview." Still nothing. She hadn't looked at me once.

"Agnes!" bellowed a deep, masculine voice from one of the

examination rooms. The receptionist—Agnes, I assumed—jerked at the sound. "Where the bloody hell is that file I asked for a decade ago!"

She became frantic in her search, piles of paperwork falling off her desk in the process.

"For the interview," I repeated. Then I pulled the Muller file she was looking for out from under one of the stacks and handed it to her. Agnes finally glanced up, her brown eyes wide, her mouth at first pursed then curving into a hesitant smile. She took the file out of my hands.

"Shit—I mean, thank you." Getting up quickly, Agnes flew to the examination room, her bright red, corkscrew curls tumbling free of the haphazard bun.

In her absence, I glanced around the overstuffed waiting room and grabbed a pen and clipboard from the desk. One by one, I went from patient to patient, writing down names and symptoms, what time they had arrived at the clinic. I was so immersed in what I was doing that I lost track of time.

"Who the hell are you?" That deep masculine voice was right behind me.

Turning around slowly, I came face to face, no that's wrong, I came face to chest with a very large man. My eyes climbed higher and higher until I reached his eyes. Not even his scowl could take anything away from this brand of handsomeness. Cheekbones high and razor sharp, full lips surrounded by a closely cropped goatee, piercing dark eyes, and a milk chocolate complexion. The only touch of whimsy that made him actually look human was a smattering of freckles across his face. As if God thought him too perfect and blew stardust on him.

"Do you speak English?" he said, rather rudely. His was very clipped.

A bark of laughter erupted out of me. Holding out my hand, I said, "Vera Horn, I'm here to interview for the physician's assistant job." He stared at my outstretched hand suspiciously. Dr. Rossetti was not exaggerating. "Dr. Rossetti sent me."

Still nothing.

His eyes examined me closely. I started to sweat a little under all that intense scrutiny. Clearing my throat, I explained, "I listed each patient here according to time of arrival." I pointed to the clipboard. "And cross-matched them with severity of symptoms. I suggest you see Mrs. Dumas next. She's seventy-nine and has the flu. I suspect she's extremely dehydrated already."

Hands on his hips, he took a deep breath and said, "Agnes, put Mrs. Dumas in examination room two." Then he turned and walked away.

"Dr. Kama?" I said baffled.

"Let's go, Horn. I don't have all day. You need to get changed. We have patients to see," he barked over his shoulder, not even breaking stride.

I scurried after him. "What about the interview?"

"We just had it," he replied without a glance in my direction.

"You don't want to see my university file?"

"Saw it a month ago." His eyes met mine, that scowl still on his face. "Where the bloody hell have you been?" With that, he pushed me into the women's employee locker room, and took off to attend Mrs. Dumas.

Chapter Twenty

THAT MORNING SEEMED LIKE ANY other. Seemed being the operative word. Little did I know when I left for the clinic everything would change. By early afternoon, Yannick had already seen most of the scheduled patients and some of the walk-ins. It was an easy day, as we liked to say, filled with vaccine shots, ear infections, and other innocuous maladies. That's why when Emilia called and asked to meet for lunch I jumped at the chance.

Sebastian's order that I not see her was pure rubbish. There was no way I would stop seeing her. She was the last tie to my old life, to my father. She'd witnessed it all—the only person I could discuss it with that truly understood what it had been like for me.

There was no getting rid of the security detail. The Department of Justice suggested it remain in place until further notice that their investigation had been concluded and subsequent arrests made. I knew Sebastian would find out about it, and I was prepared to face the consequences. I couldn't allow him to keep me in his ivory tower forever.

At the crosswalk, waiting for the light to change, I spotted Emilia sitting at one of the outdoor tables of the bistro. I knew immediately she was speaking to a man when she threw her head back in abandon and pushed her long, black hair over her shoulder, a gesture I recognized from when we were teenagers. She was laughing, talking to someone hidden behind the waiter standing next to the table. Instinctively, I glanced behind me, to make sure that Gideon and Justin were close by. I had no idea whom she had invited along, and that it may have been Yuri really annoyed me.

Gideon's eyes narrowed, his awareness sharpening when he noticed the flash of unease on my face. As I reached the sidewalk on the other side of the street, with Gideon shadowing me even closer, the waiter stepped aside.

Ten paces from the table, I came to an abrupt halt, rooted to the spot as a steady stream of pedestrians flowed around me. The bottom fell out of my world and all the air left my lungs in a blink of an eye. Seated across from Emilia, smiling casually at her, was Aleksander.

Time hadn't left a single mark on him, as if six years hadn't passed. He glanced up and his obsidian gaze caught mine. His expression sobered instantly as we stared at each other for an endless amount of time. Snapshots of our life together flipped through my mind in rapid succession, every touch, taste, and smell. An overwhelming sense of nostalgia hit me. When he stood, the spell was broken. Emilia, following his gaze, turned in my direction.

"There you are...surprise," she said with a wide smile. I was going to kill her slowly and painfully. She knew how much I hated surprises and to spring one on me of this magnitude was unforgivable. I glared back at her and her smile faded. Aleksander finally broke the stalemate, reaching me quickly and wrapping me in his arms when he realized I was about to bolt. Almost instantly, Gideon was on us.

"Back the fuck away." I had never heard Gideon use that language, or tone before and it shocked me. As much as it did Alek because he released me instantly.

"It's okay, Gideon. I know him." When he didn't react I clarified, "From Albania." Reluctantly, he backed away and after signaling to the waiter, he took a seat next to Justin a few tables down.

Alek's silky black hair was longer, tucked behind his ears, not a single silver thread to be found anywhere. Still, obscenely handsome. He shoved his hands in the pockets of his navy blazer while he studied me. From my sharply bobbed hair to the designer clothes.

"You were always a pretty a girl...but you've become a stunning woman," he said in Albanian. The compliment annoyed me beyond reason. Six years after his desertion and it was my looks he wanted to discuss? He read the resentment in my eyes easily. When I didn't acknowledge the ridiculous observation he shifted tactic. "We have a lot to discuss—don't you think?"

"No. I don't," I answered in English, drawing the line clearly. I was not the *girl* he knew anymore. I hadn't been that naïve girl in a long, long time.

"I've spent the last six years looking for you. The least you can do is allow me to explain."

Everything began spinning. For a moment I thought I would faint on the sidewalk. Noticing the color drain from my face, Alek slipped a hand under my elbow and walked me to the table. As soon as I sat down, I took a very large gulp of Emilia's water. Nobody at the table missed the way my hand trembled uncontrollably, or that the water barely made it to my lips. It embarrassed me. Two hot circles burned my cheeks. I glanced at Alek, trying to convince myself that he wasn't a figment of my imagination, and saw concern marring his brow.

"Are you all right?"

"No."

"We don't have to talk right now. I'm not going anywhere. We have time." His perceptive eyes roamed over my face in fascination. "How are you?"

"Married," I said harshly, and held up the hand wearing

the thin, platinum band.

The shock on his face evoked a pang of guilt in me. Should I have been more gentle? Was I trying to punish him? For the past six years I thought he had abandoned me. What if I had been wrong? So much I'd already thought to be true had been proven wrong. I didn't know what to trust anymore.

As if on cue, Sebastian's Bentley came speeding around the corner, Bear behind the wheel. The passenger side door swung open before the car came to a screeching halt in front of the restaurant. With all the commotion he was causing, every pair of eyes in the vicinity was on him, on us. Gideon and Justin were by his side immediately as he stalked up to the table. Fury emanated from every line on Sebastian's body, his expression arctic. His eyes skipped back and forth from me to Alek, and turned scalding with contempt when they landed on Emilia.

Having the two of them standing next to each other was surreal. The comparison couldn't be helped. Where Sebastian was openly forceful, the power he possessed to dominate straightforward, Alek was all stealth and subterfuge. His was a fox like cunning that was just as effective at getting what he wanted as Sebastian was with his force of will.

"Sebastian—"

"Get in the car." The low murmur was bone chilling. I'd never seen him like this and it made me pause, the rest of my plea eaten up by a healthy dose of caution.

Alek stood up, glaring openly at Sebastian. I started to panic. I could see where this was headed and it was nowhere good.

"Fine. Let's go," I stated. I pushed out of my chair and tugged on Sebastian's arm without any success as the two men continued to stare each other down.

"Who is this asshole?" Alek said in Albanian. I didn't answer, my nerves stealing my ability to think on my feet, a hurricane of emotions gathering strength as I watched my past and my future colliding in my present.

"Who the fuck is this?" Sebastian murmured quietly. While he addressed me, his laser sharp attention remained fixed on Alek.

"I'm her fiancé," Alek answered in perfect English.

"Sebastian, let's go," I said more sternly. By the look on Sebastian's face the proverbial crap was about to hit the fan, the tension escalating by the second. This needed to end now. Turning, I began to walk to the car.

"How can I get a hold of you?" Alek's gentle plea tugged at my heart. I replied in the same language, Albanian, to get my cell number from Emilia, who was cowering near the table with a chastened look on her face. And after directing a well-earned furious glare in her direction, I stepped into the Bentley. A beat later Sebastian slid into the back of the car beside me.

He stared out the window, his jaw locked, his hand clenched in a tight fist.

"Bear, can you please take us to the apartment?"

"Yes, ma'am," he answered, although only after his eyes connected with Sebastian's in the rearview mirror, who gave his consent with a nod. Any illusion that I had choices was just that, a carefully orchestrated illusion.

Not a word was said the entire car ride home, nor in the elevator. As soon as we entered the apartment, he stormed into the kitchen and grabbed a bottle of beer from the fridge. I threw my purse down on the couch, and watched him walk over to the wall of windows that overlooked the lake. The stiffness in his stride worried me.

Out the window, the sun hung low in a cloudless sky, the light reflecting off the water as gold crescents. The peace and tranquility of the view was in sharp contrast to what was about to transpire inside the apartment. He turned, one hand on his hip and the other clutching the bottle. Staring a hole through me, he said, "Start talking."

My eyes narrowed. "I suggest you lose the attitude. I'm no longer one of your employees, darling. Snapping and barking at me won't get you the results you want."

"Who the fuck was that?" he continued in the same tone.

I breathed out a loud sigh of frustration. The ability to reason was beyond him when he was like this. "The man I was engaged to six years ago."

He held his silence. His eyes alert in anticipation of what was to come, urging me to continue. I walked to the couch and slumped down in it, my elbows on my knees, my focus falling on my clasped hands. I picked at the nail bed of my thumb as I began telling him the story.

"I was eighteen when I saw him the first time on campus. What I didn't know was that he was my father's new teaching assistant. He was doing postdoctoral work in political science. That was when my father was still head of the Political Science Department. Alek didn't have any family left so my father kind of took him under his wing. He started spending a lot of time at the house…things just grew from there." I braved a look at Sebastian's face and found his attention riveted on me.

Holding his gaze, I continued. "We were engaged three years later. Then my father was…well, you know." Looking away, I shrugged. "Anyway, things started to escalate. The press followed us everywhere. It was a nuisance, especially on campus where Alek taught. He wanted to start over, move somewhere else." I scoffed at the memory.

My mind lost focus, wandering back in time. I could still remember the acute shock I felt watching Alek get on that train, the disbelief that he was actually leaving me. The echo of a pain I thought long forgotten found its way into my heart. "There was no way I was leaving my father. So he suggested that he travel to Brussels and find us a place to live, a teaching position, while my father's case was resolved...that was the last time we spoke, the last time I saw him before today."

I didn't have to guess what was going on in his head. Dark, blond eyebrows lowered over eyes that resembled two burning slits. The tension of his muscles spoke volumes. "The son of a bitch abandoned you?"

"I thought so..." I couldn't hold his gaze as I told him the rest of it. Because withholding any information from Sebastian was out of the question. He asked for my trust and I gave it to him without reserve. "He said he's been looking for me for the past six years."

"How fucking convenient," he spat out snidely. The bitterness in his low growl prompted me to meet his gaze.

"How so?" I asked genuinely unaware of where his train of thought was headed.

"He magically turns up shortly after you and I get married?" At the still confused look on my face he continued. "You married a billionaire, love. You can't possibly be that naïve?"

Shock. It was plain on my face. "You think this is about money?"

"Everything is about money."

My head was shaking before he finished his sentence. "No, no, Sebastian, it isn't. Alek is an academic. He's not motivated by money."

At this, Sebastian chuckled darkly and turned to face out the window. "What else did he say?"

"Not much. I was in a state of shock. You showed up shortly afterwards."

A heavy pause followed, weighed down by all the important things still left unsaid. I could feel him struggling to contain his emotions. His dissatisfaction with the conversation was palpable so I decided to squash any chance this had of festering into a serious wound.

"I'm glad I saw him."

Sebastian spun around with a look of total surprise on his face. Those expressive eyes of his followed every step I took to reach him. When I placed my hand on his chest, he flinched. Under my palm I could feel the heavy thumping of his heart, the heat burning through the fine cotton of his white shirt.

With my hand resting over his sternum, I said, "I'm glad because now I know. I'm not mad anymore. I feel nothing where he is concerned. It's like getting rid of one more suitcase with no wheels." His brow furrowed in confusion at the metaphor, at the memory of what my life had been like before I met him—all that heavy baggage I had to carry around by myself.

"If you had any idea how much I love you, you wouldn't have that look on your face."

He breathed out a heavy sigh. His hand came up and covered mine, keeping it over his heart.

"Are you going to see him again?"

"Yes." His eyes slammed into mine, though to give him credit he didn't argue. "For myself. Not for his sake. I want to know what happened."

Chapter Twenty-One

BY THE TIME I GOT home that evening, an empty home that is, I was too tired to do anything other than take a hot shower. It was eleven when I finally crawled into bed. My cell phone rang. Too spent to even glance at the screen, I absently answered, "Please tell me you're on your way home."

"Vera?"

The shaky, broken voice sounded alarm bells. I sat up straight in bed. "Emilia? Is that you?" I glanced at the cell screen and noticed it was a number I didn't recognize. The heavy silence had me on edge.

"Yes."

"Where are you? Are you okay?"

"I'm at the club…in the office." A fractured sob followed. Then a small, "No."

"I'm coming to get you. Are you safe?"

"I don't know."

"I'll be there in a few minutes. I'm in town. It won't take long."

I was out of bed and dressed in seconds. Since the case at the bank had closed, the twenty-four-hour security team had dwindled down to Bear, who had gone to the office to wait for Sebastian once he'd dropped me off at home. The cab I called was waiting for me when I made it downstairs. Ten minutes later, we pulled up in front of Fix, Yuri's nightclub.

It was Thursday night and the front of the club was

crowded with young professionals, trust fund babies, and scantily clad women trying to get into the ultra trendy club. A mountain of a man guarded the entrance. Techno music, pumping loudly, spilled out every time someone entered or left. I walked up to the bouncer and his narrowed eyes traveled from my long sleeve t-shirt down to my dark jeans. Clearly, I wasn't dressed for the occasion.

"I'm here to see Emilia." Nothing. All I got in return was a blank stare. "Yuri's girlfriend. I suggest you let me in." Still nothing. In desperation, I made one last attempt. "Do you know who I am?" And then, shamefully, I scraped up the courage to say, "My last name is Horn—as in Horn Banque." Skepticism largely remained on his face, though I could sense doubt sneaking in. The doubt stoked my courage. I took my brand-new identity card out and held it up to his bearded face. His blue eyes darted back and forth from me to the ID card. Then he stepped aside and unhooked the velvet rope. That was a rude awakening. The name of the owner couldn't get me into the club, but Sebastian's did.

Inside the music was so loud I could feel it thumping inside my chest. Neon strobe lights overhead offered only the mildest illumination. Although large, the club was packed. My eyes scanned the sweaty bodies smashed together on the dance floor. Pushing past them, I made my way to the VIP lounge. Not surprisingly, it was cordoned off, another guard, this one armed by the look of the bulge under his lapel, faithfully stood by. Seated at one of the booths with three, super thin and ultra young women was Yuri.

The problem with monsters is that they rarely look like they're supposed to. He was neither sinfully handsome nor ugly. From what I could recall he was also neither crass nor loud. He was tall and well proportioned. On the thin side. He had wispy blond hair, quintessentially Slavic cheekbones, denim blue eyes—and he wore glasses. They weren't trendy, cool glasses. They were the kind of glasses you see on an accountant, often smudged and a bit crooked. Not on a man who beats his girlfriend. Not on one that runs a serious drug operation and God knows what else. Not on one that operates as an arm of the Russian Mafia.

I stared at him with daggers in my eyes. He glanced my way once and looked away. I watched with disgust as his hand skated up the thigh and over the crotch of one of the girls who appeared to be underage. He didn't recognize me. Having met him only once—when I first arrived, when I had long hair and not a pound to spare—it wasn't a surprise. And I preferred it that way.

I had no intention of questioning him about Emilia. Stealth and anonymity were the only tools I had to work with, the only way I could retrieve her and get out without an altercation that would impel me to call my dear husband to come to the rescue.

I snuck past the table. My next stop was the bar. I figured one of the bartenders could send me in the right direction. The bar was massive, stretching the entire length of the wall. I pinched and pushed my way closer. I may have even kicked someone. Subtlety and manners were luxuries I couldn't afford at the moment. The closest bartender was a young man around twenty-five.

"Excuse me! Excuse me!" I shouted, fervently waving an arm at him. Even as I screamed at the top of my lungs, my voice could barely be heard over the music. He finally glanced my way and came over. Cupping my mouth, I screamed in French, "Do you know Emilia Gani?" He nodded. "Where can I find her?"

"I don't know. In case you haven't noticed, we're kind of busy."

"Well, can you at least tell me where Yuri's office is?"

He gave me a skeptical look. Scanning left and right he

said, "Why do you want to know that?"

"Because I have to find Emilia and I think she's in his office. Look, this is *kind of* an emergency."

He raked his fingers through his dark, shoulder-length hair. I could tell he was anxious, that he wanted no part of this—or me. And yet I could also see that he wanted to help Emilia. His eyes met mine again. "Go to the back, make a left, then two rights. If anyone stops you, tell them Stefan sent you to get more singles."

"Thank you, Stefan."

He nodded again. "Be careful." His dark eyes held mine for a fraction longer. "And take care of her."

"I will."

I pushed through an endless supply of bodies. Packed tightly on the dance floor, the sweat pouring off of them landed all over me. The neon lights coupled with the techno music made me dizzy. Just before I reached the end of the dance floor, I spotted a familiar face. It took me a minute to place her. Sebastian's neighbor, Lucinda. She was sandwiched between two very young men who were grinding against her. Cupping the head of the one behind her, she brought him closer and stuck her tongue down his throat. I kept walking.

The hall was not empty. There was a woman leaning against the wall and a man on his knees with his mouth fastened onto her groin. Neither one of them noticed me walk right past them, too busy celebrating their party of two.

"What you doin' here?" A thick Russian accent stopped me in my tracks. I turned slowly, taking the time to gather every drop of courage I possessed. Before me stood a man that was easily six feet seven and all of it pure muscle, the kind of exaggerated muscles that have veins popping out all over the place.

My eyes climbed up to his surprisingly refined features. It almost seemed that the muscles were an attempt to balance a face that could've easily been described as pretty. That's not what held my attention though. It was the dagger tattoo drawn on his collarbone. A tattoo signifying he'd been in the Russian prison system and committed murder; no doubt he was wearing the tank top as warning. I swallowed, unadulterated fear clogging my throat.

"Stefan sent me."

"Stefan?"

"Yes, Stefan. Are you hard of hearing?" Where the hell that came from, I'll never know. "He sent me to get singles in Yuri's office."

Muscle man just stared right back at me. Most unnerving. Sweat beaded on my forehead as if I was running a marathon across the Arabian Desert.

"No need to be bitch." He stepped aside and let me pass. Instinctively, I reached up and rubbed the diamond cross hidden under my shirt. I didn't breathe again until I reached Yuri's door.

Without knocking, I opened it. Emilia was sitting on the floor with her back against the wall, her arms wrapped around her bare knees, the micro mini she wore gathered around her waist. Her face was red from crying, her shoulders hunched over in defeat. My gaze immediately zeroed in on her swollen cheekbone. She glanced up then. When our eyes met, a fresh set of tears ran down her face. I was at her feet, crouching down, a moment later.

"You okay?" I whispered, wiping away the tears still running down her face. She nodded. "We'll talk later. We need to move fast. Are you hurt, or can you walk?"

"I can walk," she mumbled in a timid voice. As I placed my hands under her arms to help her up, she winced. "Don't look at me that way."

"I'm not angry at you. I'm angry with him. But we don't have the luxury to sit around and chat right now." Something told me we were running out of time, the danger escalating every second we remained inside the walls of the club.

The hallway was blessedly empty. "If we run into anyone, I'll say that we're going to find Yuri," Emilia instructed. We reached the end of one hallway and turned down another—where muscle man was apparently busy watching the woman deep throat her companion. With his back to us he didn't notice anything until we had passed him and the couple.

"Where you go?"

"To find Yuri," Emilia answered over her shoulder in Albanian. Every second of silence felt as if my head was being held under water.

"Send Vlad. I need break." Neither one of us turned to look at him; Emilia simply nodded. We didn't utter a word until we reached the main part of the club.

"Thank God, I didn't speak Albanian," I said anxiously.

"A lot of these guys are part of the Albanian Mafia. They're working together now."

"Drugs?"

Emilia's troubled eyes met mine. "Girls."

"Let's get out of here." If we didn't get out in the next few seconds, we stood a very good chance of becoming *someone's personal fuckpet* as Sebastian had put it.

Holding onto her wrist, I pulled her through the melee of bodies on the dance floor bouncing up and down with the music. Suddenly she was yanked out of my grasp, most of her scream blotted out by the deafening mix of music and people surrounding us. I turned swiftly to find Yuri holding onto her upper arm in a cruel grip, while Emilia, plastered to him, had her chin tipped down and her long black hair hanging in her face.

"Let go of her, you bastard." I put as brave a face on as I could considering how my pulse raced. If it weren't for the chaos swirling around us, he would have easily noticed how scared I was.

His impassive, blue stare jumped from her to me. He whispered something in Emilia's ear that made her cower even more, her bony shoulders curving in.

"How did you get into my club?" he calmly asked, only a hint of a Russian accent to his English.

"If you don't let her go, I will call the police."

"You've caused me quite a bit of trouble. First the police are in my house and your boyfriend screams in my face. Then Etienne, my best man, is arrested because of you. And now you want to steal my girlfriend."

"You hurt her—repeatedly. She doesn't want to stay with you any longer."

"Nobody screams in my face." It was the lack of anger, of any human emotion that frightened me most. He turned his attention back to the woman cowering next to him. "Emilia, tell this troublesome friend what you want."

"Emilia, let's go," I said, talking over him, because I knew where this was headed. Emilia's voice was barely audible. I moved to grab her other arm, but he jerked her closer to him. "Emilia, let's go," I shouted.

"I'm going to stay," I heard her mumble. Her chin tipped down, she wouldn't look at me. He'd thrown a proprietary arm around her neck, his thumb caressing the bare skin of her collarbone. The threat camouflaged by tenderness. It made me sick. I didn't know what to do. I couldn't leave her there. The punishment he would inflict on her was something I didn't dare contemplate.

Yuri's gaze moved beyond my shoulder. I was too petrified to look. God help me if it was muscle man. Slowly, the people crowding around me bled away and a halo of space opened up. I was just thinking how grateful I was not to have all those bodies smashed up against me when a very tall and very familiar one walked up beside me…

His Highness to the rescue. I'm ashamed to say that on the inside, I was screaming in unabashed glee.

He barely spared me a glance. The cold, hard look on his face was all for Yuri. "We're taking her with us," was all he said.

"No," Emilia replied. Head shaking, she pressed herself closer to Yuri as if seeking shelter from us—as if we were the enemy. "No. I'm staying here." It didn't take a genius to figure out that she was terrified of him.

Yuri petted Emilia's hair. "There, you see, this was simple misunderstanding," he remarked, his English faltering. I wondered what that meant.

Sebastian's jaw clenched, his nostrils flared. He tipped his chin at me, continuing to avoid my gaze. "We're going." Grabbing my arm, he turned to leave.

"I'm not going anywhere without her," I screeched. Then his eyes crashed into mine, burning with barely contained fury. I'm surprised I didn't drop dead from the glare alone.

"We. Are. Leaving," he ordered through clenched teeth, a staccato of words fired at me like bullets. He yanked on my arm, dragging me away. Bear, right next to us the whole time, brought up the rear. I hadn't even noticed his presence until that moment.

"Get leash for that one." Yuri's accent was more pronounced, his grammar falling apart. "She's wild, not broken—yet."

Sebastian stopped walking. For a moment I thought he would turn and go back for Emilia, but I was wrong. After a beat he exhaled harshly and kept walking, dragging me along with him.

Outside the club, the bouncer watched us curiously as Sebastian shoved me into the back seat of the Mercedes. I glared at him for the shove, though his attention remained ahead so little good that did. The tires screamed as Bear hit the gas, driving us out of there quickly.

"Did I *not* tell you to stay THE FUCK away from her?!" His voice escalated with every spoken word. I jumped in my seat, my nerves hypersensitive. And still, he wouldn't look at me. The dark did nothing to obscure the vein throbbing at his temple, the tight edges of his mouth. Shutting his eyes, he took a deep breath and exhaled loudly.

Any other time I would have apologized—he already had too much on his plate to contend with—however, this was a matter of life and death. I couldn't say for certain that Yuri wouldn't kill Emilia. Was he capable of it? My mind didn't want to go there.

"He beats her. She called me in hysterics again. And then you walk in and let him intimidate her into staying?"

His head swiveled in my direction, his wide, fiery eyes locked onto mine. "What would you have me do? Start a war with the Russian Mob for a woman that would most likely crawl back to him by morning?"

He had a point there. I hated it when he made sense. Last time I'd tried prying her away from Yuri, after he'd given her a broken rib, she ended up giving *me* the cold shoulder for weeks. I exhaled in frustration. Sebastian's glare softened. We were both silent for the rest of the ride.

Bear pulled up to our building and dropped us off. Not a word was said as we made our way up to the apartment, the space between us loaded with tension, charged with conflict. I could see by his eyes how tired he was, that his leg was bothering him. It made me feel terrible. I reached out, but he stepped away. For the first time in our relationship, he wouldn't let me touch him.

Chapter Twenty-Two

ONCE WE WERE INSIDE, HE headed straight for the shower, his strides swallowing up ground. He avoided looking at me more than was absolutely necessary. I was in our bedroom, undressing, when he returned wearing a towel hanging low around his hips. He finger-combed his wet hair back and watched me peel the jeans off my legs with a mixture of irritation and pure animal attraction.

My greedy eyes, drawn by natural instinct to his quintessential masculine beauty, moved over those spectacular traps, down his broad chest, and over a six-pack that rippled every time he moved. Dark blond hair peeked out over the top of his low-slug towel, now tenting as a result of where his apparent thoughts were headed—and taking me right along with him. The ache between my legs was increasing by the second.

It made me furious. I had absolutely no dominion over myself when it came to him. No matter how many times I tried to harness this heat living between us, to contain it, it bucked every attempt to be managed. Although I should've known better, since it had always been that way between us. This undeniable imperative to come together hadn't diminished even a small fraction since the day we met, reducing my self-control to a punch line, a bad joke. I always considered myself strong, determined, in charge of my own fate. But I hadn't been since the day he found me on my knees.

Come to think of it, that seemed about right. Because I was a willing slave to him.

When my eyes climbed back up to his face, his eyes were heavy-lidded, full of lust…and anger. There was no ignoring that. He moved fast—with impunity.

Grabbing my wrists in a firm grip, he pushed me down on the bed and fell on top of me, all two hundred and fifteen pounds of him. He made no attempt to break his fall. The air rushed out of my lungs. My wrists were pinned above my head. He held on with one hand while the other gently skated over my throat, onto my throbbing pulse. His erection pressed hard and hot in between my thighs, stoking my arousal. The heat quickly turned into a raging fire.

He nudged me twice and a low moan escaped my lips. That's all it took for the electric sensation to move through me, a branch of pure pleasure lighting up the farthest reaches of my body. He knew me, knew my body like a treasure map he'd studied over and over. He knew my weaknesses better than I did. That thought made me pause.

Spurred on by my reaction, he ground himself against me, encouraging this frenzy, this fervent, insatiable need I had for his touch until I stopped thinking altogether.

"Sometimes I want to fucking strangle you."

My eyes floated open to find his face inches from mine, frustration and desire taking turns flashing in those rust colored eyes. They darted from my eyes to my mouth. His breathing grew erratic. I watched him fight to gain control of it. He kissed me roughly and I knew desire had won.

His free hand moved lower, hooking under by bent knee. He jerked it up until it was practically resting near my head. "Sometimes I wish I *could* put a fucking leash on you."

Desire is a strange and complicated affair. What you would find repulsive under any other circumstance can become a total turn-on when done and said by the person you love—the person who brings out the best and worst in you.

I locked my mouth onto his and devoured him, consumed him, let the kiss say everything I couldn't communicate in words. Because I didn't have the courage to tell him what those words from him stirred in me. He didn't have to question it for long though. Releasing his grip on my wrists, he ripped away his towel. Skin to skin now, he brushed his fingertips back and forth over my nipples, pinching, teasing them up. Barely able to move, I squirmed chasing his fingers.

His arm, still under my knee in a cruel and punishing hold, had my hip flexed at a brutal angle. He pushed my soaked underwear aside and caught the unquestionable evidence of my arousal, the scent of my body telling him I was his to do with as he pleased, more than ready for him to take me. A brief smile appeared on features so perfect they were both a blessing and a burden.

"Can't have you running around with my heart in your hands," he muttered, rocking his hard body against my soft and willing one.

He pinched my nipple hard and my body bowed off the bed. He scraped the delicate skin at the side of my throat with his teeth. A wild thing staking his claim. But I was already his. It had happened quietly, without me noticing. He'd dug under my skin and written himself into my DNA...just as he said he'd wished to do.

When he pulled away I cried out, bereft, cold where he had been. A moment later he drove his hips against mine, fitting himself inside of me to the root. The air swooshed from his lungs while I sucked in a breath. The broad head of his erection hit the back of my womb and a spot so sensitive it sent a shockwave racing up my spine. The initial twinge of pain melted into pleasure, coalesced into ecstasy, and grew into a state of arousal I hadn't quite experienced before. Tears welled in my eyes as the sensation grew stronger and stronger. His eyes, catching every detail, lost some of their hardness...love shined through.

I cupped his face as he began to rock deeper and deeper, pushing me towards an epic climax. With my knee bent, I couldn't do anything other than submit. To his needs, to his force of will. It was intentional and I knew it. I let it happen.

He picked up the pace, driving faster and faster. Tipping his chin, he watched his body invading mine, taking possession, making us one. A dark smile curved his lips.

I was getting close, struggling to adjust to the right angle. "No," he barked, and pulled out of me. I screamed in frustration loud enough for it to echo throughout the apartment.

In one swift move, he flipped me over onto my knees, my face pushed into the mattress. "My way—understood?" The command was forceful, backed by impatience. He stroked his large hand up and down the length of my spine, in between the cheeks of my rear end. I jerked at the sensation. "Easy. Not tonight," he murmured.

The other gripped my hip with a force that I knew would leave a bruise. His erection, hot and slippery, settled between my cheeks, his hips pinned to my rear end. One hand cupped me, his fingers teasing and torturing me while the other hand held me down by the neck. I squirmed to get his fingers where I wanted them.

"Beg me for what you want. Beg me, and I'll give it to you."

Part of me wanted to buck him off, fight him every inch of the way. The rest of me ate it up, craved it, lusted after it; an addict needing a fix.

Without warning, he thrust his hips, filled me up again. "I want to hear you beg me," he commanded in a tone as sharp as broken glass, angry enough to gain my full attention even when the sound was mellowed by desire. He slammed into me harder, faster. My muscles pulled taut, quivered from the insane amount of pleasure he was giving me. Though at the same time, not enough. "I'll give you what you want. I'll give you things you didn't even know you wanted. But first I want to hear you beg."

Whines and desperate moans came bursting out of me. I was on a straight trajectory to the most powerful orgasm he'd ever given me—and that was saying a lot. What troubled me was the *why*. The bruising hold on me, the filthy words whispered in my ear excited me beyond measure. *Make me... go ahead and make me,* the devil in me whispered.

"Let go and give me what I want," he demanded, each word punctuated by a deep and powerful thrust of his hips. "And I'll give you what you need."

I couldn't resist any longer. I couldn't fight anymore. I stopped trying to control my body, my mind. I stopped seeking, and received what he wanted to give me. Pleasure. So much pleasure a river of tears ran down my face.

"I'm begging, Sebastian, please..." My voice faded away, my mind grew quiet.

"I'll give it to you, baby. I'll give you everything you need, always." And he did. He kept his promise and pushed me over the edge. I fell from the stars and landed in an ocean of euphoria.

I came...and came...and came.

Muscles expanded and contracted. I screamed his name, the sound muffled by the blanket shoved against my mouth.

Sebastian thrust one last time and stilled. Muscles turned to rock, spine curved around mine. He bit the space where my shoulder dovetailed with my neck and growled as he emptied himself inside of me. It launched me into a second orgasm.

And I came...and came...and came.

Love has a sound. It sounded like the rush of my husband's breath by my ear. Love has a feel to it. It felt like the warm slip of sweat between our bodies, and the squeeze of his hands on my breasts as he held on in comfort. Love was all those things and more. It was the intimacy expanding between us into an unfathomable place where we were no longer two, but one.

To be so vulnerable should've frightened me to death, should have sent me screaming from the room. I was hanging over a cliff, trusting him to catch me when I fell. Relinquishing control was the hardest thing I'd ever done. Placing myself in his hands meant trusting him without reserve. In the farthest, darkest corners of my mind, a voice called out, told me to run and hide, to get away. Instead, I turned and wrapped him in my arms, and held him as he fell asleep.

Chapter Twenty-Three

TRUST IS A HOTHOUSE FLOWER. It needs to be tended, nurtured, protected. It needs all your attention to help it thrive while at the same time it takes very little to erode it…to kill it. One wrong move, and weeks, months, even years of hard work and care can be wiped away in the blink of an eye.

I accepted my fair share of the blame. I will admit that my actions didn't exactly inspire trust in him. Though in my defense I didn't do anything on purpose. But his own issues, which had everything to do with his upbringing, sabotaged it as well.

"I'll be home after dinner tonight. It's the only night of the week we see patients."

Sebastian came out of the walk-in closet wearing only his underwear and socks, his pants hanging from his fingertips. On cue, my reaction practically Pavlovian, my eyes roamed over him in appreciation. When they climbed back up to his face, I didn't like what I found.

"I thought you were volunteering. That this was only going to take up a few days of your time?"

I really didn't like where this conversation was headed. My attention descended to the shell buttons of the blouse I was busy closing. "It was at first, but Yannick—"

"Yannick?" he said, interrupting me. "Who the fuck is Yannick?"

"My God, Sebastian—language." His scowl didn't lessen

one iota. "Dr. Kama. The attending physician. It's his clinic."

Four weeks had passed since I'd started working at the clinic. Sebastian had been so busy restoring order at the bank that he hadn't noticed the long hours I had been working. All that had changed in the last week. The bank was back to running as smoothly as ever, and my husband was back home earlier than usual. Russet colored eyes met brown ones, the brown ones wide with anticipation.

He looked uncomfortable, on the verge of saying something...important? "I thought you would..." He swallowed. "Now that the case is closed."

"Would what?" My skin prickled with awareness.

He looked around. I could practically see the wheels spinning in his mind. "I thought we could try again," he said, his eyes glued to the pants he was holding.

My heart dropped. I heard it fall to the floor. Things were finally back to semi-normal (whatever that was) between us. My job at the clinic was everything I had hoped and more... and he wanted a baby. How could I tell the man I loved more than anything in this world that I didn't? Not right now, anyway. Sensing that an oblique attack would be most effective, I immediately went in that direction.

I walked up to him and placed my hand over his heart. "Darling, I'm just now getting acclimated to a life where no one wants you dead, and I'm not going to spend the rest of mine in prison. I love you. I love being married to you. I also love my new job. Can I possible enjoy that for a little while longer before we throw a baby into the mix?"

By the time I was done with my little speech the side of his mouth had curved up in a sweet, adorable smile. He nodded briefly and placed a soft kiss on my lips.

"Why don't you meet me at the clinic and we can go out to dinner from there?"

That seemed to smooth his ruffled feathers. His expression

relaxed. I exhaled the breath I was holding. Crisis averted. At least, for now.

***

My days at the clinic had fallen into a comfortable routine. And what I mean by that is that we would examine patients and discuss the diagnosis and treatments. Then, outside the examination room, Yannick would fire off a thousand other potential diagnoses, quiz me on those symptoms and what my course of treatment would be—all this while I was being timed. It was like facing a firing squad every day. And I loved every minute of it.

By 7 p.m. we were almost done with scheduled appointments. A young woman, no older than twenty-one, walked in. Under her olive skin, there was a pallor to her that concerned me. Hunched over and walking slowly, she was clearly in pain. Agnes noticed as well and immediately escorted her to an examination room while Yannick finished up with another patient.

I entered the examination room ready to take her information and found her lying down on her side. When I tried asking her in French what her name was, she stared back at me with a blank expression. I tried asking her again in English and received the same vacant stare.

Yannick walked in then.

"I don't know what language she speaks but it isn't English or French." His dark, intelligent eyes assessed the woman on the examination table. Her eyes were closed, beads of sweat collecting on her brow.

"Signora, come ti chiami?" I asked in Italian. Her eyes blinked open and she answered. My eyes connected with Yannick's.

"Italian."

"Her name is Arabic," he added. A couple more questions

and we had ferreted out that she was in Switzerland illegally and she had gotten pregnant. We didn't pursue the topic further, however, it was easy to deduce that she was in the sex trade.

Looking at her, small, long dark hair, the similarities in our stories was not lost on me. Could I have ended up like her if I hadn't met Sebastian? The question sank in bone deep and rattled me.

After a thorough examination, Yannick concluded that she had had a miscarriage. She categorically refused to go to a hospital so Yannick did his best to make her comfortable.

In the now empty lobby of the clinic, we waited for her to get dressed. "What's wrong? You look pale."

Distracted, I glanced up and found Yannick watching me strangely. I'd never seen him look concerned before but he was at the moment.

"Nothing. She just reminds me…" My voice got lost in the midst of all the memories that came rushing back. "I could have been her." I shrugged. "If I hadn't met my husband—who knows what would have happened to me."

Yannick looked thoughtful. "He's a good man?"

That made me smile. "The best." I looked at the man standing before me. He was a good man. He had also become a good friend. "He wants a baby."

Yannick scowled. "What about your career?"

"That's the problem. Can I do both, and not have both suffer from neglect?"

"Tough question."

"Yes," I exhaled deeply. "Thank you for listening."

Yannick placed his large comforting hand on my shoulder. "Anytime."

"Get your fucking hands off my wife."

It was as if a cold bucket of ice water had been dumped on my head. We both turned to face the growling voice. Yannick's eyes narrowed. The two men squared up. While on the outside I remained frozen, on the inside my heart was beating savagely inside my chest.

And then it happened all at once…I couldn't believe my eyes. Sebastian launched himself at Yannick and grabbed him by the lapels. I sprang into action trying to separate them while Yannick gave as well as he got. I was sent sprawling onto my rear end by the two titans trying to shove each other around.

They only stopped and separated when the chair I fell against toppled over. Sebastian came over and hauled me to my feet. Glaring viciously, I pushed him away.

"Yannick, I'll see you tomorrow." I measured my words, afraid an avalanche of foul language was about to come tumbling out. Wiping the sweat off his brow, he nodded in answer. I walked out without looking in Sebastian's direction once.

✷✷✷

In the interminable ride home, we were both silent, the air heavy with disbelief and disappointment. I spent the time trying to school my temper into something manageable. A wave of relief washed over me when he pulled the Bentley into the underground garage and parked. I tugged on the door handle twice and still it remained locked.

"Do you want him?" The words registered slowly. I turned to take him in. He couldn't possibly be serious? His unblinking gaze was fixed ahead, his nostrils flaring, his jaw pulsing with tension. All the usual signs of irrational anger were there.

"Do you hear yourself? Do you hear how insane you sound?"

"Answer my question."

His voice was too cool for my liking. I wanted him to lose it so we could go straight to dealing with the insanity he was currently experiencing. "I'm going to say this slowly, so there's no misunderstanding...go fuck yourself."

His head whipped around. A deep frown was carved into those patrician good looks. I'd never spoken to him like that, but desperate times called for desperate measures. And after being humiliated in front of my boss, a colleague I respected enormously and a friend, he needed to understand that I wouldn't tolerate this irrational jealousy ever again.

"Watch your mouth," he murmured in a hair-raising tone.

This time when I pulled on the door handle, it thankfully sprang open. I stalked to the elevator, and without waiting for him, took it up to the penthouse. I knew I was going to pay for it upstairs, and yet at the moment I couldn't have cared less, all that mattered was getting as far away from him as possible.

Once inside the apartment, I went straight to the windows overlooking the lake. The absolute stillness of the water was visible even in the dark—in direct contrast to the turbulence of emotions swirling inside the home we shared, a storm brewing closer to that of a category five hurricane.

Footsteps intruded in the silence, measured, unhurried. When they stopped not too far behind me, I wrapped my arms around myself, staving off the tremor that had taken a hold of me since the altercation at the clinic. No doubt the effect of the adrenaline running through my veins.

"I can't believe you did that. I can't believe you would humiliate me that way."

"I can't believe you would let him touch you," he snapped.

My eyes went straight to the ceiling, where I begged God to grant me the patience and the words to get through to him.

"I'm chaffing, and not in a good way. You need to loosen the choke collar, Sebastian. I'm not a pet you take out whenever you feel like it."

I turned and leaned my back against the glass for support,

my knees turning liquid under his intense scrutiny. He'd removed his jacket and tie. With his hands neatly tucked in the pockets of his slim, gray slacks and his air of superiority, he was every inch the lord of the manor I met not so long ago.

"I take care of what's mine."

Bewildered, I stood up straighter. I stared back for an undetermined amount of time trying to judge how far he'd gone off the rails. "I'm not a thing, an object, one of your assets to manage. I'm not something to be possessed!"

"I believe the words were honor and obey," he taunted in a low voice.

I began laughing like a deranged lunatic, no humor in it. "You can't be serious."

When he stalked toward me, I stood my ground, even though I'd never seen him look quite so menacing before. Slowly lifting his hand, he reached out and ever so delicately stroked my throat with the pads of his fingers. My pulse jumped, my skin coming alive at the sweet sensation.

"I do possess you. As much as you own me. So you will do as I say—"

"The hell I will—"

"You will do as I say!" he shouted over me. Shoving his fingers through my hair, his grip on it tightened painfully. And then he swooped down, and kissed me. He kissed me hard. A kiss meant to punish, meant to dominate. Except I didn't push him away, as I should have. I only pulled him closer. My mind begged me to stop him while my body insisted I meet his passion in equal measure. The friction caused sparked something inside of me, fueling the heat between us. He slanted his head and held me in place while he deepened the kiss. His hands were everywhere at once. His fingers dug into my butt cheeks and pulled my pelvis into the rock-solid erection pushing against his gabardine slacks. I shoved a hand over the swollen head, cupped him, and he gasped into my mouth. I pushed past the wet stain spreading at the top of his zipper and squeezed his sac. I knew I was tempting the devil, and yet I didn't care.

I was unceremoniously hoisted up and carried into the bedroom with my ankles locked around his hips. We began tearing at each other. My pencil skirt and my shirt were the victims of his next attack. The first, bunched up at my waist, the latter, half ripped open. My thong was shredded to bits in a one-handed grab. His shirt met the same fate. Buttons began flying. There wasn't going to be one left on a shirt in all of Geneva if we kept this up.

He threw me down on the bed and barely got his pants past his rear end before he shoved himself inside of me, in his enthusiasm driving us both halfway up the bed.

It wasn't lovemaking, and it wasn't intended to be. It was two sweaty, lust-crazed bodies crashing into each other, taking their anger and frustration out on one another. The alpha imposing his will on everyone and everything under him. Part of me welcomed it. The deranged part, that is. But the part that could still reason knew this would never stop, the noose would only get tighter if I didn't put an end to it immediately.

My climax was sharp and fast. He came with a roar, and triggered another seismic event in my body. Afterwards he collapsed on top of me. As I fought for breath, he nuzzled the side of my neck. All the tenderness I felt in his touch kicked my anger up. Grabbing a fistful of his hair, I pulled his head back to stare into his eyes. I wanted him to see the determination on my face when I spoke.

"You aren't going to fuck me into submission, darling. I can take anything you dish out."

A wicked smile flirted at the corners of his mouth, all the anger now leeched out of him by an epic orgasm. "It's not going to stop me from trying though."

"I'm not in the mood for your jokes. Get off of me." I pushed and pushed until he rose up on an elbow. Then I watched him grab his still hard penis and rub my thighs and intimate parts with his seed. I'd never seen anything so blatantly possessive in all my life.

"Enough!" I shouted, pushing him off.

He rolled onto his back while I sat up, my legs dangling off the foot of the bed. My fingers searched for the buttons on my lavender, silk blouse and discovered that all but one were missing. Demoralized. Defeated. I was all those things and more. I could no longer justify his actions to myself. This was either a lack of respect, or a lack of trust. Either way, it had to stop.

"I'll be sleeping in the next bedroom tonight and tomorrow I'm moving to a hotel until you develop the ability to reason like a sane individual."

"The hell you are," was his warning reply. I glanced over my shoulder and found him leaning back on his elbows. His chest bare, his eyes narrowed. His pants and underwear were still pushed down his thighs. He made no move to cover himself up.

Beast. A gorgeous one. In the privacy of my mind I entertained all sorts of filthy things I wanted to do to him. But that's as far as it went. There was no way I was actually going to let him fuck me into submission. And it killed me that with all the issues hanging over our heads one glance at him had the power to turn my insides into utter chaos. The look on my face must've tipped him off because his lips curved into a smile worthy of the devil.

I went straight into the walk-in closet we shared, grabbed something to sleep in and tried to fix my hair. I was certain I looked like I'd been mauled in a dark alley. When I walked back into the room, he was in the same position I left him in, still lounging lazily like a big cat after the hunt.

"When you come to your senses, you can find me at the clinic," I told him.

The smug smile dropped right off his face. His expression morphed into a silent threat. But just in case I wasn't paying attention, he said, "You walk out that door, and you'll be sorry." His voice was super quiet. Goose bumps swept over my flesh.

"I already am," I answered just as quietly. And with that, I walked out of the bedroom we shared as man and wife without a backwards glance.

***

The next morning, I left for the clinic extremely early, before Sebastian was even awake. I found Yannick in his office, sitting behind his desk with only a desk lamp illuminating the sharp angles of his movie star face. Bent foreword with his chin resting on his fists, he stared at the chessboard as if he were waiting for the pieces to move themselves.

"You're playing by yourself?" I said, pushing down a smile.

He glanced up. "Do you play?"

"Yes, but very badly."

"Perfect, take a seat. My ego needs a stroke."

"I highly doubt that," I replied, sitting in the armchair on the other side of his desk while he rearranged the chess pieces.

"I don't know what else to say except I'm sorry. He's always been possessive, but he's never crossed the line like that before." Yannick's large soulful eyes held steady. "He's been under an extraordinary amount of stress lately." I diverted my gaze, too embarrassed by what I heard coming out of my mouth. A bad excuse.

"Has he ever hurt you?"

My eyes snapped to his. My expression of surprise switched to a defensive one almost instantly. "Never, never, he's not like that. He's...he's emotional, yes...but he's more likely to hurt himself," I vehemently argued.

"I had to ask," Yannick replied in the same low, butter-soft voice he used to comfort patients. That said more to me than his words.

"I have to look for an apartment tomorrow." The weight of his perceptive eyes was on me again while mine remained on the board. Yannick being Yannick, he didn't ask any more questions.

"There's a studio apartment on the top floor. I keep it for late nights and such. Move in there. It's clean. I just had the bathroom and kitchen remodeled."

"No. I couldn't impose." Any further objections were stalled by his words.

"You can and you will. I'm not discussing this further." We drifted into silence for a while.

"Yannick, can I ask you something?"

"I don't think I can stop you."

"How did you raise the money to build this clinic? The machines are almost brand new."

"I'm obscenely wealthy," he deadpanned.

I glanced up to examine his face. "Are you joking? I can never tell with you."

His intense gaze remained on the board. "I never joke about money. My grandfather owns chain of furniture stores. I'm his favorite."

"So modest," I mocked, chuckling.

His eyes slammed into mine. "What has modesty ever done for anyone, other than get them a place at the back of the line. The man who thinks like a pauper will never be king."

That quelled my amusement instantly. I considered what he said and couldn't find fault in it. "Who said that?"

"I did." I studied the fascinating man sitting across from me. Dedicated, driven...a force of nature. If I didn't know him personally, I would think he was too good to be true, a fictional hero in a romance novel.

"You know, Yannick, if you were just a fraction sweeter you'd be the catch of the century."

He looked up then, his dark eyes bright and mischievous, his sensual lips curving up wryly. "Who says I want to be caught?"

"The harder you fight it, the harder you'll fall," I teased.

After a beat, his expression sobered. "Like you did?"

It was pointless to dissemble, Yannick had an instinct for people that was unrivaled. Maria Rossetti had been right about that. "Exactly."

Chapter Twenty-Four

AUTUMN HAPPENED ALL AT ONCE. Almost overnight leaves turned from bright green to deep orange. A crisp bite in the air. The smell of burning wood.

I received a text from Alek the subsequent day. We were so busy at the clinic, I managed to ignore it for an entire morning. The iPhone I carried in the pocket of my medical coat was suddenly ten pounds heavier, a physical reminder of what had to be dealt with sooner or later. By late afternoon, it might as well have been blasting cannon fire.

Part of me wanted to know what happened all those years ago. I'd berated myself for so long for having had bad judgment when it came to men that it was a relief to consider that I may have been right all along, that Alek was the person I thought he was when I fell in love with him. Reason said there was no harm in getting the whole truth. My instincts, however, told me to focus ahead, to put the past to rest. Caught between my past and my present, it felt like I was being stretched on a medieval rack.

I walked into the restroom and paced nervously. This was a man I'd known most of my life, had been intimate with. Rationally, I should've been able to meet with him, let him say his piece and, with a clear conscience on both our parts, walk away. But something told me it wasn't going to be that simple. That there were land mines on the road up ahead…and I couldn't shake the feeling.

I splashed cold water on my face and reluctantly pulled the phone out.

> *I really need to see you. Give me the opportunity to explain. I know you've moved on and I don't blame you, but give me the opportunity to do the same. Give me closure and let me go.*
> *Alek*

Closure—that's what I needed. No explanations. No hashing out the ugly details. I texted back.

> *Fine. Tomorrow afternoon. I'll come to you.*

Alek's hotel room was near the train station, in one of those hip and inexpensive chain of hotels. I exited out of the back of the clinic and caught the tram. Bear had been living in my pocket since I moved into the flat above the clinic and I didn't need the complication of having him around.

When Alek opened the door to his room, the anticipation coupled with the brief flash of joy I caught on his face made me feel unbearably guilty. He didn't deserve my wrath or distrust, even though I'd spent the last six years believing that he'd deserted me.

He wore jeans and a navy blazer with a crisp white shirt. His designer moccasins looked expensive. He seemed to be living a comfortable life. Alek had always been vain. He'd always spent more time on his appearance than I did on mine and today was no different. It was an aspect of him that never sat well with me, so I tended to ignore it.

"How did you find me?"

I entered the room, taking in the neatly made bed, the suitcase in the corner, all his toiletries lined up like little soldiers on the dresser. He was always so meticulous. Long forgotten memories hit me all at once, with them came a pang of nostalgia.

"It's good to see you, too," he replied, nothing in his voice pointed to anything other than mild amusement.

"Alek, I haven't got time for this." My impatience asserted

itself. The wounded look on his face though, transformed it into guilt almost instantly. "I'm sorry. I...this has been a bit of a shock."

"I understand."

"How did you find me?" I reiterated.

"I've been looking for you for six and a half years," he said in a soft voice. I turned to search his face for the truth, to get a better read of his intentions, but he had always been good at hiding from me. That reminder shored up my resolve.

"You couldn't have been looking too hard. For the first month you were gone doing God knows what, I was home being interrogated and harassed on a daily basis."

Instinctively, my hand flew to the diamond cross. I fiddled with it as I tended to do when I was nervous, or irritated. Alek's black irises followed the motion of my hand and came to rest on the diamonds.

"Did he give that to you?" I didn't miss the bite in his voice, the possessiveness he had no right to. He stuffed his hands in the pockets of his jeans and cocked his head.

"Who, my *husband*? Yes, he gave it to me."

"What about your mother's cross? Was that not suitable for the wife of a billionaire?"

Fire shot through my veins, my blood boiling at the accusation. And yet he had just handed me a gift, granting me absolution from any guilt I may have felt for believing the worst of him. "He loves me unconditionally. My mother's cross was lost when I was running from the police. I woke up weeks later in the hospital and it was gone."

Chastened, Alek's eyes moved off. After nodding twice, he walked to the window. A freight train was pulling into the station in the near distance. The screech of its brakes however didn't drown out Alek's next words. "I wish...I wish it had been me to save you. I wish I could've given you gifts like that."

"I don't need saving, and I've never needed gifts. You knew that. I needed you. I needed your support. You denied me the one thing you had in your capacity to give—the one thing I needed." I didn't like the sound of my own voice. It reeked of resentment, as if he still had the power to hurt and disappoint me when, in fact, nothing could have been farther from the truth.

"I know," he said, his brow furrowed, his wide mouth tight. "I've regretted leaving you every day for the past six years."

He looked around, a little lost, disoriented. "I'm sorry I don't have anything to offer you. Would you like to go to the bar in the lobby?"

"I won't be staying that long."

His head whipped around and his eyes slammed into mine. "I thought you drowned in a ferry crash. I thought you were dead." His words were clipped, an implicit accusation in them as well as his eyes. The truth of his confession stared back at me, rooting me to the floor where I stood. "There wasn't a trace of you to be found anywhere. Do you know what that was like for me? Do you have any idea what that did to me?"

Sympathy followed in the wake of the guilt stabbing me in the chest.

Walking towards me, the flash of heat in his eyes cooled and his expression grew aloof, distant. "And then I'm having coffee one morning, reading the paper as always, and a small article in the finance section catches my eye. A wealthy banker, a Swiss-American who inherited the oldest privately-owned bank in Switzerland, had married an Albanian medical student. And in black and white, there it was—your name… imagine my surprise." He began chuckling, the sound caustic. It scraped my already raw nerves.

He'd been looking for me. Everything I thought to be true

about Alek over the last six years had been wrong. My breathing grew rough and forced. I felt myself shaking but I wasn't certain if it was just a figment of my imagination. I had to get out of there. Away from the truth, away from all the feelings pushing me over the edge. I'd been wrong about everything. My feet started moving quickly, rushing towards the door.

"I'm still in love with you. I never stopped loving you." Ringing loud and clear, his words stopped me dead in my tracks.

When I turned around, he was already an arm's length away and closing the distance quickly. His long-lashed, dark eyes roamed over my face, taking in every detail. Slowly, he reached out and ran his index finger in the hollow spot at the base of my throat. His touch felt plastic, a little clammy, stirring absolutely no feeling in me. Then, before I could stop him, he kissed me. He grabbed my face and held me in place as his lips fastened onto mine, his tongue a battering ram trying to push inside my mouth.

Memories came storming back with a vengeance. I had kissed this man in the same way a million times and yet this time I felt absolutely nothing. His teeth sank into my bottom lip, drawing blood. The sting ripped me out of my mental wanderings and propelled me into action. With all my might, I pushed him off. Inadvertently, he'd helped me wash away the remains of any responsibility or loyalty I may have still harbored for him.

Then I said the words that I knew to be true in my heart. "I don't love you anymore. I haven't loved you in a long time. I love my husband. Go on with your life, Alek. I have."

I opened the door and walked out. There was no need to look back. I heard the door close behind me. I wiped the blood with my thumb and licked the cut on my lip. The taste of my own blood, of my past, was bitter.

Closure. I'd gotten what I'd come for.

***

The resolution of my past, dissolving all the pain and blame I carried around for years, should have been cause for celebration. Unfortunately, the state of my marriage was causing me grief. We were at an impasse. And apparently I was married to an ox because he wasn't budging. Which meant I needed to make a move, or this could continue ad infinitum. I hadn't spoken to him in a week…an excruciating week. I must've picked up that cell phone a thousand times to call him, however, I knew that if I didn't stand my ground he would forever be riding roughshod over me. I'd fought, scraped, and struggled for every inch of my independence. I wasn't about to willingly walk into a prison and hand the keys over to any man—even one that I was madly in love with. His impending birthday gave me the perfect opportunity to offer an olive branch and end this stalemate.

As soon as I stepped into Horn & Cie. curious glances followed me throughout the building. I could count on one hand the times I'd been inside, and most of those times under inauspicious circumstances. Therefore it was not a surprise that the people that worked for him found me either a person of interest, or an oddity. One of his two executive assistants, two very sweet and thankfully very middle-aged ladies, kindly escorted me to his office, my heart thumping harder and faster with each step I took.

She knocked before she opened the solid maple door. I wondered if she could see how nervous I was. Inside I found him seated behind his desk, which at the moment seemed a million miles away from where I stood.

The navy suit he wore sharp as a blade, his jaw closely shaven, not a hair out of place. He made no move to get up or speak. He was as still and remote as the day I met him, an unbridgeable island. But man cannot exist alone. He should've known that by now.

His eyes roamed up and down the length of my body in an indifferent inspection, as if I were a business associate he was taking the measure of. Between the super intense examination and the silence, I didn't know which was making me hotter—and not in a good way. Sweat blossomed over my upper lip. I tried to lick it away and failed.

"Happy Birthday," I said, walking to his desk.

He continued with the lifeless stare. It was clear he wanted to make this as painful as possible. I was actually surprised by how cold he was being. Did he expect me to crawl on hands and knees and beg?

"I haven't celebrated my birthday since I turned twenty-one." I ignored the cool tone.

"Well, maybe we can start a new tradition…I brought you something." I placed the tiny birthday cake I made for him on the desk. When he didn't even bother to glance at it, I knew I was in for an uphill battle.

"What exactly is there to celebrate?" The apathy with which he spoke killed the last shred of hope I had that this would work.

"Sebastian." He held my gaze but didn't indulge me further. "Why are you making this difficult?" For this, he had no reply. "I miss you. Don't you miss me?" His narrowed eyes moved away to the window. When they returned to me, they were no longer shuttered. They were bright with a fresh dose of anger that seemed out of character, even for him. It confused me.

"I have a lot to get done today." He glanced at his watch then. "If you don't mind…" He was fighting this, fighting me.

I walked around his massive desk to where he sat. His eyes languid, unblinking, followed every move I made. By the time I leaned my rear end against the desk, he looked starched, uncomfortably stiff, so much so that I felt awkward reaching for him. *My* husband—I felt awkward touching my own husband. He looked almost scared to have me so close. The first crack in his resolve appeared. A tick below his eye.

I glanced at the tiny chocolate cake and said, "I didn't know what to get the man that has everything."

His head swiftly turned to face me. "Not everything," he said cryptically. However, what really snagged my attention was the sharp, accusing glare he tacked on the end.

"What's that supposed to mean?"

He stood then, and without hesitation, grabbed my face and kissed me. The kiss was forceful, meant to dominate, maybe even intimidate. There was no pleasure in it. His lips smashed mine, his tongue thrust down my throat. I tried to pull back and got nowhere. Only when I stopped fighting him did he come up for air.

"I don't have this," he said, his voice ominously low. He pushed his hips against mine. The unmistakable shape of his turgid and solid sex pressed into me. "I don't have my wife in my bed because she's too busy fucking her ex-boyfriend."

He might as well have struck me. It certainly felt that way. All the air left my lungs at once. Squeezing my hands into the sliver of space between us, I shoved harder at his chest this time. Not an inch, not even a centimeter. Trying to break loose of his hold was an exercise in futility.

"Get off of me!"

"Are you denying it?"

"There's nothing to deny! You're being absurd," I nearly spat in his face. "Get off!"

"The problem with that, *lover*," he said, practically snarling the pet name, "is that I know what you look like when you've been fucked. I saw the pictures of you coming out of his hotel room."

Scanning my memories of that day, all I came up with was

the bloody lip and the messy hair. The fight left me all at once. I went limp in his arms. As soon as I did, he let go of me and stepped back, hands on his hips, his eyes still twitching from the effort it took to contain all that emotion.

"I told you I was going to see him," I said in a much more subdued tone.

He stopped trying to control his anger. It boiled up and over, apparent in the hard lines of his body, the fire in his eyes threatening to consume him.

"You didn't mention you planned on letting him stick his dick in you."

My breathing turned shallow. "You actually believe that?"

The moment of truth. It always came back to this. Trust... the third rail between us. Would he trust me, or his own eyes? The look on his face told me that doubt had gotten a foothold.

"I saw the pictures," he repeated, softer this time, with much less conviction. Dejected, my entire body sagged under the weight of defeat. Because if I thought his controlling ways would inflict damage, then what would the lack of trust between us do?

The silence stretched eternal. He looked like he wanted to say something. Though he never did. In the end, I'm the one who spoke. "Happy Birthday." He didn't answer. And he made no attempt to stop me when I walked out.

✸✸✸

I didn't know what to do about us. Therefore, it was easiest to push my problems onto the back burner and funnel all my energy into my job. All I'd gotten for my attempt to heal this rift between us was an accusation of adultery. That he would believe that about me stung—I won't deny it. Three days later, I was leaving the clinic after a long and fulfilling day of work when I received his text.

The Horn Foundation is holding an event. A Black and White ball.

Saturday night at the Grand Theater. As my wife, I expect you to be there.

It was another slap to the face. Rage, the likes of which I haven't ever felt, blazed through me. I stared at the text in disbelief. No courtesy. No love. Not even any advance warning. Apparently I didn't even warrant a phone call. I texted back.

What do I wear, my love?

Kill him with kindness, I repeated over and over to myself. Seconds later, I got my reply.

An evening dress. I opened accounts for you at all the stores in town.

So much for small talk. Any attempt I made was met with resistance. With only two days to come up with a dress, I wasted no time hitting every store on the Rue du Rhône until I found what I was looking for at Armani. On a whim, I decided to walk into La Perla—if all is fair in love and war then I needed every weapon in the arsenal. After trying on a number of different outfits, I settled on three. I was in the middle of taking off a champagne colored bustier and garter set I'd decided to buy, when I heard two women talking right outside my changing room.

"Are you going to the Black and White this weekend?" said the salesperson.

"Yes. I can't wait!" Something about the voice of the woman that answered sounded vaguely familiar. I quickly slipped on my dark Helmut Lang jeans, my black sweater, and waited.

"I don't know who this mystery man is but he's a lucky guy. He's going to go nuts when he sees you in all these outfits," the sales girl continued excitedly.

"God, I hope so. He's amazing. I'm crazy about him."

It was the longing and desperation that struck a chord, that helped me put two and two together.

"Show him these and he won't leave your bed for a month."

"That's the plan."

I stepped out of the dressing room and stood there waiting for their inevitable embarrassment. The sales girl noticed me right away. Caroline Pruitt took a second longer.

"Will that be all, *madame*?" the sales girl asked after glancing at my wedding band.

"Yes." I handed her the garments while holding Caroline's arrested, bright blue gaze.

"Charge them to my husband's account, please. Sebastian Horn." The look on the sales girl's face was irritating. She looked like someone just informed her she'd won the lottery. "Of course, *madame*," she added in a super polite tone and hurried off to ring up the garments.

"Hello," Caroline finally said, her tone insinuating she couldn't recall where she'd seen me before. Her transparent eyes betrayed her words however.

"Vera—Sebastian's wife," I said with satisfaction—heavy emphasis on the word wife. "You're Caroline, right?"

"I know who you are," she answered, dropping the charade. She looked around nervously, fighting some internal battle. I knew which side won when she began speaking. "I also know that the two of you are separated." The taunt lacked as much conviction as she lacked backbone.

"You shouldn't believe everything you read in the tabloids."

After a beat her expression transformed from uncertainty to purpose. "I have money—a lot of it...I could give it to you."

It took me a minute to grasp what she was proposing, the notion so ridiculous that I had to make sure I'd heard her correctly. "You can't be serious?"

She lacked the courage to repeat the offer. A hint of guilt passed across her sun-kissed features. "He's my husband. I love him more than life itself and you think you can *'give me money'* for him like he's a thoroughbred stud at auction." I started to giggle at the lunacy of it. My amusement spurred her on.

"I've loved him since we were kids." Sheer desperation stared back at me. Whatever tentative control she had on her obsession had broken loose. "I've waited for him all my life," she hissed, making her case with wide blue eyes and a ferocious determination. It would've been comical had it not been so sad. "I'm his equal. You two aren't right for each other. I understand what a man like that needs."

"This is the most..." I pinched the bridge of my nose, trying to soothe the dull pain growing there. "You are out of your bloody mind. And you have no idea who he is, or what he needs." With that, she buttoned everything up, her face once again a pretty, blank canvas. "You people and your money." I chuckled humorlessly, my head shaking. "Let me give you some free medical advice, Caroline—see a therapist. My husband has never had, nor will ever have any interest in you outside of the investments he makes for you."

"We'll see about that," she fired back, turned on her Jimmy Choo heels and walked out of the store.

Chapter Twenty-Five

THE NIGHT HELD PROMISE. OR so I thought. After lengthy debate upon lengthy debate with myself, I'd come to a decision. It was clear that waiting him out wasn't working. The stubborn ox had no intention of coming to his senses any time soon, and I was afraid of what would've remained of us when he finally did get around to it. The situation had become untenable, so the decision was an easy one. My pride could suffer the hit. My heart, however, could not survive the loss.

The Armani Privé gown I had chosen was an elegant, body contouring sheath that fastened over one shoulder. Sexy and understated, all I could hope for was that it was enough to catch my husband's attention. The earrings he would recognize immediately—the pave diamond ones from JAR he had given me on our first real date. The ones that reminded me of our wisteria tree. *Ours*...funny how I thought of it that way now.

"Have fun," Bear teased. I glanced behind me, ready to reply to his sarcasm with an eye roll, and found him unapologetically leaning his big body against the Mercedes with his arms crossed in front, his biceps bulging beneath the sleeves of his tux.

I wasn't surprised to see him parked in front of the clinic when I came down from the flat. I'd tried a million times to argue that since there was no longer any threat to Sebastian's life, his babysitting duties were obsolete. To no avail. It was impossible to budge him.

"Don't get too comfy."

"I won't," he answered with a cocky half-grin.

By the time I was walking up the steps of the Grand Théâter de Genève, the event was well under way. All the streets around the theater were congested four rows deep with luxury cars and limousines, the steps of the theater littered with paparazzi. The security personnel outnumbered the guests. With the security measures being so tight, it took me forty minutes to get inside. I was almost certain someone royal was in attendance.

Inside it was a crush. Bodies spanned the foyer from wall to wall. It seemed most of Europe's elite and some of America's were in town for the event. I looked around dazed by all the glitz and glamour. You hear and read about people living this kind of lifestyle, you just don't really understand it until you've experienced it. At least, I didn't. For once reality far eclipsed my imagination.

I was disappointed not to find Sebastian waiting for me. Although nursing my wounded ego would have to happen later. At the moment I needed to find the man I loved, the only man for me—regardless of everything that had transpired. I pushed the thought aside and elbowed my way through the crowd on a mission, hustling up the marble stairs to the main room. In spite of its size a cloud of humidity from all the body heat billowed up, the scent of flowers and expensive perfumes riding on it. Gathering up the train of my dress, I walked around, scanning all the tall, blond heads in search of the man in question. When I finally spotted him across the room, my stomach dropped, the sight of him wreaking havoc on my nerves.

So handsome…and so alone.

Wearing a tux that hugged every perfect angle on his body, he stood in the midst of a large group of people begging his favors, none whom I recognized. He was the calm in the middle of the storm, his expression placid, detached. To the untrained eye he wore all that power effortlessly, but it was only a ruse. Even if it was a beautiful one.

One hand clutched a glass of alcohol while Caroline Pruitt occupied the other, hanging on his arm as if she paid rent. Reluctantly, I had to agree that they made a striking image. Her black hair to his blond. Her blue eyes to his golden ones. They belonged—they were bred for this *circus* while I was just a visitor, an outsider, and would forever be thought of as such. She threw her head back and laughed at something one of the other guests said. Then leaning into Sebastian, she whispered something in his ear. Nothing registered on his face, not even a twitch. The brooding intensity only added to his allure.

By some sixth sense his head turned in my direction and our eyes collided. Neither one of us looked away for a very long time. He looked haunted. For a moment I saw past the shutters, where the pain and fear lived. Somewhere, in there, he still loved me. I knew it in my bones. He took a step towards me, away from the crowd, but then he paused and his expression slammed shut again. I had no pride left where this man was concerned. If he wasn't going to meet me halfway, then I was prepared to cover the entire figurative and literal distance between us.

Taking a fortifying breath, I made my way over to him, bracing myself for his inevitable chilly reception. His eyes tracked every step I took to cross the room. He didn't blink once, his lids heavy while his gaze roamed over my body and up to my face. When I reached him, he stepped away from the people gathered around him, each of who gave me the once-over. Not a single smile to be found anywhere.

"I said it was a Black and White ball." The Armani gown was a cascade of silver, the entire dress hand beaded with delicate *paillettes* that captured the light and returned a soft glow.

"I didn't want you confusing me with all the other women in the room."

The guilty expression that crossed his countenance warmed my chest. At least his moral compass was still working properly. My eyes took him in like a junky finally getting a fix. The streaks of pale gold in his hair reflected the light from the massive crystal chandeliers overhead. He'd gotten a haircut. It was neatly combed back, not a hair out of place. It did nothing to hide the dark circles under his eyes though. "You look like you haven't slept in weeks," I stated, both my voice and my expression concerned.

He frowned. I wanted to smooth the lines of worry etched on his face away. "It's work."

"I know I haven't," I added, ignoring his dismissive attitude. His gaze slammed back into mine, assessing me closely. I seized my opportunity. "I miss you. I miss you so much."

He averted his eyes, his jaw clenched as tight as a vise. I'm surprised it didn't shatter. I was getting through to him. I could read it on his face. The indifference he'd hidden behind all his life never worked on me. Cracks were appearing on the walls of his fortress, and I was prepared to take it down brick by brick with my bare hands if I had to.

"Don't you miss me?" I pressed softly. When I touched his arm, his eyes lifted once again, the conflict present in his burning gaze. He was about to speak when Caroline stepped in. A flimsy smile spread on her face, glowing with a healthy tan. She smoothed her hands down the sides of her gown, a black strapless with a long train, beautiful in its severity.

"Sebastian, I need to introduce you to one of Daddy's old friends," she said, her bright blue eyes shifting nervously between Sebastian and me. The current between us was unmissable. I'm sure she felt it, too.

"In a minute," he answered, his eyes never leaving me.

"Caroline, you remember my wife?"

"Yes. Hello, Vera." Not even bothering to extend a hand, she added, "It's nice to see you again. I mean, last time we met you were still working for him, I believe." Her feigned ignorance was pathetic. So was the veiled insult. Did she think I was ashamed of my past?

"Yes. That was back when I was working as his housekeeper," I said, smiling brightly. Nothing genuine about it. "Could I have a moment with my husband?" Her eyes nervously shifted to Sebastian. When he neither looked at her nor disagreed, she stepped away.

"Are you still working at the clinic?" His tone and demeanor told me the spell had been broken. He was back to being an ass again.

"You know I am." Bear was practically living in my shadow. I was certain he was reporting back every detail of my life. Not that there was anything to report—even if Sebastian was still under the false impression that I had slept with Alek. "Look, I don't know what you think you saw in those pictures, but you should know that nothing happened." Eyes narrowed, his gaze shifted to a point beyond me. "He tried to kiss me—" The rest of my explanation was stalled by the fierce scowl directed my way once more.

"What did that motherfucker do?"

"He tried to kiss me, but I pushed him off. I told him how much I love my husband, and that he needs to move on with his life."

Somewhat mollified, he breathed out sharply and rattled the ice in his glass. "This isn't the time, or place to discuss this."

"Then what should we discuss? The fact that you're drinking?" His haunted gaze was on the move again, back to a faraway point. "And what are you doing with *her*." My tone was less careful this time, my possessiveness getting the best of me. His expression hardened, meeting mine in full force.

"That's my business," he growled. The fact that he didn't answer my question didn't worry me—I knew he had less than zero interest in that woman—it was his anger that did. He was still so furious. My shoulders fell on a deep sigh. It was impossible to reason with him when he was like this.

"I love you," I said in a last-ditch attempt. My words missed their mark and fell to the floor.

"You sure have a funny way of showing it."

"Sebastian," I implored in the most pathetically dejected voice.

"People are waiting on me. I'll see you later." With that, he walked away, leaving me standing in a crowd of strangers to nurse my aching heart.

***

I wouldn't give Caroline the satisfaction of leaving with my tail tucked between my legs, so I hung around a little longer, watching from the periphery of the room. I spotted Shay on the other side. It was impossible to miss her. She was the embodiment of a 1950s Hollywood star, wearing a white, strapless gown that hugged every exaggerated curve on her body and ended with a fishtail. Add to that the red lips, nails, and Veronica Lake waves in her hair, and she made one stunning bombshell. As soon as she saw me skirting the edge of the room, she came over.

Placing her hands on her hips, she said, "You look like you need to get wasted." A bark of laughter erupted out of me. "That bad, huh?"

"It was pretty bad."

A frown marred her gorgeous features. She sidled up next to me, and the two of us enjoyed the theatrics taking place in the massive ballroom for a bit. "I'd regularly start you off with mixed drinks, but this looks like a straight-up tequila night to me."

"Caroline Pruitt is hanging all over him. I'm afraid she may try to crawl onto his back and beg for a piggyback ride soon."

"I can't stand that bitch. Did I tell you that she sent me for coffee the first time we met?"

"No." I bit my bottom lip, schooling my amusement. Knowing how proud Shay was, I could imagine her reaction.

"I'm the executive vice president of the bank and she asked *me* for coffee—not the twenty-year-old male intern standing next to me. That woman could single-handedly set back the women's movement fifty years."

"Doesn't seem to bother my husband," I muttered, a touch of bitterness in my voice I didn't even attempt to hide. My eyes scanned the crowd for them. If he was within sight, it was impossible to keep my attention on little else. In the middle of the crowded room Sebastian was doing a great impression of a marble statue while Caroline perched on him like a filthy pigeon. I had just cause to be snide.

"It bothers him, trust me, but that bitch happens to be worth two billis so eat shit from her, we both will."

My eyes were as wide as saucers. "Two billion?"

"Yep."

I noticed Gideon staring at us. The true definition of tall, dark, and handsome, he wore his tux like he was made for it. All that quiet intensity cut quite the elegant figure. He gave me a quick nod in greeting and I smiled back. "There's a very handsome and very mysterious man watching you from across the room," I murmured suggestively.

Shay's gaze surveyed the crowd until it landed on Gideon. A small smile lifted the corners of her ruby red lips. "You mean my date?"

"I thought you two hated each other?"

"I was so sick of coming to these things alone. Besides, he's the only man that doesn't run away when I shout at him, like the only one—seriously." I was laughing so hard tears spilled down my cheeks. "Now are you going to come get a drink with me, or are you going to continue to lurk in dark corners like some pale, goth heroine in a Tim Burton movie?"

"I'll have you know I'm skulking, not lurking," I replied, fighting the smile stretched across my face.

"Suit yourself. Send up a flare if you change your mind." With that, she smacked a kiss on my cheek and wiped the lipstick off with her thumb before she walked away.

Shortly afterwards the concert began. I watched for a while, even though I was too distracted to enjoy it. At some point I decided to make a trip to the ladies' room. The long corridor was empty, everybody in their seats. Who could blame them when Sting was performing.

"Vera." The raspy voice softly calling me reached inside and warmed the chill residing near my heart. Relief. I felt an overwhelming sense of relief sweep over me. In gratitude I reached up to rub the diamond cross sitting on my sternum. I turned and watched him walk to me with only the barest hint of a limp. So stoic when he was in pain. My gaze climbed to his face as he drew closer. He looked conflicted, struggling with words and feelings.

"Where are you going?"

"Back to the flat. I was just on my way to the ladies' room before I…" My voice faded as we stared into each other's eyes. Accusations, heartache, broken promises—it was all there. Then again, so was mercy. "I've seen enough," I quietly finished, holding his gaze, challenging him to take a single figurative step forward and I would come the rest of the way.

It happened all at once. He grabbed my face with both hands. The kiss was a wild thing, full of passion and desire, anger and love. So much love. I grabbed a hold of his wrists and kissed him back as fervently as he kissed me. Our hands were everywhere, sliding around each other, pulling the other one closer. This undeniable thing between us, drawing us together in pleasure and in pain.

"Vera?"

Oh no, no, no, no, my mind screamed. Sebastian pulled away, his eyes narrowing at the intruder standing a few paces behind me. I looked over my shoulder and found Yannick looking a bit guilty, while to anyone else he would've appeared aloof and disinterested.

Sebastian's eyes jumped between Yannick and me. The veil of indifference fell over his face once again. My heart sank. I knew what was coming. Swallowing, I pleaded, "Sebastian—" But I never got the chance to finish because he ripped his wrists out of my hold and stalked away from me.

Swiveling on my heels, I glared at Yannick. "Has anyone ever told you that you have the *worst* timing? What was that about?"

"I just wanted to make certain you were alright." His voice tight, his English extra clipped.

"I'd like to know what it is about me that makes your gender think I can't take care of myself!"

Tugging on his cuffs, looking every inch as gorgeous and sophisticated as ever, he raised an eyebrow and said, "You're in a mood. We'll talk tomorrow." Before I could get out another word, he'd walked away.

My best laid plans had been blown sky high. An evening that had started with promise had ended in complete disappointment, the gap between Sebastian and me wider than ever. It was time to retreat and regroup.

***

I was in the ladies' room, deep in thought about how best to deal with my husband, when I stepped out of one of the stalls and came face to face with my worst nightmare. Paisley was in the lounge area. Bent over at the waist, she was snorting razor sharp lines of cocaine off the marble countertop. I froze, nailed to the spot on the floor while every instinct in my body told me to run. My heart beat so fiercely I was pretty certain she could hear it trying to break out of my chest.

She glanced up and stopped short when it dawned on her who I was. Straightening slowly to a full height of practically ten feet with her platform shoes on, she placed her hands on her whippet thin hips and glared a hole through me. She was much thinner than usual. Impossible to fathom, though true. Her designer dress hung off the sharp angles of her bones, her eyes flat, her skin dull. She'd been living hard and fast since I last saw her outside the doctor's office and it showed.

"You fucking bitch." Her voice was a low, angry sound, similar to the primal warning a wolf makes right before it sinks its teeth into your throat. "You fucking, whoring cunt!" The aggressive step she took towards me snapped me out of my trance. There wasn't much I could do, however. She stood inconveniently between me and the exit. "You cost me everything! My money! My husband—" I didn't fail to notice she'd placed her money above her husband in order of importance, her volume descending on the latter. "Sebastian!" she added belatedly, ending on a high note.

"You did that to yourself," I spat out, finally locating my voice under all the bewilderment. She lunged for me quicker than I could anticipate and managed to hook her claw-like fingers at the top of my dress, near my collarbone. Then, with her face screwed up in a demented scowl, she yanked with all her strength.

The dress came apart. The one shoulder strap holding it up snapped, beads went flying in every direction. I grabbed onto the front, to keep it from sliding off, and while defenseless, she slapped me across the face, the sound echoing off the wall-to-wall marble.

"What is going on here?!" shouted a feminine voice with a distinct drawl. The assault in progress stopped instantly. My formidable knight in tarnished armor wore Chanel and a glare that could freeze fire.

Diana Redman stood inside the entrance of the bathroom in a column of black Chantilly lace that looked painted on every square inch of her sleek body. It started at the top of her neck and descended all the way to her toes. Never in my wildest dreams could I ever have imagined that I would be happy to see her—but I was. I just hoped my joy wasn't misplaced.

Her almond-shaped eyes shifted from me to Paisley, and back to my dress. "What have you done, Paisley?" she calmly said, punctuating it with the arch of a blond brow.

When Paisley glanced over her shoulder, I grabbed the opportunity to scoot out of her reach. "I'm giving this bitch her due."

Diana crossed her slender arms in front, a posture I'd seen her son assume when he was ready to do battle. "Step away from my daughter-in-law."

"What?"

"You heard me. And clean yourself up while you're at it—start with the powder under your nose."

Wiping away the traces of cocaine with the back of her hand, Paisley shouted, "You hate her as much as I do!"

"No. I don't. And you forget a very important detail, sugar. She's a Horn. Now run along. I don't want you bothering them again. You know I'm still real friendly with your daddy. If you want to get in his good graces again, you'll do as I say, or one well-placed word from me and you're done—for good this time." The clear threat was delivered with a lethal smirk.

The indecision was all over Paisley's gaunt face. A moment later she stomped to the door in defeat, one predator recognizing the other as the larger, more dominant one.

"Bye, now," Diana drawled as Paisley walked out. When the door closed, Diana rushed over to me. Reaching up, she cupped my face gingerly. I couldn't help it—I jerked back. Only months ago this woman hated me enough to see me wind up in the hospital, and now she was my protector?

She scanned the state of my dress. Her brow remained perfectly line free while her tight mouth telegraphed her anger. She tipped up my face with her fingers under my chin, turning it left and right while she inspected the cheek that was still burning. "Come, sit down," she gently ordered.

Holding my dress up, I shuffled to the boudoir stool in front of the expansive mirror and sat. I almost didn't recognize the gasp coming from my own lips. A red welt, the outline of four distinct fingers, streaked across my porcelain skin, my sharply-bobbed hair was a disheveled mess, red scratch marks were on my chest and neck.

"I can't leave like this," I said more to myself.

"No, you can't."

I glanced up at Diana, who was running a hand towel under the sink, and whispered, "I don't know what to do."

She wrung it out and placed the cold compress on the cherry red mark. "I'm sorry." Her eyes met mine briefly, before they fell to the floor. "You have no idea how sorry I am. Can you ever find it in your heart to forgive me?"

What was I to say to that? I could forgive, but I would never forget. "You had nothing to do with this."

"I mean for everything else—although I'm sure Sebastian will find a way to blame me for this, too." She was right, knowing Sebastian he would. However unfair, she still didn't deserve my sympathy, or lies to allay any guilt she may have felt or pretended to feel. When I remained silent, she continued, "Will you accept my apology, Vera?"

I looked up, into her subdued expression. "Yes." Hope

made her eyes light up. "But that does not mean I'll forget." The light dimmed once again. She reminded me of a little girl, reacting in real time to every single feeling she had. "You have a long and arduous road ahead of you. If you really want to make amends, start with your son."

"I know," she agreed, her tone sullen. "I'll do whatever it takes. I'm not promising to change overnight. I know not to have those kinds of expectation—at least, that's what my therapist tells me." There was true longing in her voice, an earnest vulnerability that I knew was unusual for her. "I want to be part of this family. I'll do anything to be part of this family again."

I didn't know what to say. I had problems of my own to worry about, and at present, a big one to deal with. The unfocused look in her eyes transformed to determination. "This is what we're going to do…"

Fifteen minutes later she finished zipping me into her Chanel dress while she wore mine, her bodyguard's tuxedo jacket draped over it. Her dress was three inches too long for me, otherwise it fit. After applying powder to my red welt, I left the bathroom in search of Sebastian.

It was well past 2 a.m. The concert had ended and people were steadily departing, the stairs crowded with everyone trying to beat the traffic. For twenty minutes I searched in vain. Frustrated, I finally decided to walk back to the car in the hope that Bear could tell me where to find him.

Leaning against the car, Bear straightened when he saw me approaching. His eyes roamed over me. His brow wrinkled while he curiously studied my dress, though he chose to remain silent.

"Have you spoken to Sebastian?"

"Yes." He opened the car door and said nothing else.

"Well, where is he? Did he leave?"

"Yes."

Something in his tone made the hair on the back of my neck stand up. "By himself?" I asked while my stomach churned with suspicion and fear.

"No."

A shockwave moved through me, arresting my breath. *He couldn't be right. This couldn't be happening.* "With whom?"

The long pause before his answer told me everything I needed to know. "Caroline Pruitt."

My heart collapsed. It was as if the scaffolding that held it together gave way all at once. Any hope I had was crushed. Doubt took up whatever space was left.

Chapter Twenty-Six

THE FOLLOWING DAY I HAD to force myself out of bed, my body and my will drained of strength. Any hope I may have had of salvaging my relationship was in steady free fall, dwindling by the minute. The evidence of my sleepless night mocked me in the bathroom mirror. Drifting in a fog of depression, I don't even know how I managed to get out of the shower and dress myself.

The first text came in at 8 a.m.

I need to talk to you. Call me.

The nerve...the bloody nerve of him. I ignored it of course. Instead I called Yannick to inform him I wouldn't be making it into work that day. He refused to hear of it. Therefore, after drinking a triple shot of espresso and making myself semi presentable, I headed to the clinic. Which turned out to be a wise decision in the end because flu season had hit all at once. By the time I made it downstairs, the waiting room was filled wall to wall with at-risk patients, such as children and the elderly.

It was late afternoon when I finally made it out. An ominous, graphite gray sky hung overhead. Fat cumulous clouds pregnant with moisture threatened to unleash a torrent at any minute. Seemed about right, considering my mood. Somewhere, out there, there was a bottle of vodka with my name on it and I was determined to find it. Red wine had always been off limits. I had a strong allergy to sulfites, which would've heaped a migraine onto my already basement-dwelling spirits.

As I headed to the market down the street, a brisk wind zipped over my skin and a shiver crawled up my spine. I stopped to put on the sweater I always carried in my tote and spotted the Bentley parked across the street. He stepped out of the car and stood with one hand stuffed into the pocket of his trousers and the other clutching a bouquet of flowers, his jacket and tie already discarded. Even from across the street I couldn't fail to notice the apprehension on his face, the simmering anger from last night conspicuously absent.

Mine wasn't however.

I was seething, the pressure between my eyes increasing exponentially with every step he took. When he finally reached me, he stood there without saying a word, thoughtfully examining me like I was one of his bank accounts he couldn't quite balance. My eyes traveled to the enormous bouquet of black magic roses that he made no move to hand me. I snorted.

"What are you doing here?" My prickly demeanor confused him. It was all over his face.

"I'm your husband. Do I need a reason?"

"You sure have a funny way of showing it," I spat out, slapping him with the same words he used on me the night before.

"What's that supposed to mean?"

"You know exactly what it means."

His eyes fell on the thin platinum band around my finger, following the anxious movements of my fingers tapping the strap of the Balenciaga handbag he'd surprised me with one day when he overheard me compliment Shay on hers.

"You didn't call me," he stated, his tone neutral, his countenance not giving anything away.

"What a keen mind you have."

He exhaled loudly, his frustration palpable. "Can we speak?" he said, and scraped his hair back repeatedly. "Here," he said, handing me the flowers as if they were a cumbersome thing he no longer wanted to carry around.

The nerve...the bloody nerve. Ignoring his outstretched hand, I walked past him without another glance in his direction.

"Some other time. Right now, I have an appointment," I threw over my shoulder.

An appointment alright—with sweet oblivion.

A beat later he was at my side again. "An appointment? With whom?" The possessive tone he used ratcheted up my sense of injustice.

I wheeled around. "None of your goddamn business! Sound familiar?" He jerked back, surprised by the force of my anger. The flow of people on the sidewalk turned to stare curiously at the scene we were making.

The sky, reflecting what was happening down below, broke open and rained down on us, the wind kicking the heavy downpour sideways had us soaked in minutes. While he was on his heels, I took off down the street. Before I had a chance to get anywhere, a large hand wrapped around my upper arm and spun me around.

"Slow down, Mrs. Horn. I'd like to have a word with you first," he drawled in an awful voice. I fought to break free of his grip without success. The water hit our faces hard. Both of us blinked rapidly, though neither one of us made a move for cover. The bouquet, still in his hand, sagged under the force of the rain coming down. "I...I want to apologize." He wouldn't look at me as he spoke.

"Apologize?" I laughed without a drop of joy. "*Last night* would've been a good time for an apology. We're closed for business today. Apology not accepted." I took a few more steps, but moving quickly, he cut me off.

"Okay...okay. I was an asshole to you last night." His brow

furrowed. His eyes, suddenly pleading, captured mine. "Let me make it up to you."

He went home with another woman and he thought I was going to *let him make it up to me*? Was I living in an alternate universe where this was acceptable behavior? My mind turned black with rage. "Get the hell out of my way."

"Let's play nice, folks," a deep baritone bellowed from a few feet away. We both turned in its direction. Sebastian leveled Bear with a glare that should've turned him to a pillar of salt, while Bear, standing next to the SUV under an umbrella, simply smiled back at him.

"Get in the car," he had the nerve to order.

"No."

"Vera—get in the car. We're soaked. It's cold. I don't want you getting sick."

My mouth went slack in disbelief. "You certainly didn't care what happened to me last night!"

"Last night? What about last night?"

"Stay the hell away from me! I trusted you! You asked me to trust you and I did and look at where it got me!"

The look of utter confusion on his face didn't earn him any points. He managed to get a hold on it before I walked on.

"Why did you sign the prenup?" Those words stopped me dead in my tracks. The impact was like getting hit by a freight train, devastating, knocking all the wind out of my lungs at once. "I saw David."

Oh my God. Did he want a divorce?

I turned then, slowly, my heart beating viciously, my knees turning to jelly while my eyes reflected all the pain I was feeling. He watched me expectantly.

"Did you think I wouldn't? Did you think I ever cared about any of this? This," I said, waving my arm around like a crazy person. "Is half the problem. I never wanted any of it. I just wanted you." With that, I turned and ran, disappearing into the night, into the rain, leaving everything that I loved behind.

***

The next day I received an unexpected visit. I won't deny that when the doorbell rang a burst of hope swept through me. Even after everything, I missed him like crazy. There was a black hole where my heart had once been.

I opened the studio door to find Marianne standing there dressed in a stylish gray swing coat, holding a pastry box. I took one look at her face and burst into tears. Not the cute kind either—the ugly, body-racking kind that makes your face look like a tomato on steroids. She wrapped her free arm around me as we made our way to the tiny kitchen table. Twenty minutes later the tears were mostly dry and my stomach was filled with three quarters of a large raspberry tart.

"He left with her," I said, my cheeks stuffed. "He went home with her."

Marianne's sympathetic gaze held mine. "Are you certain? It doesn't sound like him. Caroline has been sniffing around him for years. He was never interested in her."

"I know. That's why I wasn't worried when I overheard her in the lingerie store. But then Bear told me he left with her."

"You need to ask him. I'm turning sixty-six this year, and if I've learned anything it's to be direct—subtlety and insinuations will get you nowhere good." Taking a long gulp of tea, I swallowed the dessert stuck in my throat and told her the rest of the story.

"He went to see David...I think he wants a divorce." A fresh set of tears surged up as the words left my lips. She frowned, her plump lips pursed tightly. I wiped the moisture away with the heel of my hand.

"Did he say so?"

"He said he went to see David."

"But did he say he wants a divorce?"

"Well...no, not exactly." Any more of her interrogation and she would have me doubting my own name.

"You're jumping to conclusions, *chérie*. I suggest you ask him plainly. I suspect you will get a very different answer than the one you are presuming."

Her words gave birth to a new sense of hope. Maybe I had jumped to conclusions. In truth, I was scared of the answer. Because what would I do if she was wrong?

"Have you heard from Charlotte?"

The troubled look on her face gave her thoughts away. "No—you?"

"Nothing," I said, head shaking. "When should we start to worry?"

Contemplative, preoccupied, her round blue eyes moved away from me. "Soon."

***

One day rolled into another. Before I had a chance to sort out what to do next, another ten days had passed. Work kept me busy. I didn't have much time to think until I went upstairs and got in the shower. Every evening the hot water washed away my armor, leaving me naked and exposed, vulnerable. And each night, I cried myself to sleep. I didn't get a minute of sleep otherwise. My imagination ran wild, conjuring a million dreadful scenarios of what he was doing and with whom. I was paralyzed by indecision.

"What the fuck," a tall, busty redhead exclaimed—it was definitely an exclamation. Wearing a black Jill Sanders suit and a look of total determination, she stood near the front desk of the clinic with her finely manicured short, red nails tapping on her curvy hips.

"Hello to you, too," I greeted, pushing my smile back down when I realized she wasn't in a mood to appreciate my sarcasm.

"Don't give me that, Mrs. *Horn.* Or have you forgotten you're married?" Her tone sharp, her voice angry—Shay's version of tough love.

Turning my attention to the girl at the front desk, I said, "Agnes, I'm taking my break." Shay was hot on my heels as I made my way past her and down the hall. "No, I haven't. Though I'm not certain if he has."

"What's that supposed to mean?"

"Ask your friend. Better yet, ask Caroline Pruitt next time you see her, which should be often."

"V—" Shay grabbed my shoulders and spun me to face her. "What are you talking about? Caroline Pruitt? I haven't seen Sebastian in a week."

Her words sliced my heart into ribbons. My breathing turned shallow. Had he spent the week in her bed? Like she had told the shop girl at La Perla? The nausea hit me instantly. Any moment now I was going to vomit.

"He hasn't been to work. He won't answer any of my texts or phone calls." She marked off the list with her long, tapered fingers. "I'm doing the best I can, keeping business on track, but I can't do this without him for much longer."

My marriage was over...I couldn't believe it. Breathing deeply, I steeled myself against the onslaught of pain. "I can't...I can't talk about this...I need to be alone." Aimlessly, I started walking away from her.

"The hell you do. You need to go stop your husband from killing himself," she shouted after me. Her words stopped me cold. My head whipped around.

"What did you say?"

"He's holed himself up in that apartment and he's drinking himself to death." There was an unmistakable note of alarm in her voice. For as long as I'd known her I'd never seen Shay scared, rattled. "And God knows what else. He won't speak to any of us. Marianne tried yesterday—fat good that did." At my rapt expression, she continued her rant. "Fuck's sake, I thought he was stubborn, but your pride is megalithic."

Whatever she said next was drowned out by the loud ringing in my ears. Panic, that he was hurting himself, spurned me into action. I pivoted on my heels and began hustling down the hall, back to the check-in desk. "Agnes, tell Yannick I had a family emergency." The sweet-faced girl gave me a short nod.

"Where are you going?" shouted the bossy redhead.

"To talk to my husband," I shouted back over my shoulder.

"'Bout fucking time," I barely heard her say, her words fading away quickly. Because I was already out the door, not willing to waste another precious minute.

Chapter Twenty-Seven

I WAS IN A MAD rush to get to him and completely oblivious to my surroundings, my senses clouded by heavy thoughts. That's why I didn't notice the woman that stepped into the elevator right behind me. You would think I would've learned my lesson on elevators by now.

It was her overly sweet perfume that pulled at my attention. I looked up into deep, blue eyes and recognized her immediately. Sebastian's neighbor, Lucinda. Everything about her screamed trophy wife from a mountaintop. Her face was completely frozen. I'm surprised she retained the ability to blink with all the Botox in her face.

This was the person who had set in motion the chain of events that contributed to Sebastian's car crash. That killed a woman and a child. She didn't own all the blame, of course not. However, had she not instigated the fight with what I suspected was a well-placed and well-timed lie, the course of all our lives might've been different.

She greeted me with a disingenuous smile before she turned to face ahead. "He's not home."

I wasn't about to let this predator insinuate herself in my business. "You would be the last person to know the whereabouts of my husband."

She turned to me then, a smug smile on her overly filled lips. "I know I haven't seen you in at least a month, which means this marriage is over."

"It's funny you should say that because although you may not have seen me, I definitely saw you." Armed for battle, I turned to look her squarely in the eyes. "At Fix—about a month ago. Does your husband know you have a taste for boys?"

A crimson stain surged up her neck and covered her face. The elevator door chimed and opened on her floor. She placed her foot in the doorway and forced it to remain open. Her blue glare was electric. "He'd never believe it."

"Not my word, no, you're right about that. But I have friends in low places. Which means I have access to all sorts of...*information*." I let that hang between us. There was no way she could know I was totally bluffing. Six months ago I wouldn't have dreamed of threatening a fly, and now I was ready to wage war with just about anyone to protect the one I loved. "So from this day forth, you will mind your own business, and not bother my husband anymore with your lies. He told me what you said about a man coming out of the apartment when he was married to India."

This was a fishing expedition. I wondered if she'd take the bait, if she would deny it, or stay silent. She removed her Louboutin pump from the corner of the elevator and stepped back.

Silence it was.

My heart thundered inside my chest. I didn't look away. However, as soon as the doors shut, my entire body sagged in relief, drained from the adrenaline rush. I entertained the thought of telling Sebastian only for a moment. It wouldn't do anybody any good to resurrect the dead. I wasn't a hundred percent certain whether India had cheated on him or not. Either way, I now knew for certain that I had to keep him as far away from that woman as possible.

***

The lights did not turn on automatically when I entered the apartment. That was the first sign that there was something very wrong. The atmosphere was that of a funeral. A miasma of grim energy hung around, so thick it was tangible. Darkness covered every corner of the room, drapes pulled tight, the air stale. The silence was absolute. Only the heavy beating of my heart and the air I labored to pull into my lungs could be heard.

Then there was the mess. Pillows were scattered on the floor, clothing strewn about, furniture out of place. That's not what made my breath catch and my stomach flip. It was the trail of empty bottles that led to the bedroom. Taking one timid step after another, I followed them to the doorway. There I stood, scanning the room for a sign of life, when a low, raspy voice pulled my attention to the oversized chairs near the window.

"What do you want?" Barely visible, he was seated with his head leaning back on the cushion and an arm hanging over the armrest. In his hand was a glass flask.

All the wounded feelings I'd been nursing for the past month dissolved in an instant. What had I been holding on to? My principles, or my pride? The answer came crashing down on me with a large dose of shame. My pride was costing me the love of my life. Instead of trying to reason with him, I'd let him push me away. I should've known he wouldn't do anything to harm me, that he would only harm himself. And I'd let him. I might as well have sanctioned it.

I'll admit that I was nervous. The situation was as unpredictable as the man sitting in the chair. With great trepidation, I walked over to him and sunk to my knees, facing him, forcing him to look at me. I almost didn't recognize the man staring back. There was nothing left of the bright, funny charmer that had stolen my heart.

His eyes moved away from me, at a point in the distance.

Now that my sight had adjusted to the dim light filtering through the crack in the drapes, I could see his eyes rimmed in red, purple shadows painted under them. His hair was dirty, hanging in his face. He wore at least a week-old beard—and he smelled. My God, he smelled. By the look of his t-shirt and sweats he hadn't taken a shower since the last time he had shaved.

"Tire of your boyfriend already?" He refused to look at me—and knew how to push my buttons all too well. The snide insult raised my hackles and pricked my pride, but I schooled it into submission. This is what had gotten us into this mess in the first place.

"He was never my boyfriend, you dolt. Stop trying to hurt me."

The erratic tick on his cheek told me I had hit a nerve. He wasn't as far gone as he wanted me to believe. "I don't want you here. Get the fuck out," he growled. But I'd heard it, the crack in his voice, in his resolve to push me away and out of his life.

"I'm not your subject, darling. You can't decree I leave you alone and expect me to obey."

His eyes finally met mine, narrowed, burning with anger. I was so grateful the *Walking Dead* look was gone I didn't care what he threw at me. "If you're here to ask for a divorce you can forget it. I'll never give you one."

The pain I felt grip my chest was not for me. It was for him. He thought he was threatening me. How had I allowed it to go this far?

"Good—because I'll never give you one, either. You're stuck with me, so you better make peace with it." If the circumstances hadn't been so tragic, the look on his face would've made me laugh. I desperately wanted to kiss the shock and confusion away. However, I knew I had to go slowly or he would fight me tooth and nail. His suspicion and distrust would overrule his intellect.

"Why not?" His unblinking gaze held mine. I could've sworn he stopped breathing. It took me a minute to figure out what he was asking. In the pause I gave his question serious thought.

"Because you're the only one that's ever really understood me, who's ever cared enough to climb the walls I hide behind. Because you're the other half of me—sometimes the better half. Because I love you all the more for the faults you don't hide from me, not in spite of them. Because I never realized who I was until I met you. Because I can't sleep without you, I can't think without you…there are a million different reasons I want to be with you, and I can't think of a single one to justify being without you."

His devastated gaze darted away to the drape-clad window, blinking repeatedly.

"How much have you had to drink today?" I kept my voice as gentle as possible.

"What's it to you?" he forced out through a clenched jaw.

"Everything," I answered. Brushing the long, dirty hair out of his face, I tucked it behind his ear. He flinched. At first I thought he was going to slap my hand away, put distance between us, but then his eyes fluttered and his jaw trembled and I couldn't stop myself from crawling onto his lap, wrapping my arms around his neck, and holding him tightly. Something inside of him broke loose. No longer able to contain all that toxic emotion, his entire body shuddered and didn't stop. His arms lay limply by his side while the rest of him shook, as if he didn't have the strength to hug me back.

"You know what else I won't let you do? Destroy yourself. This has to stop."

His chest heaved as he grappled to measure his breathing. When he finally managed to gain some control, the words that were log-jammed in his throat came out all at once. "I'm sorry.

I'm so fucking sorry," he said, sounding like he'd swallowed broken glass. I felt the words on my skin, on the lips tasting me. I felt it when he buried his face in my hair and inhaled deeply.

"I'm the one that's sorry," I murmured in his ear, his face now resting on the curve of my neck. "I let my pride get between us." His arms slowly snaked around my waist and crushed me to him with a force that would leave a bruise. "Both of us have a lot to make amends for, and I intend to start right away."

We sat like that for hours, neither of us wanting to break the intimacy, frightened that the connection would disappear if untethered—that it was all just a dream. "Don't take this the wrong way, my love, but you smell God-awful. I'm going to get a bath started. Try to get some rest meanwhile."

He didn't rest. Instead his eyes followed me around the room while I stripped the bed and tidied the destruction. It was as if he was scared I would disappear somehow. By the time I had the drapes and windows open night had fallen. The air was warmer than usual for this time of year. A wind kicked up, carrying with it the scent of wood burning and pastries from the bakery in the building next door, the sound of people strolling on the street below.

Slowly, I undressed him, his eyes never leaving me for a moment. He barely blinked when I pulled his t-shirt over his head and his sweatpants down over his lean hips, much leaner than they were only a month ago. It made me nauseous to see how much weight he'd lost. He remained completely still while my fingers traced the lines of his throat, over his Adam's apple. It rose and fell on a nervous swallow. I glanced up and found his gaze burning brightly as my fingers traveled down over the muscles of his chest and abdomen, carved in frightening relief with the absence of a normal amount of body fat. When my hand skated over his thigh, he stopped me, his hand resting gently over mine. He exhaled harshly, his jaw pulsing. I wasn't sure whether it was in pleasure or pain.

"When was the last time you ate?" I asked, my frustration abundantly clear.

After a beat his shadowed eyes moved away and he mumbled, "I don't remember."

I fought to rein in my temper. "First bath, then food. Did you take any pills?" With his history, it would've been irresponsible for me not to ask. A tide of relief washed over me when he shook his head, the breath I was holding hissing out. "Sebastian, how much did you have to drink?" Taking his hand, I pulled him up out of the chair and wrapped my arms around his waist. My shoulder wedged under his armpit, he leaned his two-hundred-pound frame onto mine.

"I finished the last bottle this morning. I was about to order more when you showed up."

"Are you nauseous?"

"Yes," was his quiet reply.

Once I had him in the tub, I undressed. His eyes, large in his face, devoured the flesh each article of clothing I peeled away revealed. When I was done, I slipped in behind him. He hummed, his eyes drifting closed. I wrapped my arms around his waist and washed his chest, his stomach, between his legs. He gripped the sides of the tub. I pushed him forward and soaped his back, lathered and rinsed his hair.

"We still have a lot to talk about," I said softly, running my fingers through the hair at the base of his skull. I stroked down the back of his neck and followed the long, elegant line of his now more pronounced spine. Melting into my touch, he leaned back into me. Quiet. So quiet it worried me. "Not now though," I added. "Now I just want to hold you and take care of you…and show you how much I love you."

✼✼✼

It was like watching the same horror movie twice. Except without remembering where all the scary parts were. That's what it felt like. I spent the next few days emptying vomit-filled buckets, changing sweat-soaked t-shirts and sheets, and holding him when his body shuddered. By day three the cold chills had largely dissipated, though all the other symptoms remained.

"Can you forgive me?" His quiet voice found me in the darkness, the question cautious. Well past midnight, I was curled up in the stuffed armchair I'd pulled up next to his side of the bed. Although my eyes were closed, I couldn't sleep. "Please," he murmured.

My eyes blinked open to find him lying on his side with his arm tucked under his head, watching me as if the fate of his life was in my power. I stroked the side of his hip and thigh, the body parts within reach, and answered him.

"For what?"

"For treating you the way I did. For saying those things to you." His scowl was directed at himself. "Nothing happened with Caroline. Nothing," he adamantly repeated, his expression tortured.

His growing agitation galvanized me into action. I crawled out of the chair and over him, straddling his hips when he rolled onto his back. With my face inches from his, I placed my hands on his lean cheeks and said, "Hey—I believe you."

"Marianne said that you thought—"

I shut him up with a gentle kiss. "I did. And I'm sorry I didn't give you the benefit of the doubt. Do you forgive me?" I rolled off and lay beside him, rising up on an elbow so I could gauge his reaction. And then, sifting my fingers through the hair at his temples, I waited.

"There's nothing to forgive." His eyes jumped all over my face. It was clear he was working up to say something. "I—I don't know why you want to be with me."

I knew what it took for such a proud man to make himself vulnerable. "Because being without you is intolerable. We're part of each other, for better or worse. There's a reason they put those words in that little speech we had to recite. Let's not kid ourselves, this isn't the last time we'll hurt each other. Just don't ever stop fighting for us."

His jaw pulsed, his eyes blinking rapidly. He wrapped a large palm around my neck and brought me down to his mouth. "There's nothing on this planet more important to me than you. Don't let me fuck this up."

"I won't," I whispered. I felt ready to split at the seams, my body no longer capable of containing all the love I had for him. He sealed the promise with a kiss. And for the first time since I walked back into his life, he slept soundly through what remained of the night.

✳✳✳

By the end of the week the color had returned to his face and he could actually keep solid food down. Our midnight heart-to-heart may have dispelled any lingering hurt between us, but it also pushed us into what I like to call "the polite zone." It drove me crazy. I wanted to shake some feeling other than contrition out of him. He constantly wavered between staring at me as if he'd seen a ghost, to not meeting my eyes at all when we spoke. With each day that passed and his health improved, the need to clear the air and discuss what had happened hung over us like a blade, the tension steadily rising.

I was on the couch reading when he walked in. Hair disheveled from his afternoon nap, jeans hanging low and revealing the absence of underwear. He was ridiculously handsome, much too handsome for someone who had recently been to hell and back. Standing in front of me with his hands stuffed into the front pockets of his jeans, he shifted awkwardly.

A desperate need to erase every cubic square inch of air between us came over me. I held up my hand and he took it without hesitation. The minute his body blanketed mine, all the tension I was feeling gave way to comfort, his heat seeping into my bones. He settled between my thighs and hugged me, placing his face on my chest, over my heart.

"How do you feel?" I asked. I brushed his hair back, and he exhaled deeply.

"Better—because you're here." The suddenly hard appendage pressing against the inside of my thigh validated that statement.

"I would say so." I laughed and he looked up, sporting a crooked smile I hadn't seen in ages.

"I missed you. I miss that smile."

Moving with intent, he crawled up my body and kissed me, his hands holding my face in place while he devoured my mouth. A slew of emotions were on the lips that met mine: passion, relief, love—apprehension. He pulled back and his eyes traveled over every salient point on my face, from my cherry-stained lips, to my eyes filled with love and regret for all the reasons that had kept us apart.

"We need to clear the air."

"Nothing happened with Caroline. I drove her home because she said her limo was stuck in traffic." The light, sexy mood morphed into a serious one. I sat up, running my fingers through my hair, and he followed. Judging by the expression on his face, he looked like he was about to shatter waiting for my verdict. "You believe me, right?" In his eyes was the indisputable truth. I could always find it there.

"Of course, I do. But that's not the issue." I straddled his lap and held his face. "You asked me to trust you and I have, I do—but you never gave me yours in return." I watched him wrestle with those words, arguments coming to the forefront and receding. I knew exactly the moment he capitulated in his mind because his gaze fell down between us, a deep v insinuating itself between his brows. "Stop doing that. I don't want your shame or regret. I want your trust—and your love." I lifted his face, forcing him to meet my eyes.

"You'll always have that," he quietly replied.

"It didn't feel that way this past month."

"I don't know why I said those things." He looked away again, his mouth pinching, his head shaking. "I didn't mean any of it. My anger got the best of me. And by the time you left my office, when you came to see me for my birthday, I realized how badly I'd fucked up." His voice descended to a low murmur. "I couldn't deal with the look of disappointment I saw on your face." Closing his eyes, his head fell back on the sofa cushion. "I'm just like her," he added, his voice full of self-loathing. I'd never heard him sound hopeless before that moment. My temper asserted itself.

"Your mother? Are you? Because if that's the case then we might as well go our separate ways now."

His head snapped back up, eyes wide, a spark of fear following surprise. Almost immediately it changed into determination. By now I knew that nothing centered and propelled him into action quicker than a challenge.

"Give me another chance. You don't have to move back in if you don't want to," he said, his face twisting in agony on the last few words. "Just let me show you that I trust you. Let me prove it."

Unconditional love. I never believed in it. I'd always thought it was rubbish. Love was completely conditional on how one person treated the other. Looking into his eyes, however, I understood it. Apparently I needed the lesson as much as he did. He didn't have to ask for my forgiveness because he already had it, he didn't need to prove his trust because I already believed him. Regardless of what happened,

I would always love him, conditions be damned.

"Do you know how I feel about you?" I asked, my eyes trained on every slight nuance of his expression.

"You love me." His answer sounded more like a question.

"Beyond measure."

Large eyes full of regret studied me. "After everything?"

"Forever," I told him, my voice emphatic. "Don't ever doubt it."

The wonder in his expression made it hard to say the next few words. But I knew unequivocally that if I didn't, our marriage would never survive. "I'm not moving back in—not immediately." Those impossibly wide shoulders sagged. "You *will* have to prove it. To yourself, not to me. Otherwise we don't stand a chance." Brandy colored eyes connected with brown ones. After a curt nod, an agreement was reached, a challenge issued.

※※※

Something woke me in the middle of the night. His side of the bed was empty. I ran a hand over the Pratesi sheet and found it cold. His scent, sandalwood and something else, something subtle and rich, drifted up from the ivory super fine cotton. It's a credit to my steely nerves that I didn't instantly go into full-blown panic. The remnants of sleep evaporating instantly, I went in search of my husband. The empty spare bedroom made a small nervous flutter in my stomach kick up. So did his empty study and the den. I breathed a loud sigh of relief when I found him in the main living room, facing the wall of windows that overlooked the lake. Naked, he stood with his back to me, staring out the window.

The light that the harvest moon cast outlined the angular edges of his body in silver. With his head resting on the glass, he was lost in thought, a million miles away.

"Sebastian," I softly called out.

He turned and watched as I walked up to him. In his gaze was a lifetime's worth of longing. We stood before each other frozen, neither one of us brave enough to make the first move. Gathering the U of Texas t-shirt I had worn to bed, I pulled it over my head and dropped it. It was like a switch was flipped.

He moved first. Lips crashed together, bodies slammed into each other, almost painfully so. He was already hard. I could feel every beautiful inch of him pressed between us. Instinctually, my hips pushed into him. He moaned. I sighed. Fingers shoved through hair. He tugged my head back, exposing my neck, and nipped the delicate skin there, then placed a string of kisses along my collarbone. I melted into him, offering myself to him without reserve. Grabbing my lacy panties in both hands, he pulled them apart.

"I'll buy you another pair," he said with a half-grin.

"You owe me ten," I teased.

He picked me up as easily as if he'd never been sick at all. My back was pushed against the cold glass. A shiver shot up my spine. In front of me, his skin was on fire, my nipples hypersensitive to the heat coming off of him. Under different circumstances I might've checked for a fever. I leaned in closer, took every inch of warmth and safety he offered. His heart, beating strongly, gave me everything else I needed and wanted.

His erection pressed against my body exactly where I needed him. I hooked my heels into the beautiful, round muscles of his rear end and rubbed against him. His hands left my face and burned a path down my body, squeezing breasts, skating between the cheeks of my rear end and lower. He pushed his pelvis into me, spread me wider. His fingers, slick from my arousal, rubbed all the way down to where our bodies met, teasing me into a state of sexual madness. Too long...it had been too long since I'd had him inside of me. He pulled back far enough that the broad head of his erection breached my entrance. His supplicating eyes connected with mine.

"You're the only reason I keep breathing," he murmured in a rough-hewn voice. He watched me closely to make sure the words sunk in, that I understood the gravity of his admission.

The harvest moon wouldn't let us keep any secrets, didn't allow us to hide any of our most intimate thoughts and feelings behind the cloak of night. It cast a spotlight on the tears welling at the corners of my eyes—and his. Without further delay, he drove his hard body into mine, filling me so completely that I felt a twinge of pain at first. Tangled up in each other, he held me securely while he pumped into me over and over, pushing me faster and faster towards sweet oblivion.

"I'm a bastard, and a possessive son of a bitch," he rasped, grunting with each determined thrust of his hips. "But I love you more than life itself, and there isn't anything I won't do to keep you." The pressure building in my body coiled tighter and tighter until I was whimpering encouragement and incoherent nonsense. "Come for me, baby," he murmured in that sweet, sexy voice of his.

At his command, demanding me to take my pleasure, the coil unraveled, a Catherine wheel spinning out of control, sending sparks of pleasure shooting through my body. I screamed his name out and dug my short nails into the muscles of his shoulders. He shoved home one more time and shouted at the point of release. Breathing heavily, we stayed glued together for a long time, long after I stopped feeling the cool glass on my back, long after he softened and slipped out of my body. When his legs began to tremble, he carried us to the couch where we crashed for the rest of the night.

"Don't let go," he whispered right before we fell asleep.

"Never again," I whispered back.

Chapter Twenty-Eight

I STAYED AT THE APARTMENT as long as I could with the excuse that I wanted to make certain he was eating properly and gained back most of his strength. Truth was, I didn't want to leave. How I accomplished it for a month was beyond me. How I existed before we met was even a greater mystery.

The day I moved back to my flat he was super quiet, following me around the apartment as I tidied up.

"When are you going back to work?" I asked. Sitting at the counter, he watched me organize the freezer with the meals I had prepared for him.

"Tomorrow."

"So soon?"

"I can't stay in this apartment another minute...especially now that you're leaving." In the silence, I glanced at him and found him looking like a whipped puppy—or maybe more like a whipped tiger. "You don't have to go," he argued quietly.

"I expect you to eat everything. The containers are labeled." This was the most difficult part, holding to the plan when every cell in my body rebelled at the thought of being separated from him. "I have to. You know I do." The forlorn look on his face almost had me rethinking my decision. Almost.

"When can I see you?"

"You're my husband. You can see me whenever you want."

That seemed to appease him, the tense look on his face relaxing to some degree.

"I'll pick you up for dinner at the clinic." His words hung in the air, a challenge, a promise—definitely not a question. I stopped what I was doing to see what his face told me. The look he wore made me smile. Determination. It was all over him. His strength of will had always awed me. When he put his mind to something, he was an unstoppable force.

"I'll expect you by six thirty," I doubled down, and the predatory glint that I saw in his eyes told me he was up for the challenge.

"I'll be there."

***

With his hands on his hips in a defiant stance, Yannick glared—there's no other way to describe it, it was a glare—at my beloved husband. The same husband that only a moment ago looked all soft and in love, at present looked like he was about to commit bloody murder.

"What's he doing here?" The sweet inquiry was leveled at me with a deep v etched on Yannick's brow.

"He's my husband. He can hang out here all day if he damn well pleases." My push back seemed to do the trick. I pressed my case. I knew that if I didn't assert the rules firmly, these two dolts would've gone at it ad infinitum. "You two need to sort this out. I am sick and tired of drama. I love my job and I love my husband. Those two things are not mutually exclusive. I'd like to keep both. I would also like to get through a single week without any yelling, accusing, or fighting going on. Are we clear? NO. MORE. DRAMA."

A long, contemplative pause ensued. And then Yannick turned his formidable attention on said husband. "Are we going to have a problem?"

"I don't know—are we?" Sebastian stood a little straighter,

his arms crossed in front. I noticed as soon as he walked through the door that he didn't have his cane with him. I'm pretty certain that was not a coincidence.

"Because I can't afford to lose her. I lose everybody and I won't lose *her*." I could feel the faint prickle of heat on my collarbone.

"Same goes here."

An epic silence followed, along with a lot of staring each other down and sizing each other up while I sat by clueless. Was this some kind of native masculine language that females weren't privy to?

"Make yourself useful, and help her change the bed linens." And with that, Yannick turned on his heels and marched to the next examination room.

Sebastian's confused expression made my lips curl between my teeth, fighting the laughter that threatened to burst out of me.

"He always like this?"

"Always," I confirmed, fully chuckling.

"Let's get going."

"Certainly—after you help me with the bed linens," I chided. He grumbled the whole time we worked. But when we left later that evening, arm in arm, a big smile lived on his face.

✳✳✳

By early morning, the snow was already falling steadily, dampening the blast of car horns and the vroom of buses. Fat, fluffy snowflakes, some the size of a fist, turned the busy city into an enchanted wonderland. By late afternoon it was up to my knees and still coming down hard. With cashmere hat and gloves on tight, I took my time walking to the corner store to do some grocery shopping, enjoying how romantically beautiful the city looked. Tilting my head back, I let the snowflakes cover my face and hang on my eyelashes, laughing as I licked them off my lips and replayed the scene that had transpired that morning in my head.

Sebastian moaned. His arms overhead, he stretched his back from side to side. "Do you have any fucking idea how many beds we own? Or, for that matter, how many king size mattresses? But here we are, squeezed into this shitty double bed."

I couldn't help but snicker. I'd made the decision to move back home today, a surprise he would get later. Throwing the covers off, I mumbled, "Somewhere there's a triple shot cappuccino with my name on it."

"I've got something right here with your name on it," he drawled, then took my hand and pressed it against the erection bursting out of his boxer briefs. I poked him as I got out of bed because, as usual, he was making me late for my shift at the clinic.

"Ouch. That hurt, Dr. Mengala," he said, rubbing the side of his gorgeous chest. In the three weeks since I'd left the apartment he had already gained back most of the weight he'd lost.

"You're such a baby," I replied over my shoulder, and hurried to put on my underthings. He leapt out of bed and wrapped his arms around me from behind, enveloping me in heat and a hundred-proof testosterone. When he rocked his hips into me, I almost rethought my decision.

"It's your fault I'm soft and sensitive there, woman," he murmured seductively in my ear. I rolled my eyes and elbowed him there again for his corny reference to Adam's rib.

"You better go take a cold shower because I'm late as it is."

"Fine," he grumbled. After which, I got a hard slap on the ass and watched him squeeze every naked inch of his six-three frame into my tiny shower.

"How the fuck does Yannick shower in this thing?" I was

certain it was a rhetorical question. Then, more muttered insults directed at the poor shower.

My resolve had been fading since the day I'd moved back to the studio apartment. I never wanted to be apart from him ever again, plagued by a constant craving to feel him, hear him, touch him. Every night he came over, and every night we would spend hours talking and making love. Even my skeptical self had to admit that it felt like something had shifted within him...between us.

I'd read somewhere that a relationship cannot survive if either of the two people in it held anything back, that love was nourished by revealing yourself to the other. That intriguing piece of information stayed with me for a long time because I never really understood it. For so long we had both been trying to protect ourselves from the world at large that we had to learn how to trust all over again, how to let someone in...to reveal ourselves to one another. We had to almost lose everything, to realize that the only thing worth protecting was the love we had for each other. Without it, nothing else mattered.

A bling alerted me to the text. I fished the iPhone out of my pocket quickly, expecting to see one from Sebastian. We were going to dinner and a movie that evening. I'd been looking forward to it all day. What I found instead turned the hot blood in my veins to ice.

It was a picture...a picture of a bloodied and bruised Emilia. Naked and lying on a dirty cement floor, her hands and feet were bound together with rope like an animal being prepared for a spit. An instant later I couldn't see the picture anymore. My hands were shaking so violently that my phone fell, landing in a soft pile of snow on the sidewalk. I dropped to my knees, my heart beating a mile a minute as I frantically dug in the snow until I found it.

That's when a second text from an unknown number came

in. The bling hit me in the gut. I was terrified to look.

> 6 p.m. The train station. Platform 3. Alert the authorities or your husband and I'll send her to you in small pieces.

The weight of the world came crashing down on me. I knew in my bones that whoever had her wasn't bluffing. My first instinct was to call Sebastian. But I might as well have signed her death warrant, so instead, with great trepidation, I dialed Yuri's number.

"I haven't seen her in a week," Yuri casually claimed. "The bitch probably ran off with that bartender she was always shaking her ass at. He hasn't been to work either."

"I swear to God, you deplorable piece of shit, if anything happens to her I will make it my life's mission that you spend the next half of yours in jail!"

"I'm telling you I don't know where she is." After that, he promptly hung up on me.

Gathering all the sense I had left, I started to form a plan. In an hour Sebastian would be showing up at the flat for our date—on time. He was always on time. Loaded down with the groceries I had just purchased at the market, I began to sprint home. Slipping and sliding in the snow, I slammed into people crowding the sidewalk like a pinball. And still, I kept running. Because nothing was going to prevent me from being on platform three in an hour.

Chapter Twenty-Nine

IF I HADN'T BEEN SO anxiety stricken, I would've stopped to consider what this would do to my marriage. As it was, I didn't have the luxury of time. Or contemplation, for that matter. Marching as fast as I could in deep snow, I strained every muscle in my legs running back to the flat. The snow was still coming down, accumulating on the sidewalks, on the streets, heavy snow, soaked with moisture and hard to move. I think it took everyone in the city by surprise.

Some primal instinct told me to prepare for the worst. I changed into jeans and layered my clothing. I slipped a small, and very sharp paring knife into the sturdy, high ankle winter boots I was wearing. I was a doctor after all. I knew where every vital artery was. All I needed was a small sharp instrument to end someone's life—and possibly save my own. I hoped it wouldn't come to that, however, my past had taught me never to discount anything.

I was leaving without a word to Sebastian. I could only imagine how he would feel when he found me missing. Any minute he would show up at the flat and go into full-tilt panic. The melee of feelings that thought invoked was too much for me to bear.

After making sure the ringtone of my iPhone was on mute, I headed out. As soon as I ripped the front door open, my heart skipped a beat. Standing with his fist raised in the air, ready to knock, was Alek. Both of us stood there, staring at each other in shock for an undetermined amount of time.

"What are you doing here?"

"I have to talk to you."

"Not now, Alek!" I shouted, slamming the front door shut. My nerves were so frazzled it took me three tries to get the key in the lock and turn it.

"Did you get a picture, too?"

My breath stalled. I whipped around and examined his handsome face. He looked...I don't know, worried. The cloak of superiority and nonchalance he was never without was presently missing. "Emilia?" was all he said, all that needed to be said.

"Yes, I have to go. I have to be on platform three by six. That's in twenty minutes. I'll barely make it in time in this weather." Walking right past him, I marched double time down the long hallway, headed for the stairs.

"I'm coming with you," he said, keeping pace, his voice right behind me.

"No."

"There's no way I'm letting you go alone. Besides, they're expecting me."

I looked over my shoulder, sizing up his intentions. "Fine, but let me do the talking," I fired back. He jerked in surprise. His brow furrowed at my delivery.

"You've changed." This was no compliment. His tone reeked of disapproval.

"Yes. And I have you to thank for that." Pushing the door of the building open, I stepped out onto the sidewalk with Alek right behind me.

"Vera?"

I never thought the sound of that voice could ever hurt, never fathomed that hearing my name on his lips could devastate me. And yet, I felt all those things and more. I turned slowly. Sebastian stood on the sidewalk, snow halfway up his jeans-covered calves. He was dressed casually for our movie night, a gray cashmere beanie hanging right above his eyes, eyes that jumped back and forth from me, to Alek. Lips parted. Bewildered. He looked like I'd plunged a knife in his chest, like I had betrayed him.

The night sky, glowing with the light from street lamps reflecting off the still falling snowflakes, gave everything a romantic appeal when in reality a nightmare was unfolding.

"Let me do the talking," I murmured to Alek in Albanian.

Shoring up my resolve, I took one step closer. A woman's life depended on what happened next.

"Alek showed up. I'm going for a quick drink with him."

"I thought...we had plans," he croaked. He did nothing to hide the pain, the gaping wound in his heart. It nearly killed me to see him in such a state, but time was running out. I had to go at him hard and fast, leaving him no room to argue, otherwise he'd never let me go.

"Change of plans," I stated. "Don't make this difficult, Sebastian. I'm not in the mood for any of your crap. We're only grabbing a glass of wine. I'll call you when I'm done." Somehow I managed to push all my love for him behind a closed door, my expression one of total indifference. I didn't give him a chance to respond. Walking back to Alek, who had been patiently waiting and watching in the wings, I grabbed his upper arm and pulled him along, leaving Sebastian standing in snow—and confusion. But I couldn't say for certain, because I never looked back.

✳✳✳

The streets were mostly empty. I pulled the hood of my down puffer coat over my head. Eyes shifting furtively side to side, searching for danger, I probably looked like an inept criminal.

"Do you think he'll follow?" Alek asked after a solid fifteen minutes of heavy silence. The look on my face had probably warned him to keep his mouth shut.

"No."

No, he wouldn't…not after my implied threat. Sebastian knew that one more broken promise, one more perceived breach of trust would have ended our relationship for good. And I had used it against him. Rage ran through me. At myself, at life. All I wanted was a quiet life with the man I loved, but there was always an obstacle thrown in our way, the universe conspiring to make it impossible.

"Are you getting a divorce? Why aren't you living with him?"

The muscles in my legs were weak from trudging through the snow. It was still falling steadily, all the roads in the city eerily deserted.

"Because of you, thank you very much," I snapped. That wasn't entirely true. Though for reasons I couldn't explain, I wanted to hurt Alek. I wanted to make him feel as bad as Sebastian was feeling right now. "And no, we aren't getting divorced if I can help it. He's the only man I ever really loved. The only one that's ever really loved me." I stole a sideways glance to see if my bullets had hit their intended mark. Sharp, scruff-covered jaw tight. Lips pursed in a straight line. My success only managed to make me feel worse.

"I don't know why you seem to think I'm the villain here."

"That little stunt you pulled…" Alek's expression was completely blank. "With the lip biting, almost worked. Almost," I explained, my tone caustic enough to burn.

He turned then, grabbing my arm to stop me. "I spent years looking for you. Beating myself up for leaving you there." The tortured look on his face did nothing for me, not even a sliver of sympathy did it evoke.

I continued walking, the snow as treacherous as quicksand. The effort it took to pull my legs out of it with each step was getting to me. And then…finally. I spotted the train station up ahead. My anger with Alek faded away. My heart was suddenly stuck in my throat. I swallowed, but it remained exactly where it was. That's why I didn't scream, why I couldn't scream when a sudden, overpowering force hit me from behind and pulled me out of the snow, almost out of my boots, and off the street. The next thing I remember was a sack being placed over my head. The smell of gasoline and cow shit. And something else, some other...chemical. Then, nothing, only absolute black.

***

Untethered, I drifted on a dark and dangerous sea—a sea of fear. A jolt, my body bounced. Curved in a fetal position, it pressed against metal, not smooth but ridged. Then, pain. A lot of pain, in my shoulder, my head, my legs. It grew stronger as I slowly ascended from the depths of hell I was visiting only moments ago, back to consciousness, back to the hell I would be experiencing in reality. The smell of gasoline and cow crap made me nauseous. My stomach heaved. I tried to take shallow breaths, but that only made me hyperventilate. I coughed and coughed, vomit rising up with it.

"She's going to throw up, take that thing off," said a distressed voice—a familiar one. The fumes were making me so lightheaded I couldn't remember how I knew it.

"Give her another shot. Knock her out again. We have another two hours to go." A Russian accent? The needle stung...and then I faded away.

***

Someone was slapping my face. I winced. Slap, slap, slap in rapid succession. I winced again, my face screwed up in protest. Still foggy from the drugs, I didn't have it in me to even muster the appropriate amount of fear. I knew two things for certain: I had just been kidnapped, and I had been transported to God knows where. The pain was everywhere, and intolerable. There was so much of it the slap on my cheek was more of an annoyance in comparison. A mosquito buzzing in my ear. Except that mosquito was probably two hundred pounds and armed to the teeth.

My eyes cracked open. Realizing the room was dark, they ventured open all the way. It took me a minute to examine my surroundings. I was alone, lying on a dirty floor. No Alek. And no sign of the man who had slapped me, and a man it definitely had been. A stab of fear pierced my heart. Was he taken as well, or did they dispose of him right away? Alek was an intellectual, not a fighter. I wasn't certain he'd ever been in a fist fight once in his entire life. He could talk himself so brilliantly out of any trouble that he didn't need to raise his fists.

Composure. I needed to keep my composure and gather information. I was in a house. Dark, and dirty, and dank. Dilapidated. Windows covered up with sheets. Abandoned. The few pieces of furniture were either broken or covered with inches of dust and dirt. I was sitting on a wood floor stained with oil and…was that blood? The singing of birds drew my attention to the covered windows. The house was in a wooded area. Maybe a forest?

The good news was that I was still dressed. The bad news—my wrists were secured with plastic ties behind my back. Without the use of my arms it was a struggle to sit up. My shoulders were burning, burning with the intensity of a thousand suns. I must have had my arms bound for some time. On the other hand I hadn't lost feeling in them yet, the blood supply wasn't totally cut off. There was your silver lining. It was also cold, so cold the tip of my nose felt frozen.

Someone moaned behind me. With great effort, I turned my aching head and found Emilia lying on her side, close to the wall. Dirty, bruised, ankles and wrists bound by the same plastic ties as mine. My heart sank even further into despair. Scooting on my rear end, I turned my body and did a crab crawl over to her.

"Emilia." Her eyes fluttered. "Emilia, wake up. Open your eyes. It's me, Vera," I begged, my voice rising, my composure slowly but surely unraveling.

Her eyes blinked open. What seemed like an eternity later, she finally focused on me and said, "Vera?" I could tell from the dilated pupils that she'd been drugged too. With what, was anyone's guess.

"Good. You're awake." Entering through a door at the other end of the room were three men. The first one was no surprise, Yuri. The second made my blood run colder than it already was, muscle man. But the last, the last was the one that held my attention. My blood went from ice cold to fire hot in the blink of an eye.

"How could you?"

His dark eyes met mine for only a moment. He diverted his gaze, staring at anything other than me. His hands stuffed in the pockets of his jeans, he rocked back and forth on his boots.

"Look at me, you bastard! Look at what you've done!" I don't know where I found the strength to scream so loud.

"Shouting, shouting, shouting," Yuri very calmly said. "I don't like it." His English was perfect again.

My eyes zeroed in on Yuri. "You said you hadn't seen her. If you ever cared for her, even a little, get her some medical attention." Considering the circumstances, begging him was not beneath me. I was no naïve princess. I was acutely aware that there was a very good chance I wasn't going to get out of this alive. I figured it wouldn't hurt to beg them to spare Emilia's life.

Yuri cocked his head. "You poisoned her mind against me. She wasn't the same. She was going to run away with the boy, the bartender."

Stefan. I sucked in a breath. As each piece of the puzzle came together, my fear grew proportionally larger. My body shuddered from the cold, mostly though from the knowledge that Stefan was probably already dead and buried. "Why am I here? If you plan on holding me for ransom, you'll be sorely disappointed. My husband and I are separated. I don't think he'll even notice me missing."

"She's lying. He cares. He cares quite a bit. I saw it myself."

"You disgusting piece of shit," I spat out.

"Enough!" Yuri interrupted. He was about to speak again when his cell phone rang. Glancing at the screen, he motioned to muscle man, and they both walked back out the same way they came in. Only one man left in the room. Alek.

Chapter Thirty

"They were going to kill me."

I looked up into supplicating eyes, his expression full of regret. Faithless coward. This was the first time in my life I could say that I was sorry I had been right all along. I shifted my sore legs, flexed my foot, and felt it. The small knife was still tucked into my boot. Stupid, stupid men. It never occurred to them that I may have been carrying a weapon. Now all I needed was the use of my arms.

"I can't feel my arms anymore, Alek. You have to cut these ties...please." Plan A was kill him with kindness and understanding, appeal to his ego. Plan B was...there was no plan B.

"I can't, *Zogu*. They'll kill me." The sound of the Albanian term of endearment—a pet name that he knew my father always used—launched me into an indescribable rage. Had my hands been free, I could've plunged the paring knife into his neck at that moment. I did my best to tamp down the anger.

"Why would they kill you? What did you do?" The words were forced out between a tight-lipped grimace.

"Loans..." He looked like he wanted to say more but stopped. This was a game I had to play very carefully. Alek's true weakness was his arrogance. He dazzled me when I was a stupid young girl, easily taken in by a few big words and a pretty face. As a woman, I saw him for what he truly was—a narcissist through and through. He couldn't resist the opportunity to showcase his brilliance. I waited patiently for him to speak again of his own accord. "I borrowed against our money."

"Our money? What money? We didn't have a goddamn *lek*. They are going to kill me, Alek," I persisted.

"No, they won't. Tomorrow we'll get the money waiting for you in Montenegro, and then you and I will disappear." His expression changed the more he spoke, the unease and doubt subsiding. Arms crossed in front casually, nose tilted slightly up. His arrogance, unable to stay hidden too long, came up for air in its full glory.

"Did you say Montenegro?" The last shred of hope I held that I could change his mind went down the proverbial crapper.

"Banks are funny like that. They won't give access to a bank account worth three million to just anybody. You were meant to be *my* wife."

"So this was your master plan all along?" I said, my voice rising, rage and dismay taking turns flashing in my eyes. He met my accusation without so much as a hint of remorse. His unflinching expression not only confirmed it, the smug bastard actually seemed proud of his accomplishment.

"I underestimated how impulsive you could be." His countenance turned pensive, as if I was a riddle he couldn't quite figure out. "Running away? In the middle of the night? You surprise me. Wish you would've been that adventurous when we were fucking."

"How?"

He shrugged. "It was absurdly easy. He trusted me with the combination of his safe. I ran his errands for years. I transferred money all the time for him. He never assumed anyone else ever gave a shit about money because he didn't. Very small minded of him, I always thought. He disappointed me in that."

A dormant volcano of rage exploded within me. "You betrayed a man that treated you like a son—loved you like a son."

"Do you remember what we did on our first date?" The bastard had the nerve to smile wistfully, as if this was some pleasant trip down memory lane.

"I've worked very hard to forget everything about us," I ground out, straining not to lose it completely on him. I had to keep him talking, stall him. I needed time to assess my surroundings, to figure out if there was any chance to escape.

"We pretended we were in Paris," he continued, unaffected by my contempt. "We both wanted a better life."

"Yes! But not at the cost you're willing to pay—let me rephrase that—you're willing to cost *me*. Your greed killed my father!"

"No." He charged forward, stopping close enough that I automatically shrank back and curled into myself, afraid he would hit me. I didn't put anything past him anymore.

"Good old-fashioned pride killed your father," he drawled in an awful voice. "He couldn't bear to let his friends see him as anything less than a bastion of moral rectitude, of everything good. He could have told the authorities, he could've turned me in. He and I knew I had access to the money. But he didn't." He chuckled darkly. "He didn't because he was ashamed of what it said about his judgement."

I stared at him with pure hate in my eyes.

"We all could've done a little bit better! Except for your father, and the high fucking horse he rode in on." His hands curled into claws that looked ready to choke the life out of me.

And then a monumental realization crashed down on me. My mind finally caught up with my gut instincts. The knowledge crawled over my skin like an army of red ants. "Oh my God...was *any* of it real? Did you ever love me, or were you going to marry me only to get access to the money?"

"Of course, I loved you. I was even faithful in the beginning."

His dark eyes fell on the diamond cross peeking out from my half open coat and narrowed. I knew what was coming. His face screwed up in a snarl and he yanked the cross off my neck, the thin platinum chain digging into my skin before breaking free.

"You won't be needing this. I'll buy you a new one once we get to Russia."

Russia?

Muscle man suddenly appeared in the doorway. "We have company," he announced, his tongue tripping over his accent.

Our Father
Who art in heaven
Hallowed be Thy Name
Thy kingdom come...

The cavalry had arrived.

"In here!!" I screamed at the top of my lungs. Which produced a coughing fit, my throat still raw from the chemicals they had used to knock me out when they took me. Muscle man stepped closer into the room. He reached behind him and pulled out a serrated hunting knife as long as my arm.

"Make her be silent, or I will," he barked at Alek while his cold, dead eyes remained on me. Alek bravely stepped in between us and held his hands up.

"I will, I will." No doubt he couldn't afford to lose his golden goose. Quickly, he produced a cotton handkerchief out of the inside pocket of his down jacket and roughly stuffed it into my mouth, jamming it down my throat. It made me cough even more violently. The scent I recognized as uniquely his brought back every memory of us. Another wave of nausea hit me.

Pop, pop, pop. Gunfire. I knew what it sounded like now. More of it. A lot more. Muscle man hurried out the door, handgun drawn. Alek's eyes darted around. The more gunfire rained, the more anxious he became. Moving swiftly, he grabbed me by the elbow and yanked on my arm. I screamed in pain and launched myself up onto my feet. My legs were barely able to support me. I was still weak and dizzy, probably dehydrated. The sound of men shouting in English and Russian outside the house increased while the gunfire lessened.

"Let's go," he said, wrapping an arm around my waist. I glanced down at Emilia. She was still out cold. I said another prayer for her.

We were headed for the back of the house, exiting onto a rickety covered porch, when a familiar voice said, "Get down! Face down on the ground! Now!" Ben Winters and Gideon Hirsch stood at the back entrance of the abandoned house with their guns aimed at Alek.

***

The faithless coward released me at once. As soon as he did, I collapsed onto my knees. Slowly, Alek went to his, then down on his belly, palms in the air in surrender.

"Hands behind your head," Gideon growled and placed a knee on Alek's back.

"Wish this motherfucker had been armed so I could've shot him," I heard Ben mutter to Gideon. My arms were suddenly free of the plastic ties. I cried out in pain and Gideon began massaging my wrists, working his way up my arms. With no strength left in me, I sat back on my heels.

"I won't tell," Gideon replied in that soft voice with the rolling Rs.

"Sebastian?"

"We had to uh...restrain the sunuvabitch. Pardon—*him*."

He's in the car," Ben answered.

"Is he okay?"

"He? It's you I'm worried about."

Wrapping his arms around me, Gideon gently lifted me to my feet. Ben was much rougher with Alek. My gaze slid sideways to the man I once thought I loved. The man I had vowed to spend my life with. I was looking at a total stranger. A stranger who didn't have the courage to meet my eyes.

"Where are you sending him?"

"Interpol will take custody. They're sending him back to Albania, where he'll be residing in a six-by-eight cell."

"Emilia!" I belatedly remembered.

"Let's get you inside while Interpol wraps this up," Gideon added.

I took a moment to glance around. The house was surrounded by a heavy forest. Gray and bare, the trees were not covered with snow. Nothing else stood out except for the armed men with official-looking uniforms traipsing through.

"Where are we?" I asked, beyond confused.

"Croatia—border of Montenegro."

I watched Ben take Alek away. He didn't look at me again.

***

Clad in riot gear and heavily armed, police officers swarmed the property inside and out. Two of them were assisting Emilia when we walked back into the house. They had released her bound hands and feet, but didn't move her. I walked over and crouched down close. She didn't make a peep as I checked her pulse. Two EMTs rushed over to help.

She raised a hand and gripped mine. "Vera?"

"It's me," I murmured. "You're safe. You're safe. I have you."

Gently, I stroked her hair. No doubt she was in shock, both mentally and physically beaten down. It would take a while for her to accept that Yuri was willing to sacrifice her without so much as a second thought. She tried to get up, but I wouldn't let her. I was certain that with the beating she took, she sustained a number of broken bones.

The EMTs lifted her gingerly onto a gurney. I squeezed her hand, murmuring in Albanian that I loved her and would see her soon. After that, they whisked her away.

"You're next," Gideon softly ordered.

"Not yet," I answered, my gaze elsewhere, scanning the room filled with people doing their job. My eyes bounced from police officers and medical assistants, to Sebastian's private security team.

I found him, then—a blond, disheveled head above everyone else. He glanced around nervously. Even from afar I could see the anxiety in his gaze as he searched the room for me. When our eyes connected, mine welled with tears. All the fear I had pushed down and locked up came bursting forth with a vengeance. A loud sob broke out of me. A moment later I was in his arms, enveloped in love, smothered in kisses and tender caresses. I buried my face in his chest and wrapped my arms around his waist in a death grip, while my body convulsed uncontrollably.

"Shhh, I got you...I got you," he whispered close to my ear. "I'll always come for you." Between kisses, he muttered some more nonsense I couldn't make out—something about handcuffing me to him, I think.

"You know I didn't mean a word I said to you the other day." I wiped my snotty, teary face in his shirt.

"When I got back in the car, I remembered you mentioned wine, and knew something was wrong. I know you love me. I know you wouldn't hurt me like that...I trust you with my heart," he finished in a gruff voice.

A shiver rocked my body. He unzipped his down jacket and wrapped it around the both of us, cocooning me in his warmth and reassurance. A short time after that I was hooked up to an IV and resting in Sebastian's lap. I closed my eyes, drawing strength from the man I loved, my home—the only place I belonged was with him.

"How did you find me?" I asked. I was awed by my good fortune. It was almost too good to be true.

After a pause he answered, "The cross."

"My cross? What does my cross have to do with it?" In reflex, my hand flew to my breastbone and found empty space. "Alek took it."

"There's a chip imbedded in the platinum frame. A tracking device."

"A tracking device," I repeated absently. As the knowledge began to seep into my tired brain and register, I looked up with a mixture of amusement and outright fury that had me wavering between laughing and punching his lights out. At least, he had the grace to look sheepish.

"You've been tracking me all this time?" I asked, downright incredulous.

Did I want to be mad about it? Yes. But there was also no doubt in my mind that I wouldn't be alive if it weren't for his possessive tendencies and questionable tactics. "You psychotic, control freak..."

He kissed me quickly, interrupting my mini tirade.

"*Your* psychotic, control freak," he murmured in a low sexy voice. "You own me, baby. All of me. Even the psycho parts. For better or worse, remember?" I looked up into his solemn face. Sweet, impossible man.

Everyone defines love in his, or her own way. Through trial and error, pain and pleasure, together we'd decided that our love was going to be defined as unconditional, beyond measure—no matter what.

"I love you, my psychotic control freak."

"I love you more," he mouthed.

Tired beyond anything, all I wanted to do was go home, crawl into bed, and let him hold me. Unfortunately, I had a nagging suspicion that we would be spending hours getting debriefed by Interpol. Ben walked up and inspected my person, his head shaking. "She needs to get checked out at a hospital." He directed this at Sebastian as if I wasn't standing between them.

"I'm fine," I cut in.

"And you're needed at headquarters," Ben continued.

"The fuck, I am." Before the words were out of his mouth, he was already pulling me away, out of the musty, cold house.

"Where are you going?" Ben shouted in exasperation.

"Home. So I can make sweet, sweet love to my wife."

"Wishful thinking. We're at least sixteen hours away by car," I reminded him. He smirked.

"Don't ever underestimate me, lover." No...I would have to be a total idiot to ever underestimate this man. The look on his face told me not to bother arguing.

Outside, the sunlight was blinding. My eyes narrowed into two slits. I trudged through the mud slowly while Mr. Six Foot Three pulled me along. He finally gave up. Hooking his arm under my legs, he carried me the rest of the way, overriding my very vocal objection.

The rhythmic beating of helicopter blades gained my attention. It was sitting in an open field, next to the house.

"But what about—" I stuttered. He held the door open and pushed me into the back of the helicopter while Bear, sitting in the pilot seat, looked over his shoulder wearing a big, fat smile on his face.

"Uh uh, nothin' and I mean *nothin'* is going to stop me from getting you home and gettin' inside you," he drawled in my ear, his accent as thick and sweet as honey. "But first, a quick pit stop to see Yannick and get you checked out."

I stared into the eyes of my best friend, my lover, my

lighthouse in this crazy storm that was my life. I crawled onto his lap, wrapped my arms around his neck, and raked my fingers through his hair. "I know what we could make," I murmured, smile stretching from ear to ear.

His lips hooked up on one side and his head tilted, his eyes burning with mischief. "What's that, darlin'?" He brushed my dirty, matted hair back and tucked it behind my ear.

"A baby."

I should've known better than to pose it as a challenge.

Epilogue

SEBASTIAN

"Babe? Baaaabe!" I walk into the foyer and listen for voices.

"*Mon Dieu*, stop shouting."

"Hey, Marianne. Have you—"

"Out back," she tells me, waving to a point behind her.

"Where?" I walk across the foyer and past her without pausing.

"In her favorite place—but I'm warning you," she says with a strange inflection in her voice.

My steps slow and I turn to face her. I can feel the frown forming on my face. Worry rears its ugly head. "Is everything okay?"

It's gotten better the last couple of years, thanks to my wife—she seems to know exactly what I need before I know I need it—but it'll always be a part of me.

"She's fine," Marianne assures me. Her voice fades away as I move as quickly as I can on one fucked-up knee down the hall. These walls don't haunt me anymore, the ghosts of my past evicted by the love that lives here now. We've made this house ours.

Rushing out the French doors, I cross the wide slate patio. The sun, shining brightly, reminds me what an amazing life I'm living. I know how lucky I am. Not a day goes by that I don't look at the people I love and thank the good Lord for giving me this gift. If I wasn't a religious man before, I sure as fuck am now. Things with Diana are still touchy. Vera has a better relationship with her than I do. I can't seem to forget. Just not as forgiving as my beautiful wife, I guess.

I roll up my shirtsleeves and loosen my tie as I walk past the conservatory, and cut across the meadow—our meadow. I've made love to my wife here more times than I can count. I can't even smell the scent of fresh cut grass anymore without getting hard. It puts a smile on my face every time I think about it. Christ. I have to adjust myself in my pants now.

Finally, I reach the wisteria tree she loves so much. She says it reminds her of us, of how it all began. And then I see her and smile. She's asleep on the lounge chair. Her arm hangs over the armrest, a book on the ground below it. I stop, not wanting to wake her yet, and just watch. I'll never get tired of this. Fuck, it's the most beautiful sight in the world. I'm no poet, or songwriter. Pretty words and melodies won't ever come out of this mouth. But I know what I feel, and I know how lucky I am to have it. I've led a life that most men only dream of, and I'd trade it all to spend only a second with this woman. Where she is concerned, I have no pride, no vanity. There are no rules or laws I won't break to keep her safe and happy. She's everything. It begins and ends with her.

Her eyes blink open and her head turns my way. That beautiful mouth curves into a smile just for me.

"Get over here, you handsome peeping Tom."

She doesn't have to ask twice. I walk up and bend down to kiss her gently. Then I kiss my son's forehead. His plump lips gape open as he sleeps pressed up against his mother's breast, his hands fisted on his chest. Lucky little dude. Make sure you enjoy every minute of it, buddy.

"What I wouldn't do to be in his place right now," I murmur, careful not to wake him.

"You can be," she tells me and wiggles her eyebrows.

"Later tonight."

"Promise?" Shit, I'm hard already with the way she's looking at me. I pet my son's silky, dark hair with my index finger. His baby mohawk is irresistible.

"You have this strange obsession with his hair," she giggles quietly.

"It's the coolest thing ever."

"Don't you dare wake him," she says more seriously. "I'm going to have to go back to work just to get some peace and quiet."

"Quiet is overrated. Speaking of your work, I just saw Yannick. He hired another doctor, and the new MRI machine was delivered today."

Yes, my wife built another clinic with Yannick. Yes, it still makes me uncomfortable even though he's become a close friend.

"Really?" she says, a little too brightly. And now I'm annoyed. She reads my mind perfectly, grabs the back of my head and pulls me down for another kiss.

"Daddyyyyyyyyyyyyy!"

We break apart and my wife rolls her eyes. "Here comes the tyrant. It's scary how alike you two are." I chuckle at the resignation on her face. We both know what's coming.

"Should I be offended?"

"She never asks," my wife barrels on, one dark eyebrow raised. "She just makes demands and expects everyone to fall in line. Does that sound like anybody we know?"

"Daaaaaaaaaaaad!"

I look over my shoulder to find my daughter running ahead of Olivier, all skinny arms and long legs. She launches herself into my open arms and wraps her arms tightly around my neck, her wet bathing suit soaking my shirt and pants—the little brute. Startled awake, my son starts to cry while my wife shakes her head.

I push the wet tangle of long blond hair off my daughter's face while she chatters on about how many laps she swam, and how she wants me to time her while my son screams at the top of his lungs, which at the moment seem to be much larger than his small body. My wife's warm, brown eyes meet mine. There are no words, just a profound understanding of what a gift we've been given.

"Is this what you wanted?" she asks, her question barely comprehensible over the sound of our children.

"This is everything," I say as I stare at the woman who brought me back to life, who erased the quiet with laughter and filled the emptiness with love.

"You better amend that edict," she mutters cryptically.

Panic sets in. So does a weight pressing down on my chest. "What? Why?"

"Because I'm pregnant again, that's why."

"Holy shit." The panic vanishes only to be replaced with a hot lump of fuck knows what that gets stuck in my throat. I take two deep breaths. But damn, I gotta get a handle on this shit.

"Daddy," my daughter scolds. "You said another swear word."

"I'm sorry, love. How much do I owe the swear jar now?"

"A lot—like *a lot* a lot." My daughter's face is very serious. I try like hell not to smile. "It's okay, Daddy. If you don't have any more, Mommy can help you," she tells me while she pats my cheeks, not very gently by the way. One glance at my wife and I know she's desperately trying to look serious and failing. And then I start laughing, and she laughs right along with me.

Thank You

I sincerely hope you enjoyed reading Sebastian and Vera's story as much as I loved writing it. If you would kindly take the time to write a short review, I would really appreciate it!

Thanks Again,
P

Stay tuned for…

Cold, Hard Winters. Ben and Charlotte's story.

About The Author

P. Dangelico loves romance in all forms, shapes, and sizes, cuddly creatures (four legged and two), really bloody sexy pulp, the NY Jets (although she's reconsidering after this season), and to while away the day at the barn (apparently she does her best thinking shoveling horse crap). What she's not enamored with is referring to herself in the third person and social media so don't expect her to get on Twitter anytime soon. And although she was born in Italy, she's been Jersey Strong since she turned six.

Instagram –PDangelicoAuthor
Goodreads
Twitter
Facebook –PDangelicoAuthor
Pinterest
www.pdangelico.com

CPSIA information can be obtained
at www.ICGtesting.com
Printed in the USA
LVHW102140110922
728121LV00018B/299

9 780692 919705